PENGUIN BOOKS

HOME BOY

'*Home Boy* is a slam-dunk for H. M. Naqvi' *USA Today*

'Naqvi's smart and sorrowful debut is at once immigrant narrative,
bildungsroman and New York City novel, with a dash of the picaresque
... *Home Boy* is a remarkably engaging novel that delights as it disturbs'
The New York Times

'Sharp, sleek prose, a tightly wrought structure and a slam poet's instinct
carry this book to the top of the heap' *The Hindu*

'A stunning debut' *Literati* (*The News*)

'A marvellous literary achievement shaped by a refreshingly humane,
irresistibly cool, and distinctly curried sensibility. From the word go, *Home
Boy* is populated by larger-than-life characters and big ideas. It will make you
think, laugh out loud, possibly cry, and at times, dance with joy. You won't
even notice that H. M. Naqvi has redefined South Asian literature'
Lee Siegel, author of *Love in a Dead Language*

'A fast-paced and evocative coming-of-age-tale' *San Francisco Chronicle*

'H. M. Naqvi takes your breath away ... [*Home Boy*] is urbane and chic but
in his portrayal of the brown man's burden he cuts close to the bone'
Daily News and Analysis (India)

'Naqvi's prose is evocative of Nabokov, in its immense energy ... a treasure
trove of illuminating language' Anis Shivani, *Huffington Post*

'This is prose with panache, culturally *au courant* and with an eye for the
absurd – a cross between early Jay McInerney and Gary Shteyngart, with
subcontinental seasoning. It incorporates underground music, fashion and
intoxication-producing substances as well as [a] translation of Faiz Ahmed
Faiz and home-cooked seekh kebab and biryani' *Indian Express*

'A genre-busting, page-turning debut, *Home Boy* fuses street slang and
literary discourse, pop culture and politics, history and comedy,

ABOUT THE AUTHOR

H. M. Naqvi has worked in the financial services industry, run a slam venue and taught creative writing at Boston University. He has received the DSC Prize for South Asian Literature and the Phelam Prize for poetry. Ensconced in Karachi, H. M. Naqvi is working on his second novel.

Home Boy

H. M. NAQVI

PENGUIN BOOKS

For Aliya

PENGUIN BOOKS

Published by the Penguin Group
Penguin Books Ltd, 80 Strand, London WC2R 0RL, England
Penguin Group (USA), Inc., 375 Hudson Street, New York, New York 10014, USA
Penguin Group (Canada), 90 Eglinton Avenue East, Suite 700, Toronto, Ontario, Canada M4P 2Y3
(a division of Pearson Penguin Canada Inc.)
Penguin Ireland, 25 St Stephen's Green, Dublin 2, Ireland (a division of Penguin Books Ltd)
Penguin Group (Australia), 250 Camberwell Road, Camberwell, Victoria 3124, Australia
(a division of Pearson Australia Group Pty Ltd)
Penguin Books India Pvt Ltd, 11 Community Centre, Panchsheel Park, New Delhi – 110 017, India
Penguin Group (NZ), 67 Apollo Drive, Rosedale, Auckland 0632, New Zealand
(a division of Pearson New Zealand Ltd)
Penguin Books (South Africa) (Pty) Ltd, 24 Sturdee Avenue, Rosebank, Johannesburg 2196, South Africa

Penguin Books Ltd, Registered Offices: 80 Strand, London WC2R 0RL, England

www.penguin.com

First published in India by HarperCollins Publishers India
in a joint venture with the India Today Group 2010
First published in Great Britain in Penguin Books 2011

Printed in Great Britain by Clays Ltd, St Ives plc

A CIP catalogue record for this book is available from the British Library

ISBN: 978-0-241-96150-6

www.greenpenguin.co.uk

Penguin Books is committed to a sustainable
future for our business, our readers and our
planet. This book is made from paper certified
by the Forest Stewardship Council.

Of course all life is a process of breaking down, but the blows that do the dramatic side of the work—the big sudden blows that come, or seem to come from the outside—the ones you remember and blame things on…don't show their effect all at once. There is another sort of blow that comes from within—that you don't feel until it's too late to do anything about, until you realize with finality that in some regard you will never be a good man again.

—F. Scott Fitzgerald, 'The Crack-Up'

I ask my vagrant heart: 'Where is there to go now?'
No one belongs to anyone at this hour. Forget it.
No one will receive you at this hour. Let it go.
Where can you possibly go now?

—Faiz Ahmed Faiz, 'The Hour of Faithlessness'

This is how it should be done/
This style is identical to none.

—Eric B. & Rakim, 'You Got Soul'

ONE

We'd become Japs, Jews, Niggers. We weren't before. We fancied ourselves boulevardiers, raconteurs, renaissance men, AC, Jimbo, and me. We were self-invented and self-made and certain we had our fingers on the pulse of the great global dialectic. We surveyed the *Times* and the *Post* and other treatises of mainstream discourse on a daily basis, consulted the *Voice* weekly, and often leafed through other publications with more discriminating audiences such as *Tight* or *Big Butt*. Save Jimbo, who wasn't a big reader, we had read the Russians, the postcolonial canon, but had been taken by the brash, boisterous voices of contemporary American fiction; we watched nature documentaries when we watched TV, and variety shows on Telemundo, and generally did not follow sports except when Pakistan played India in cricket or the Knicks made a playoff run; we listened to Nusrat and the new generation of native rockers, as well as old-school gangsta rap, so much so that we were known to spontaneously break into *Straight outta Compton, crazy motherfucker named Ice Cube / From a gang called Niggaz With Attitude* but were underwhelmed by hip-hop's hegemony (though Jimbo was known to defend Eminem's trimetric compositions and drew comparisons between hip-hop's internal rhythms and the beat of Kurdish marching bands). And we slummed in secret cantons of Central Park, avoided the meatpacking district, often dined in Jackson Heights; weren't rich but weren't poor (possessing, for instance, extravagant footwear but no real estate); weren't frum but avoided pork—me on principle and Jimbo because of habit—though AC's vigorous atheism allowed him extensive culinary latitude; and drank everywhere, some more than others, celebrating ourselves with vodka on the rocks or Wild Turkey with water (and I'd discovered beer in June) among the company of women, black, Oriental, and denizens of the Caucasian nation alike.

Though we shared a common denominator and were told half-jokingly, *Oh, all you Pakistanis are alike*, we weren't the same, AC, Jimbo, and me. AC—a cryptonym, short in part for Ali Chaudhry—was a charming rogue, an intellectual dandy, a man of theatrical presence. Striding into a room sporting his signature pencil-thin mustache, one-button velour smoking jacket, and ankle-high rattlesnake-skins, he demanded attention, an audience. He'd comb his brilliantined mane back and flatten it with wide palms. He'd raise his arm, reveal a nicotine-stained grin, and roar, 'Let the revelry commence!' then march up to you, hand extended, declaiming, 'There you are, chum! We need to talk immediately!' Of us three, he was the only immigrant. While he lived day to day in a rent-stabilized railway apartment in Hell's Kitchen and subbed at a Bronx middle school, his elder sister had emigrated in '81—at the tail end of the first wave of Pakistani immigrants—and enjoyed spectacular success. A decade later she sponsored AC's green card. A small, no-bullshit lady, Mini Auntie worked at the pediatric ward at Beth Israel on East 87th, lived in a brownstone around the corner, and financed AC's on-and-off-again doctorate and studied debauchery.

Jamshed Khan, known universally as Jimbo, was a different cat altogether, a gentle, moon-faced man-mountain with kinky dreadlocks and a Semitic nose which, according to AC, affirmed anthropological speculation that Pathans are the Lost Tribe of Israel. Not that such grand themes moved or motivated Jimbo. Propped against a wall like a benign, overstuffed scarecrow, he'd keep to himself, but at a late juncture he would grab you by the arm to articulate the conversation he'd been having in his head. Jimbo was known to converse in malapropisms and portmanteaus, his deliberate locutions characterized by irregular inflexion of voice, by rhyme if not rationale. On the face of it, he was a space cadet, but we knew he knew what was what. Unlike AC or me, he had a steady girlfriend and, as a DJ slash producer, a vocation with certain cachet. But if his career trajectory opened doors in the city, it estranged him from his septuagenarian father, a retired foreman settled in Jersey City for a quarter of a century. In that time he'd raised a son and a daughter and several notable edifices on either side of the Hudson. Born and bred in Jersey, Jimbo was a bonafide American.

As for me, they called me Chuck and it stuck. I was growing up but thought I was grown-up, was and remain not so tall, lean, angular, like my late father, have brown hair, tin-tinted eyes, and a sharp nose, 'like an eaglet,' my mother liked to say. I'd arrived in New York from Karachi four years earlier to attend college, which I completed swimmingly in three, and, though I was the only expatriate among us, liked to believe I'd since claimed the city and the city had claimed me.

The turn of the century had been epic, and we were easy then, and on every other Monday night you'd see us at Tja!, this bar-restaurant-and-lounge populated by local Scandinavian scenesters and sundry expatriates as well as socialites, arrivistes, homosexuals, metrosexuals, and a smattering of has-been and wannabe models. Located on the periphery of Tribeca, Tja! seldom drew passers-by or hoi polloi, perhaps because there were no gilded ropes circumscribing the entrance, no bouncers or surly transvestites maintaining vigil outside. It was hush-hush, invitation by wink and word of mouth. We'd got word that summer when my gay friend Lawrence né Larry introduced us to a pair of lesbian party promoters who called themselves Blond and Blonder, and ever since the beau monde included a Pakistani contingent comprising Jimbo, AC, and me.

Soon Jimbo a.k.a. DJ Jumbolaya was spinning there, and when I'd arrive, he'd already be in the booth, svelte in a very Kung Fu Fighting tracksuit, swaying from side to side, hand cupped around ear, pudgy fingertips smoothing vinyl like it was chapati. Starting down-tempo with, say, a track from a cooing Portuguese lounge singer, he'd then kick it with some thumping Senegalese pop, seamlessly, effortlessly, as if the latter were an organic extension of the former. DJ Jumbolaya distilled the post-disco-proto-house-neo-soul canon in his compositions. His credo was: *Is All Good.*

When I'd slide next to him and pay respect—high five, chest bump, that kind of thing—he'd say something like 'Dude, you've come to sip martinis and look pretty 'cause you're a preena, a lova, a prophet, a dreama,' and when I'd ask what he was having, he'd say *whatever,* so I'd order a couple of cocktails from Jon the bartender, who would have his shirt unbuttoned to his navel and made drinks for us on the house. He told me he'd served in the French Foreign Legion as a chef and, recognizing me to be a man of the world, would relate news ('you hear about the latest Mai-Mai offensive?'), dispense proprietary advice ('it's best to run hot water over a razor before shaving as the metal expands'), and discuss matters of aesthetics ('that one, yeah, the one that's looking at me, she's got what's called a callipygian rump'). Leaning on the bar, drink in hand, I'd suck it all in.

Friends would show up in ones and twos, characters we knew from Tja! and here and there. There was Roger, a towering sommelier originally from Castle Hill, who'd taken classes in conversational Urdu because, he'd say, 'I dig your women.' Once he asked, 'You think they'd make with a brother? What do I gotta do, man? Like, recite Faiz?' And Ari, a curator at a Chelsea art gallery who cultivated a late Elvis bouffant, had this great story about his first day at P.S. 247 when he found himself in Dodgeball Alley at lunch: 'So, like, the black kids, and the white kids, they separated into teams, like it was 1951 or something, and there was this pencil-neck Chink and a bunch of sorry-looking Spics, and me, the Jewboy. We didn't know which side to join, and like nobody wanted us, so we banded together like the Last of the Mo's. And sure, we got our asses kicked pretty bad the first day, but man, after a couple of weeks, *they* were black and blue . . .'

By and by and arm in arm, Blond and Blonder circulated, making small talk and grand gestures—'Like those shoes!' 'Canapé for everyone!' Sometimes Jimbo's girlfriend made an appearance. A natty, masculine woman with a belly and waddle, she hailed from East Coast aristocracy, sipped berry Bellinis, no cassis, and moved with a hipster crowd— what's called an urban tribe—comprising acolytes. We all loved her and called her the Duck.

On occasion, when I'd find a girl perched on a distant barstool, legs crossed, hair wafting the scent of apple shampoo, I'd say, 'Ciao ciao, baby.' It wasn't a pickup line, just something I muttered when I was drunk. The last time we'd been at Tja!, a girl with mermaid eyes and a pronounced Latin lisp had actually responded to my tender advance with a staccato laugh. 'Next week,' she'd said before being tugged away, 'jou 'n me tan-go!' There was, I believed, great promise in the phrase, in the 'proverbial tango.'

Typically, however, I'd await AC's advent, his heavy hand on my shoulder. All bang, no whimper, he'd chat, chant, dance burlesquely, flirt amiably, and I'd stand beside him, nodding, grinning, reveling in the sense of spectacle. Once he burst in with bloodshot eyes, bellowing,

I rise at eleven,
I dine about two,
I get drunk before sev'n;
And the next thing I do,
I send for my whore, when for fear of a clap,
I spend in her hand, and I spew in her lap!

Conversations paused, a glass or two dropped, and everybody looked at each other—Jimbo at me, Blond at Blonder—like gobsmacked kids at a magic show. Then there was spontaneous and resounding applause. Bowing impressively, AC went about playing the part of the said poet, spewing, spending, and all. With him, the night always promised picaresque momentum. Jimbo would join us after he was done serving up curried riddims, and we'd palaver and drink some more, then close the place down, only to return the week after, or the week after next.

At the time we didn't think that there was more to it than the mere sense of spectacle. We were content in celebrating ourselves and our city with libation. It was later that we realized that we'd been on common ground then, on terra firma. Later we also realized that we hadn't been putting on some sort of show for others, for somebody else. No, we were protagonists in a narrative that required coherence for our own selfish motivations and exigencies.

Two, maybe three weeks later we decided to assemble at Tja! because we were anxious and low and getting cabin fever watching CNN 24-7. Moreover, we believed that there was something heroic in persisting, carrying on, in returning to routine, to revelry.

Hailing a cab, I cruised down the West Side Highway with the window half open, taking in the night. The air was warm and fishy, and the moon, brilliant and low, was torn to shreds by the jagged waves of the Hudson. Downtown seemed festive, lit up with floodlights, but the buildings obscured the mayhem, the mountains of rubble behind them. Three months earlier I'd worked on the forty-first floor of 7 WTC, the third building that went down. My colleagues escaped with cuts and bruises but brushed against the spectacle that would scar their lives.

The smell of burning wafted through the night, and in the distance police lights shone like disco balls. It was time to forget, time to be happy. There was a blur of movement inside and bursts of laughter over the music that were at once vulgar and cathartic. Blond emerged, dancing up to me in slow motion, churning her arms like bicycle wheels. She was tall, bony, and walked like a man. We embraced desperately, like reunited lovers, and said nothing of the postponed festivity. 'Where've you been, my prince!' she began. 'People have been asking after you. Think I saw Lawrence, and d'you know Hogart?'

Glancing at the booths, tables, heads, bodies arranged around the enormous bamboo bar, I didn't recognize anybody: not Roger, Ari, not the mermaid who promised to tango. And I didn't know no Hogart. 'Go on,' Blond was saying, 'get yourself a drink. You look like you need one. We all do.'

When I ordered the usual, the bartender said *you got it, buddy*, like we went back a long time, but I didn't know him from Adam. I would have liked to ask after my old friend legionnaire Jon, but he was too quick or I was too slow, and the guy next to me was carrying on bombastically. 'When I moved here, I knew I'd have to make a shitload of money, like my main man, Montana, because, he says, "In this country you gotta make the money first." So what do I do? I play the market—it was a goddamn gold rush, I tell you—and I raked it in like a mofo: got me a nice car, nice digs, a yacht, a girl that was in the glossies, and then *boom*—'

Pausing, the Bombaster turned to me, probably because I'd been watching him as if he were a street performer ingesting a saber. 'What's your story?' he asked. Offering a dubious shrug and lopsided smile, I sidled away. What do you say?

As I palliated my anxieties in a corner with a very dry, very dirty martini, the girl from last time materialized in a fragrant nimbus of face cream and lavender, swaying and swinging to the bass, and though I had rehearsed the moment for a fortnight in my head, my nerve failed spectacularly. Brushing past, she vanished like a vision. It was early but already turning out to be that kind of night, slightly out of frame, slightly off-kilter. My first drink went down easy but hit me hard. Suddenly, mercifully, Lawrence né Larry appeared, defiantly summery in a gray seersucker draped over a daffodil yellow Lacoste. He had a deep voice, a soft laugh, and the mien of James

Stewart. We embraced then examined each other from head to toe to check if the other was whole.

'What's wrong, baby?' he asked, pinching my cheek. 'You don't look like yourself. Lemme guess: *you* haven't seen the *dust bunny* yet!' Flashing a sympathetic grin, he shoved his hand into his jacket pocket and produced a tiny blue packet that he pressed into my palm. 'Come find me,' he said, gliding away.

Negotiating the bamboo alleys with the stem of the second martini glass pinched between my fingers, I passed a clique of waifs kissing each other on the cheek and a claque of swarming rakes on the way to the restrooms in the back. As usual there was a line, and as usual I waited, arms folded, back against the wall watching the doors open intermittently. Couples and threesomes emerged every now and then, laughing and stroking their swollen nebs with their thumbs. Typical bathroom banter circulated: somebody said something about powdering her nose; somebody else said, 'You say *queue*. That's so cool!' When my turn came, I entered tout seul, securing the door behind me.

Setting the glass down on the rim of the sink, I pulled the packet from my pocket and straddled the WC like a pro. I tapped powdered clumps onto the porcelain top, cut two slugs with the serrated edge of an expired MasterCard, and rolling up a fiver, inhaled through either nostril. There is solace in ritual and routine. Closing my eyes, I inhaled, exhaled, and nodded to the heavens as if in prayer. The smell of soap and liquor and sandalwood pervaded. Before leaving, I observed myself in the mirror: my hair was rakishly mussed, my nostrils dilated, and my eyes, pink and veiny around the edges. I had on a vintage black leather jacket, and suddenly it made sense to turn up its collar.

Outside I lit a Rothman, took a long satisfactory drag. I gulped down the second martini, savoring the salutary aspirin aftertaste in the pit of my throat. Suddenly, I was a party, an animal. As anybody at Tja! could have told you, Charlie stirs the inner lycanthrope, the primal imperative. Raising my glass to a girl standing on a nearby

table, teetering on heels, candle-smooth legs astride, the primal
imperative hardened. I wanted to lick her shaved armpits, taste
her immaculate toes; I wanted her, wanted every woman, Swede,
Oriental alike. Cheers of 'Skål!' rose from the booths as if to
corroborate my sentiment. It was time to find the Girl from Ipanema.
But before I could make meaningful progress, I spied Jimbo by the
turntables, like in the old days—two-tone track jacket, dreads up
in a bun above his head—except that his hands were jammed into
his pockets, causing him to slouch like the new kid hovering on
the periphery of the playground. Hugging me with his heft, Jimbo
mumbled, 'Mimsy were the hommies, dude.'

Although one could not be entirely certain what Jimbo meant
at any given time—conversing with him required hermeneutic
feats—I suspected he was alluding to one of two recent tragedies.
It so happened that between now and then he had been replaced
by another deejay, the son or brother of a celebrity whose tribal
ragga shtick had become au courant. Then the plaster and drywall
and some of the wood slats in the ceiling of his junior studio off
Liberty Street had come loose, then collapsed in the last ten days,
compelling him to seek refuge. He was supposed to stay with me,
but AC insisted on hosting him because AC, as usual, was on some
kind of trip. The arrangement was probably not easy—nothing about
AC was easy—but when I inquired why he couldn't stay with the
Duck, Jimbo waved his hand as if half-heartedly swatting a fly. 'AC's
lookin' for you, dude,' he said as if he hadn't heard me. 'Kept sayin'
somethin' 'bout *civilized human beings*. Know anythin' 'bout it?'

Shrugging, I wondered why I had not come across AC yet—he
was not one to go quietly into the night—then Jimbo pointed him
out at the far end of the bar: clad in his trademark one-button
velour jacket, his hair pulled back with Brylcreem, AC stood over
the Bombaster, in medias res, delivering some sort of disquisition,
reifying two heavy, misshapen balls in his hairy, gesticulating hands.
Leaving Jimbo to ruminate for a moment, I squeezed and pushed
and excuse-me'd to the other side.

'You remember,' AC was saying, his stentorian voice carrying over the noise, 'about twenty years ago, bands of Afghans battled the Red Army? Yeah, well, they were called rebels, freedom fighters— Mujahideen—the Holy Warriors. They fought with World War II rifles till we armed them with AK-47s and Stingers. We invited them to Washington and, ah, compared them to the Founding Fathers. They were the good guys, chum. Osama B. was one of them.'

When AC paused to take a dramatic drag, I tapped him on the shoulder. Turning around with a start, he exclaimed, 'Ah! There you are!' A lock of hair fell over his prominent forehead; he had the air of somebody doing many things at once, focused yet distracted, more juggler than ringmaster. 'Listen,' he said, putting his arm conspiratorially around me. 'We need to talk.'

'Is this about Jimbo?' I asked. 'Because you know he can always crash with me.'

'It's not that—'

'You were saying,' the Bombaster interrupted.

'I was saying,' AC continued without missing a beat, 'after the Mujahideen defeated the Soviets, they turned their guns on each other. Nobody remembers now, but tens of thousands died, Kabul was razed to the ground, and something like four million refugees left for Pakistan. Afghanistan, in effect, ceased to be a state, but by then everybody had lost interest in the region, in—if I remember correctly—what some guy in the administration called "the obscure Afghan civil war." You follow, chum?'

The Bombaster nodded intently. AC blew his nose into a cocktail napkin, then turning to me, announced, 'We need to sit down, like, ah, civilized human beings. We have plans to discuss that require consideration and quiet. It's a zoo in here. We're headed to Jake's.'

Before I could open my mouth—*What plans? Why Jake's? Why now?*—AC had returned to grand themes and a rapt audience: 'Then the Mujahideen's progeny emerged, the Taliban, the Bastards of War! You know when they swept through Afghanistan, they were garlanded, hailed as heroes? You see, they brought order for the first time in decades. But soon the proverbial shit hit the fan. They outlawed music, TV, fun. They hacked off limbs, shot women, blew up the goddamn Buddha of Bamiyan! Now they've, ah, transmogrified into the villains of modern civilization, but you know, they're not much different from their fathers—brutes with guns—except this time they're on the wrong side of history.'

Pleased with being privy to the imperatives of wild men and the goings-on in far-flung arenas of the world, the Bombaster asked, 'What're you drinking?'

'A double Wild Turkey, please, with a drop of water,' he replied before informing me, 'We leave right after.'

'I, um, need to find somebody,' I said weakly.

Turning around, the Bombaster asked, 'So lemme get this straight: you guys aren't Indian?'

'We're too handsome, chum! You can call us Metrostanis! Cheers! Skål! Adab!'

Shoving off, I said, 'I'll meet you there, yaar.'

'Ooay!' AC called, as if hailing a rickshaw in Karachi traffic. 'This is serious.' Then fixing me with a look meant to convey consequence, he yelled, 'I'll be waiting.'

Impelled, I parted the crowd like a man on a mission, circled the bar several times, and checked each and every booth and the restrooms in the back for good measure, but the Girl from Ipanema eluded me. As I knocked about, I began wondering what I would say if I ever found her, then the martinis became molten in my empty stomach. Feeling insubstantial and sick, I decided it was time to leave, but as I turned, I found myself face-to-face with a vision. 'Ciao, ciao,' I blurted, my heart beating like techno.

'¿Que?'

'Bow, wow?'

'Jou are like puppy dog?'

'Well,' I replied, 'I like to think, more like a wolf.' In an effort to elucidate, I growled unconvincingly and, summoning the rudimentary Spanish I'd picked up watching Telemundo, added, '*El loco.*'

'Jou are craysee?'

'I mean *el lobo, el lobo!*'

'*¡El lobo! ¡Ha! ¿Habla español?*'

'I can learn,' I muttered to myself.

'*¿Que?*'

'Are you, um, Argentine?'

'No!' she cried, feigning offense. 'I am of Venezuela.'

'Of course you are.'

'How jou know?'

'Because,' I replied with the astonishing fluency of a playboy, 'you're so very beautiful.' The blandishment caused her eyelids to flutter and look away as if to allow me a moment to scrutinize her up close. And in the blink of an eye I discerned the tiny, freshly bleached hairs on the edges of her pout, the slight dimple in her chin, and God's finishing touch, a crescent-shaped mole on her collarbone. In the blink of an eye, I was smitten. It didn't take much. Although I aspired to be cavalier about women, unlike AC I couldn't manage trysts in toilets, necking in cabs, the protocol of metropolitan courtship. In the four years I had been in the city, in the twenty-one and a half years that comprised my life, I fell in love routinely. It went almost entirely unrequited.

When I offered to buy her a drink, a mojito, *¿si?* she said *que rico* and repeated the query with an inflection suggesting agreement. It was a fortuitous, unexpected development, a boon. Emboldened, I grabbed her hand, tugging her to the bar where I organized refreshments.

The Girl from Ipanema spoke in a low gurgle, but even though we were close enough to kiss, I managed to miss the meat of the conversation because I was busy marveling at her bubblegum lips. And though her accent was thick and her command of the language poor, I did glean that her family had emigrated in the not-so-distant past, a decision informed by the resurgent populist neosocialism sweeping South America, in particular the radical land-redistribution policy and thuggery of the present regime: 'They take all Papa's houses. We are leaving. We are American.' I found myself thinking that if I married her, I too would become a bonafide American. In a sense, we were peas in a pod, she and I, denizens of the Third World turned economic refugees turned scenesters by fate, by historical caprice. That's when I thought I heard her say, 'Jou haf nice ass.'

Staring blankly, I considered the compliment, uncertain whether I had misheard or she had misspoken, whether this was how courtship worked in Caracas—the jaunty etiquette of a warm-blooded people—or whether it was a local matter, something to do with the phenomenon of 'terror sex' reported in newspapers and periodicals. As I tried to formulate a becoming reply, something gracious and witty, she brushed my eyelids. 'Oh!' I exclaimed, '*My eyes!* Thank you! Thank you very much.' Then she inquired where I was from, and when I told her, she asked, 'Jou not Italian?' I scratched my ear, she sucked her lips to smoothen the cracks in her lipstick, and then we wordlessly observed the bartender crush mint leaves with a fork in two tall glasses before us. Adding sugar, lime juice, rum, he topped each with club soda, crushed ice, and a garnish of lemon crescents.

'*Gracias,*' the Venezuelan said smilingly.

'*De nada,*' the bartender replied, grinning impishly.

'*Bueno,*' I chimed in.

'Now,' the Girl from Ipanema announced, 'I go to toilet,' before sashaying away for the second time that night. At that fraught moment, I didn't know whether to stay put or follow, whether she needed a Kleenex, a bump, or simply had to relieve herself. Regardless, I should have called out 'Wait!' or 'Come back!' or something like that, and later, when reviewing the episode in my mind, I recalled things to say, funny things, bold things, things men say to woo women, but just then I stood there dumbly, my hands flopping at my side. It was as if my reservoir of cool had run dry. It was time to leave. I demanded the check with a vigorous scribble in the air and settled the tab.

The Bombaster carried on: 'We're going down, but it ain't what you think it is. There's this DOD report that says that WMD aren't the biggest danger to humanity. It's nature, man! Global warming, Noah's second flood, coming at ya! You think New York's going to last? You think we'll survive? *Un*-an! We'll all become God's goldfish, baby . . .'

The doors closed on vulgar music, distant drums. Tribeca, stricken, was deathly quiet, a ghost town. The streets were empty and strewn with the usual garbage. I hurried past closed doors and shuttered entrances, farther and farther away from disaster, thinking *this is what it feels like to be the last man on earth*. Turning into West Broadway, there was the suggestion of civilization in the porters loitering outside the Soho Grand, the couple tentatively crossing an empty street, a squatting bum. There were, however, no cabs anywhere. The blocks between Canal and Houston seemed longer than usual, probably because there was a certain urgency in my stride, as if I already knew that years later, in retrospect, that night would stand out in the skyline of my memory.

TWO

We who arrived in the West after the colonial enterprise, after our forefathers, heroes, icons—the likes of Syed Ahmed Khan, Mulk Raj Anand, and M.A. Jinnah—found the east coast of the Atlantic habitable if not always hospitable, but America was something else. The weather was mostly friendly, the people mostly warm, and the premise of the nation, the bit about 'your bruised and battered' (or as AC put it in his native Punjabi, '*twaday tootay-phoothay*'), was an altogether different thing. You could, as Mini Auntie told me once, spend ten years in Britain and not feel British, but after spending ten months in New York, you were a New Yorker, an original settler, and in no time you would be zipping uptown, downtown, crosstown, wherever, strutting, jaywalking, dispensing directions to tourists like a mandarin. 'You see,' you'd say, 'it's quite simple: the city's like a grid.'

The theoretical premise of America had more tangible implications. You did not, for instance, have to explain yourself. Learning I was 'foreign,' my college roommate, Big Jack (a native of a place called China Grove, TX), inquired, 'Ain't that in South America?' Testament to the theory of symbolic interaction, perhaps, it didn't matter, because 'it's not where you're from,' as Rakim once averred, 'it's where you're at.' Sure, they said institutionalized racism was only a few generations old and latitudinally deep, but in New York you felt you were no different from anybody else; you were your own man; you were free. At any given minute, you could decide to navigate your way up Fifth Avenue to regard shiny luxury watches in shop windows, eat a kosher hot dog on Central Park South, or read *Intro to Sociology* at an outdoor café off Christopher.

And sure, independence had its dark dimensions, its lonely frequented loci, like a scarred green bench in the northwest corner of Washington Square where nobody sought you out. You would turn up your collar then, and sit with your arms folded regarding the masquerade. You were no different from the next man: bum, pot dealer, panhandler, booted malcontent sprouting gelled spikes like lacquered weeds from his head. New York could be a lonely place, but over the course of a year, these places became fewer and farther between.

There was AC's cluttered cove in Hell's Kitchen, a fantastic and fecund place somewhere between Barbarossa's private quarters and a fin-de-siècle boomtown brothel, featuring burgundy wallpaper, wall-to-wall rugs, velvet curtains cut from Salvation Army dresses, a hammock, a filthy aquarium, a bonsai collection, and shelves upon shelves of books. There were books in piles on the floor, Toynbee's twelve volumes in the bathroom, and *The Critique of Pure Reason* propped up a wobbly, termite-ridden foot of the dining table. The pièce de résistance, a functioning fountain of a pissing cherub with a chipped nose, salvaged from an estate sale, was garlanded with strings of sewn jasmine on special occasions like Thanksgiving, Christmas, 14th August, Eid. AC's landlord, a reformed slumlord, was on his case for the usual reasons—noise, late rent, no rent, no fountains allowed—but also because AC had altered the layout of the fifteen-hundred-plus-square-foot railroad apartment by erecting walls, compartmentalizing the space into a library, bar, sehen, and a random area bathed in blue light called the Blue Room. 'This is my place in the world,' he insisted. 'I'll do with it as I please.' Later I would be over, reading, playing speed Scrabble or Texas hold 'em, watching flicks from AC's collection (variously labeled *Korean Action Movies*, *Movies w/Madeleine Stowe*), or dabbling in homemade hallucinogens. During my freshman year, however, I had only been over once because AC was a man possessed then, working till six every morning on his dissertation, which he brazenly proclaimed would change the 'contours of modern discourse.'

Consequently, I frequented AC's sister's place, where there was always 'somebody if not somebody else over' and you were welcome 'whenever.' There was also the promise of a meal at the end of the entrance corridor, past the Damascene brass lamp, the colonial-era lithographs, and the silver-framed mirror in which you'd check the parting of your hair. Mini Auntie presided in the dining room like the Oracle at Delphi, her large gray eyes peering into your consciousness as you entered. 'You must eat something, child. You're cadaverous! What would your mother say if she saw you now?' If you were lucky, she'd warm up a plate of killer nihari, transporting you home, to Burns Road. Otherwise, you'd be treated to homemade pizza or a shami-kabab-and-butter sandwich. You'd also be treated to lectures on politics, love, life, the institution of marriage. 'Find a girl, child, and love her. Don't break any hearts. Mark my words: it'll come back to you.' After divorcing her husband, a 'good and proper chamar,' she fled Lahore to find her calling in pediatrics and the city. A small woman, she had subsequently been reincarnated as Mini, a one-word moniker, like Madonna, and like Madonna, she was a one-woman institution, a pillar of the city's expatriate Pakistani community. To us, children of her pals back home, she was a foster mother, especially as she had not produced progeny herself.

During my senior year, Mini Auntie's was displaced by the Duck's. The Duck lived in a swank corner apartment overlooking West Broadway, her parents' pied à terre in the city. They had another one on Fishers Island and, as far I knew, one in Aix-en-Provence. Her father's people had reportedly landed on Plymouth Rock and drifted down the coast to New Canaan, Connecticut, while her mother's mother hailed from blue-blooded French stock, though they didn't seem to take such things very seriously. The Duck certainly didn't. She would be at the door when we arrived, beckoning with extended arms, fingers clutching the air. She would hug, tug, seat us, and depending on the occasion or the time of day, pour us brandy, port, grappa. It was as if she instinctively knew what you needed. All the while the Duck's dog—a gray terrier with long silky hair and tiny black eyes—would sniff and bark like a drag queen. 'C'mon, Lyman,' she'd say, patting her thighs. 'Be nice, be polite.' Turning to her guests, she'd say, 'You're meeting special people tonight, people without whom New York's not New York! These are the famous Pakistanis!' She had a talent for introductions. In her apartment we met the veritable who's who of the city, from heiresses who wore no underwear to graying men with sharp features who would engage you with rarified lisps. And just as you were talking about the hot new band that was performing at Badlands or the Hammerstein Ballroom, they would turn up for a nightcap, manager and groupies in tow, a little tired, a little sweaty but, because of the Duck's hospitality, quickly recharged and ready to go. There'd be great revelry, epic celebration into the night. And before retiring, at six or seven in the morning, before that creeping bittersweet feeling that the world is quite wonderful but your time on it is finite, you would have breakfast with rockstars.

When there was no place to go, there was Jake's. We weren't sure whether Jake's was legit—the secrecy Jake cultivated seemed contrived, and, we mused, the authorities must have wind of it—but it certainly had the facade and the ambience of a speakeasy. There was no sign or other indication that the large black door—often mistaken for a service entrance—led to dingy quarters that accommodated a pool room and bar. The pool room was so narrow that you could not get at the table from one side without deploying the bridge, and the felt on the table was so scratched that trick shots were de rigueur. Many a night the uninitiated got hustled playing nine ball, not just nickeled-and-dimed but properly Benjamin Franklined.

A single green bulb revealed the alcove between the two rooms where we'd hang back, circumscribed by two chairs jammed together to form a love seat, a threadbare ornamental ottoman, a coffee table crudely rendered from a tree stump. Other artifacts embellished the area: a triangular construction sign featuring horizontal zigzags, a globe of the world circa Bismarck's Wars of Unification, a set of framed Harvester butterflies (the only known North American carnivorous species, which, Jake would tell you, 'will bite your head off, guy'), a wizened, oversize, wide-rimmed top hat nailed to the wall. As you'd expect, each item had an accompanying story that changed with each recitation. It was an impressive display, a lifetime's worth of clutter.

Jake would be perched on a stool at the near end of the bar, beside a small black-and-white TV with a V-shaped antenna. Gaunt, silver-haired, and raspy-voiced, Jake entertained in a crisp white shirt that revealed the meager curls on his chest and a handsome dark blazer that usually sprouted a black rose. Sometimes he assumed the figure of a capo; sometimes he assumed the persona of a pimp. If you arrived with a *ladyfriend*, he would beckon from the back, demanding an introduction and a kiss on the lips; then producing a disposable Kodak from his jacket, he would instruct you to 'step back, guy, 'n' take a snap.' Hundreds of pinned pictures featuring Jake with his skeletal arm around simpering women adorned the wooden lattice separating the alcove from the bar.

The bar was rudimentary and opened onto a hallway that did not seem to be used by the tenants of the converted brown stone off Bowery. At the end of the passage was a standing-room-only toilet where we did blow. There was an open courtyard behind the bathroom where you were not permitted to loiter but that you had to traverse on your way out. You entered through one door and exited through another, and if you didn't follow protocol, Jake would throw you out, yelling, *'Bruttoor!' 'Cattivo!'* 'NO ROOM FOR YOUS!' There wasn't much room anyway: you never found or could fit more than seven or eight people inside. It was a secret shitty little place, a clubhouse for the dissolute, the disconsolate.

As I sidled inside that night, Jake, illuminated by the glow of his TV, looked up from his perch and nodded. Twin hunched silhouettes lurked by the bar in the background while Jimbo and AC sat in the alcove up front among empty glasses, bottles of beer, and a wrinkly pack of American Spirits. Ensconced on the ottoman, Jimbo mulled the symmetry of a cigarette. After due deliberation and a persistent wheeze, he had quit cold turkey some three weeks earlier, an inopportune moment in the history of the summer. In the interest of economy, I had attempted as well but failed. AC, meanwhile, slumped, shirt untucked, as if lapsing in and out of an ontological stupor. When he saw me, he leaped up, crying, 'Where the *hell* have you been?'

'I'm sorry, yaar,' I panted, 'there were no cabs anywhere—'

'You can't do this to us, chum. We were worried. We've been waiting for hours,' he fulminated, making something of nothing, but I listened demurely, deferentially, as usual, thumbs hooked in pockets. At that instant he could have been delirious from insomnia or high or, worse, both. 'You have to remember, we have responsibilities to each other, as friends, and more importantly as, ah, human beings. We cannot allow ourselves to be cauterized. We are the glue,' he announced, waving an arm about him with rhetorical flourish, 'keeping civilization together. Without bonds and good manners, without commitments, even small commitments, we're nothing, unconnected, uncivilized, animals! Do you follow?'

I nodded and then again for effect.

'Dude, you're never sure,' Jimbo interjected, 'and you're sure you could be right—'

'I'm not interested in your, ah, pablum,' exclaimed AC.

'That like phlegm?' Jimbo wondered aloud.

'I'm sorry, AC,' I said. 'I really am.'

We settled into hard chairs and a mysteriously grim mood. We lit cigarettes, passed around warm beers, and concentrated on the floor. Although I wanted to get the Girl from Ipanema episode off my chest, I was afraid to disturb the studied silence. Jimbo, however, leaned forward, elbows on knees, verging on conversation. I could sense that grand themes didn't occupy his thoughts. Something else was on his mind, something parochial, closer to home. 'Duck's AWOL, dude,' he finally announced.

'Fuck the Duck, chum!' AC proclaimed.

'Can't, pussycat,' Jimbo retorted. 'She ain't here.'

'What's happened?' I asked.

'Dunno,' he replied, creasing his considerable eyebrows. 'She ain't returnin' my calls . . . must be pissed . . . gotta go see her.'

Grinding a cigarette into a butt, AC rose determinedly and disappeared into the back.

'What's eating him, yaar?'

'Civilized soonkers and such.'

'That's what he wanted to talk about back there?'

'No, dude, the Shaman.'

Mohammed Shah or the Shaman was dark, lanky, over the hill, and could be described as a drifter, a grifter, an American success story, a Pakistani Gatsby. Apparently he quite literally jumped ship back and subsisted day to day, hand to mouth for years, working gas stations along Palisades Parkway and Queens Boulevard. This, however, was mostly hearsay. A few things we knew for sure: he told the Long Island natives whom he courted at hotel bars that he was an Arab sheikh, and sometimes it worked. In recent history the Shaman had managed to secure a position at a top-tier insurance company, and suddenly though not entirely unexpectedly, he was on the up and up. In celebration, he had leased a scarlet Mercedes 500 SEL and mortgaged one of those rubblestone and wood houses in Westbrook, Connecticut, where he hosted ostentatious parties while slinking soberly on the periphery.

'What about the Shaman?'

'Man's AWOL too.'

After 9/11 we heard not only from family and friends but from distant relatives, colleagues, ex-colleagues, one-night stands, two-night stands, neighbors, childhood friends, and acquaintances, and in turn we made our own inquiries, phone calls, dispatched e-mails. When AC returned with a shot of Wild Turkey, he told us that he had called the Shaman, left messages. 'Something isn't right. I've the feeling—admittedly the, ah, proverbial gut feeling—that the Shaman's gone missing.'

As he gravely lit a cigarette, Jimbo and I exchanged bemused, skeptical looks, stretched, cracked our fingers. The Shaman was an unreliable character at the best of times. Known to go underground for ages, he would surface unexpectedly as you're leafing through a copy of *Big Butt* at the corner bodega. At any other time, we might have told AC to chill the hell out, but he was in a particularly excitable state that night. Jumping up, as if bitten in the ass by a carnivorous butterfly, he sent the balls whirling on the pool table behind him with a sweep of the hand. We watched the balls zigzag and rebound against the sides and against one another and roll into the pockets with hollow clunks.

'Goddamn it,' AC exclaimed, 'somebody say something!'

Jake coughed up phlegm in the background, crying '*Buono, buono!*' Then I asked, 'Don't you need more to go on than your gut?'

'Precisely, chum,' AC replied, pounding the meat of his palm with the eight ball. 'We should find him immediately—tonight! We need to go to his house, stake it out, break in, whatever it takes. We're his friends, maybe his only friends. We owe it to him . . . we owe it to ourselves—'

'He could be out of town, dude,' Jimbo interrupted. 'This one time the city was really gettin' to me—hadn't been away for like ten months—so I went upstate, with the Duck, and I wasn't stoned or nothin', but the blue and green of the sky and water like really hit me, like the colors were alive or something, maybe 'cause blue and green are in the middle of the color spectrum—I dunno—but I was like, give it to me baby, *I'm dyin' here*—'

Suddenly AC's eyes flashed, the only hint of an imminent outburst: 'I DON'T CARE ABOUT THE FUCKING COLOR SPECTRUM, CHUM! I care about the Shaman! I care about this city.' His thick, wavy locks kept falling over his eyes, and he kept pulling them back. 'Those bastards,' he continued, 'they've fucked up *my city*! THEY'VE FUCKED UP EVERYTHING!'

Again there was silence, save the susurrus of shadows from the far end of the bar and the white noise from Jake's TV. But Jake was not at his perch. He'd probably ducked into the bathroom for a line. Just then the two figures from the bar materialized. They had prominent chins, heavy shoulders, thick torsos, the waxen physiques of brawlers. Tense and unsteady on their feet, they lumbered toward us like two big bags, provoked, it would seem, by our shibboleth. 'Whatchugonnafuckup?' one of them asked; the other echoed the query in a sharper pitch as if to clarify connotation or import. Like us, they had been drinking, exorcizing their own demons.

Jimbo and I looked to AC, the seasoned bar brawler among us. Built like a wrestler, a village pahalvan, he was meaty, possessed a low center of gravity, and often claimed that he had coined the maxim, *The Golden Rule of bar fighting is the loser goes to hospital*, and its corollary, *And the winner goes to jail*. Clearing his throat, he said, 'I think you misunderstood, chum,' evenly, unapologetically.

'Misunderstood my ass,' came the reply in a tenor that suggested violence.

We all froze like dancing statues, knowing in the back of our minds that at that moment apologetic grunts could have been uttered and we could have shaken each other's hands, patted each other on the back, gone home unscathed, and slept like babies. But it wasn't happening. It was almost like we weren't just contending with each other but with the crushing momentum of history. Brawler No. 1 hissed, '*A-rabs*.'

Repeating the word in my head, I realized it was the first time I'd heard it spoken that way, like a dagger thrust and turned, the first time anything like this had happened to us at all. Sure, we'd been in donnybrooks before but for bumping into somebody in a foul mood or not letting go of a cue stick. This was different. 'We're not the same,' Jimbo protested.

'Moslems, Mo-hicans, whatever,' Brawler No. 2 snapped.

'I'm from Jersey, dude!'

'I don't care, chief!'

Then for some reason that remains inscrutable to me, I rose as if I had just been asked to deliver an after-dinner speech—throat dry, hands at my sides, notes hopelessly misplaced—and with uncharacteristic chutzpah, proclaimed, 'Prudence suggests you boys best return to your barstools—' Then there was a flash, like a lightbulb shattering, a ringing in my ears, the metallic taste of blood in my mouth. I didn't quite see the fist that knocked me flat on my back.

Gathering my senses and cigarette, I looked up to see AC come from behind and crack a Bud Light across Brawler No. 1's head. I watched his head jerk, legs buckle. I watched him topple the construction sign and hit the ground facedown, dark blood seeping from a hidden gash in his head. Just then Brawler No. 2 lunged at AC, swinging a wild, looping fist, what they call a haymaker. AC expertly pulled away, then came at him, waving the jagged edge of the broken bottle. '*Maar maar ke mitti karan ga*,' he raged in Punjabi before reverting to local vernacular: 'C'mon, you stinking son of a—'

Suddenly Jake appeared, flapping his arms like an albatross, and pushing himself past Brawler No. 2, thundered, 'GETATAHERE! ALLAYOUS!'

'We're cool, we're cool,' Jimbo said, extending his palms before him. 'We'll make things right.'

'GETATAHERE!' Jake yelled again. 'NO ROOM FOR YOUS!'

Jimbo picked me up in his arms, though there was no need, and we made our way through the hallway and courtyard and onto the street. We heard Jake cry, 'Jesus! I got fucking blood on my suit!'

Pumping his fists in the night air, AC cried, 'Niggaz start to mumble / They want to rumble / Mix 'em and cook 'em in a pot like gumbo . . .'

But we'd been kicked out of Jake's. Things were changing.

THREE

When I woke, it was dark, and for a few moments I didn't know where or who I was, but then I felt thirsty and sore, and my bearings became clear when I perceived the outline of the drawn, dust-swept blinds at the far end of my apartment. The day was either over or overcast, though the second-story walkup didn't get much sun anyway since it overlooked a concrete area framed by the discolored backs of neighboring townhouses. It did, however, have what passed as character in the classifieds: high ceilings, hardwood floors, exposed brick, and a large functioning fireplace that I never had the opportunity or inclination to use. During winter, the prewar radiator abruptly switched on, emitting noises that sounded like distant seagulls. As a result, I would often wake to the sensation of being adrift at sea.

There wasn't any of the clutter that would suggest that I had lived there for almost a year: no rug, bookshelf, toaster, ironing board, plant, or full-length mirror. Indeed, the apartment was clutterless: there was a thirty-inch TV in the center; a fancy stereo system with gold-tipped heavy-gauge cable—a purchase informed by Jimbo's technical know-how—stacked in a corner; and a striped aquamarine futon, a hand-me-down from AC, pushed up against a wall. Four identical chairs with steel backs were arranged in a semicircle, draped with trousers, ties, underwear.

The arrangement may or may not have contributed to positive feng shui, but I abided by it. One weekend though, feeling tired and bored with myself, I had managed to decorate the entrance wall with four framed pictures: me as a three-year-old, left on a rooftop somewhere to contemplate the world; my late father as a young man sporting a young mustache, his elbow resting on the balcony behind him; a photocopy of the Victoria's Secret model Yasmeen Ghauri, hugging her bare legs in a way only women with beautiful legs do; and another of M.A. Jinnah, the founder of Pakistan, playing billiards, biting a cigar.

The classifieds had not mentioned that the apartment featured an antediluvian mustard-tiled bathroom with a musty air and a flimsy door or a mustard-tiled kitchenette with fitting that suggested overuse (though I had only once prepared poached eggs and fried toast in it). Save the many empty ash-flaked cans of Coke, two mistakenly pilfered shot glasses, and some clear plastic cutlery, the kitchen was also clutterless, though the drawer above the sink housed an untidy collection of powdered spices. Ever since I had moved in, I had planned to cook, deploying the recipes my mother dispatched with unfailing regularity, but then the thought of eating home food, comfort food, alone made me shudder. And yet I had no hesitation in devouring a five-dollar burrito with extra sour cream and guacamole before the TV, or sitting on the windowsill, looking down at the accidental, communal backyard with a Styrofoam plate balanced precariously on my thighs.

Many windows opened into the courtyard, but from my perch I could only peer into the apartment opposite mine. It was also sparsely furnished, as if the tenant—a slender, squirrelly guy with close-cropped blond hair—had just arrived or was just about to move out. He spent most of his time in printed boxers lounging on an easy chair, expertly picking at takeout cartons with chopsticks, watching TV, remote clasped in hand. Late at night the apartment flickered phosphorescently, and once or twice I had happened upon desperately fumbling shadows, the brief, stirring profile of a breast. Mostly, however, we were home alone.

It wasn't as if I didn't have plans for the place, plans I would review in idle moments, sitting on the can or on the commute from work, featuring floor-to-ceiling bookshelves from IKEA, a round walnut breakfast table, a drop-open mahogany bar, a stretch fish tank, a double-knotted Pakistani carpet, a hookah, and a leather couch on which you could sit cross-legged, arms thrown back, surveying the accoutrements of urbanity. With the requisite infrastructure, I would have guests over for cocktails and after-after-hours: college pals, women, hipsters we knew from Tja! *It's all going to come together*, I kept telling myself. And it almost did.

In the bright fall of a giddy year, I became a banker, an investment banker, not because I was swept by the spirit of the age, by bullish sentiment, by the Great Bull Run, but because my mother told me to. A woman of the world, Ma was cognizant that banking and 'aiytee' had displaced medicine and engineering in the last decade as coveted careers for able young Pakistani men (and we both knew that I never quite had the aptitude for the sciences). The pursuit of happiness for us was material. Since I had no particular calling, having majored in lit, a discipline in which, I learned, anything goes, I did what I had to do: after dispatching résumés on thick paper and making some phone calls, I secured interviews and then a job at a big bank that had just become bigger. It all happened just like that, quickly, efficiently. When I received the offer, I called Ma, announcing, 'I got it,' who in turn called friends and relatives to tell them about her *Wall Street son*, adding, 'They make millions!'

That was not accurate. Starting salary on the Street back in 2000 was forty grand plus bonus—not exactly a million bucks—but ample for us. Once I began work, I transferred cash home every month via the hassle-free, under-the-table hawala system—an operation later shut down by the feds—housed at the Kashmir Restaurant near the Port Authority. And the grand plan was that after the bank sponsored my green card, a process that in those days took about three, four years, I would sponsor Ma's. Then we'd live happily ever after like a happy, all-American family, minus father figure.

Ma had gushed, 'Oh, your father would have been so happy,' though there wasn't much evidence to support the claim. Although my father was a chartered accountant by trade—traditionally a third option for able young Pakistani men—I suspected he would have rather pursued photography, his childhood hobby. This odd biographical footnote was corroborated by albums of monochrome still-life shots I had discovered as a teenager and the beautiful old Rolleiflex that rested on the armoire (alongside a miniature glass replica of the Kremlin) in our drawing room like out-of-reach testaments to a man I never knew. I am not even sure how he 'passed away.' According to family lore, he slipped in the bathtub, but I had a persistent suspicion, substantiated only by aborted conversations and skittish expressions on faces of aunts and uncles, that he committed suicide.

In any event, banking seemed grand at the time, and I looked and played the part: on the first day and every morning for just under a year, I slicked my hair back, harnessed a pair of paisley-print suspenders, my only sartorial extravagance (apart from my shoes), and donned one of my father's three narrow trousered woolen suits that had luckily returned to style, retro as it were (and, I was told, brown was the new black). I worked fourteen, fifteen-hour days, including most weekends, 'crunching numbers' and assembling 'pitch books' for multimillion-dollar mergers, acquisitions, and debt and equity issues. When I had downtime, I played Tetris glazy-eyed or chain-smoked while pacing around the block, counting the concrete squares beneath my feet.

In the odd, inspired moment, my VP, a thirty-year-old guy from Metuchen, NJ, would walk over from his office, tie slung over shoulder, or swagger—if he had brokered a deal that morning or scored the night before—preaching the gospel of prosperity: 'What do we do here? We create value, make markets more efficient.' Conversant in Street-speak, he demanded *due diligence* and *granular analysis* and insisted on mixing metaphors: 'Ball's in your court, sport. Now run with it.' Nodding, I would roll up my sleeves and dig in, feeling vaguely part of the secret, intricate, if procrustean machinery that made Capitalism tick. Even if I didn't always buy it, I figured, who ain't a slave?

By all accounts, I was well regarded in the department and in time became what is known on the Street as the *go-to guy*. If you needed a qualitative take on revised EPS projections for a company, or comps on a space that defies easy categorization, or a pitch book on acquisition ideas for a Big Pharma player in the morning, I was the man. Indeed, *Chuck it* became a sort of catchphrase, and though it may not sound particularly flattering, those in the know will appreciate its resonance. In the semiannual review, my VP wrote: 'Dependable. Conscientious. Sees projects through with min. supervision. Thinks about problems. Writes very well.' Although it was a fine assessment of a lit major turned banker by the exacting standards of Wall Street, I was by no means a Big Swinging Dick. The review went on to delineate KEY AREAS OF IMPROVEMENT: 'Needs to improve multitasking, attention to detail, grasp of financial concepts.' I had some work cut out for me. I would get there. I had time. I had the will.

A year later, however, just after Independence Day, at the beginning of the end of the Great Bull Run, I was fired. It was quick and efficient, and the pink slip was unexpectedly yellow. After I had cleared my cubicle into a shoebox, my VP was good enough to invite me into his office. 'Take a seat,' he said, kicking a chair. 'You know, this isn't personal, right?' I suppose I did; it had to do with the bottom line, the Invisible Hand. Although he must have spoken for ten minutes, I only caught his concluding remarks: 'My hands were tied. You'll do okay, sport. You're a team player. You're taking one for the team.' I nodded, then walked out, shoebox tucked under arm.

Although Ma did not know and did not need to worry—I kept sending money home fortnightly—toward the end of the summer, my savings, astutely invested in stocks with high price-to-equity ratios, in companies with anticipated future earnings contingent on clicks per page or FDA approval of some clinical drug, had been reduced to a few cents on the dollar. I cut cable, cellular service, and magazine subscriptions and began investing in lottery tickets. (*Hey, you never know.*) There wasn't much more I could do. The market had soured. I found myself in a profound funk.

On afternoons that I actually made it off the futon and out of my apartment (on average, four days out of seven), I moved from refuge to respite. I had developed a routine, a tour of the Upper West Side, really, commencing at the Moroccan-run newsstand down the street, where I purchased the *Times* and made small talk with the proprietor, pausing at Gray's Papaya for a Recession Special (two hot dogs and a Tropical Breeze for $2.99), and ending up at Central Park. Under the weeping willows of the Great Lawn, I surveyed the paper, from the pictures of affluent affection on the engagements page to the sports section, commiserating with the gritty but hapless, Ewingless Knicks. Every once in a while I would stretch my neck, watching teenagers tossing Frisbees, au pairs supervising toddlers, sunbathing. Sometimes I would listen in on conversations, cocking my head to one side while pretending to read. Other times I dozed.

On the way back, I would frequent used bookstores and record stores, and on Sunday nights, I caught flicks at the Lincoln Plaza or the Cineplex three blocks up. On Tuesday evenings, I drifted into museums because admission was free, gawking at broken Doric columns and noseless busts of Caesars at the Met, studying the likes of Goya and El Greco at the Frick, or tracing the peculiar turn in art from representation to idea at the Guggenheim, something I could never get my head around. After all, dung is dung. Once or twice, when feeling adventurous, I ventured uptown to the Cloisters or downtown to the World Trade Center rooftop, where I contemplated the world and my place in it.

Jimbo had shown up several times during my blue period like Santa in the off-season, unannounced and bearing care packages, a CD that he had remixed the night before, or a track that profoundly stirred him (and would inevitably profoundly stir me). There was a time when we would listen to Nusrat, Nina, *Jesus Christ Superstar* in rhapsodic rapture till dawn, but in those days DJ Jumbolaya was pressed for time because he was on the verge of something big: a project with that Queens-based Pakistani siren whose techno anthem had stirred us all the year before. The Duck had introduced him to her, and the two had hit it off, as she had needed a producer attuned to her sensibilities, while he had needed material and a muse.

Another time he had huffed and puffed up the stairs with this bootleg track called 'Freestyle Dive' from an electronic duo who hailed from 'the Peshawar underground scene.' It blew my mind. We lounged like geckos in the afternoon sun, inert but alert to the changes in melody and mood and light. Before taking off to set up turnstiles for a gig—vodka promotional, bar mitzvah—he would say something like 'I carry my theme music under my thumb.' It was great to have the monotony of those days broken by the sound of Jimbo.

Some afternoons AC dragged me out for lunch and pointers. Slapping me on the back, he would say things like 'Buck up, chum!' or 'Shake the world off your shoulders!' and, ingesting slice after slice of pizza, would philosophize thus: 'You know, when we break up with our girlfriends, or our parents die—or we get fired—it seems that the world has come to an end.' Placing his greasy hand on mine, to make sure I was listening, he continued: 'It's strange, this, ah, instinctive anticipation of extinction, of Judgment Day. It's irrational, but that's the way we've been configured by old Mama Nature. You follow, chum?' I barely did. Sometimes I suspected that AC was talking not only to himself but about himself. 'Arguably that's why our species has been so successful. The dodo would still be around if it anticipated its end. Mark my words: the platypus is on its way out, but we'll carry on . . .'

AC had been on sabbatical for two years, give or take a semester. Unable to summon the Olympic discipline required to complete his doctorate in intellectual history (or as he liked to say, the 'history of history'), he withdrew from the New School one fine day, then vanished into the musty confines of his apartment. Jimbo and I would call a few times a day, undeterred by his abrasive message—*I'm here but not here*—an adumbrative echo, he claimed, of some mantra of Continental philosophy. One night we even tried to break into his place to rescue him from himself, but the neighbors called the police on us. Scurrying down the stairs, however, we knew in the back of our minds that AC could take care of himself.

When AC finally emerged four months later, he sported a scrim of mustache above his lip and cited the 'tyranny of the third person, the pretense of objectivity' as an 'epistemological dead end.' Although we couldn't make head or tail of AC's rhetorical jujitsu then, the epiphany fundamentally changed him: he emerged a man of action, a self-styled public crusader, and in that effort began volunteering at soup kitchens and area churches before settling as a substitute at P.S. 67, a rough-and-tumble South Bronx school that had repeatedly failed to meet federal testing goals.

There was no doubt that AC had a talent for instruction, for edification. We learned that he organized interclass poetry slams, field trips to museums, the Botanic Garden, the Cloisters, Astroland. We learned of other aspects of his heterodox pedagogy: he was known to rap the Romantics, perform handstands to illustrate the force of gravity. He was also known to purchase books from his own pocket—by the pound, at the Strand—or, in flagrant disregard for copyright laws, photocopy entire novels from his own library as handouts. Although it was difficult for us to reconcile AC's hard-partying nights with his day job, over time he was recognized by others, garnering prizes and medals (inscribed in Latin for 'Excellence in Teaching') that he carried around with him wherever he went, pinned on the inside lining of his velour jacket.

❧

When I thought about it, remaining sequestered, hunkered in my apartment, I too awaited an epiphany, direction, a way out. And one hot, fateful weeknight in early August, I whimsically would have one. Feeling faint and forlorn circa three in the morning, I took a cab to a now-defunct twenty-four-hour dhaba in Little India popular with cabbies, bankers, kids from NYU and Hunter, and the neighborhood streetwalkers. As we neared, I noticed the wide-shouldered, walrus-mustached cabbie scrutinizing me in the rearview mirror, as if attempting to discern the color of my eyes.

'You are liking the food here?' he finally asked. I told him that the buffet was decent, but nothing beat the fare back home. 'You are Pakistani?' he inquired. I nodded. 'You are from Karachi.' Wondering how he could tell, I nodded again, but before I could get my head around the matter, he asked, 'You will eat with me?'

Glancing at the license wedged in the Plexiglas partition, which read 'Karim, Abdul,' I replied, 'I will eat with you, Karim Sahab.' I felt grateful, even touched; I hadn't been invited out to dinner for some time.

Though it was late, seven or eight other diners feasted on generous portions while enjoying an old Lollywood flick on the TV fixed above the counter, starring the legendary 'chocolate-box hero.' It harkened back to simple times and simple pleasures. After ordering nihari for two, we tore into naans and doused them into the soupy, savory dish of calf calves, waxing nostalgic about our hometown. There was much to recall: Bundoo Khan's legendary seekh kababs, picnicking in the shade of the palm trees at the Jinnah Mausoleum, riding pillion on a Honda C70, the tangy whiff of the Arabian Sea. Swept by sentiment, by the idea of driving fast and carefree at night, I heard myself say, 'Karim Sahab, I want to become a cab driver.'

It was a revelation to both of us.

Stroking his luxurious whiskers, Abdul Karim did not readily respond. Instead, he picked his teeth with a toothpick, knocked back a glass of water, rinsed, swallowed. 'It's tuff life,' he finally said, 'tuff business. You are sure?' I nodded vigorously. 'Cocksure?' 'Cocksure,' I repeated.

In an effort to bolster my case, I emphasized that I had been driving since the age of fourteen, or about a third of my life, and was in the possession of a valid American driver's license. I added that I was responsible and tidy.

Abdul Karim stroked his whiskers some more. Then, leaning into me, he told me that after years of driving, he had been on the lookout for 'sumbady nat anybady' to share the week with because he wanted to spend quality time with his family but 'all the buoys' he met were 'first-class rotters.' The stars, it seemed, were aligned. In an avuncular tone, he said, '*Tum achay bachay ho*,' which translates to 'You're a good kid,' and after delivering a pithy speech invoking unity, faith, and discipline, principles that guided his career, he offered me a job and his hand. Unbeknownst to most, especially Ma, I would become, in less than a fortnight, a bonafide New York City cabbie.

Abdul Karim explained to me that most cabbies worked for fleet operators, paying a leasing fee by shift or for an extended period of time, but he was that increasingly rare animal known in cabbie argot as an 'owner-operator'—a medallion holder who drives his own cab. I would be his one and only employee. Abdul Karim walked me through the entire process. Getting a cabbie license can typically take up to seventy calendar days, but he suggested that I opt for what the New York Taxi and Limousine Commission calls the 'expedited processing system,' whereby it's possible to secure one within ten days, two weeks.

'To be qualified,' Abdul Karim would explain, 'you must be having no history of criminal nature and no prior revocations. You must be owing no money to DMV, PVB, or TLC and you must be having letter from owner, which I will be giving.' Moreover, you must:

1. 'be at least 19 years of age';
2. 'be a legal resident of the United States and have a legal address in the United States';
3. 'be examined by a doctor and have the doctor sign and date the medical history form';
4. have a 'chauffeur's license or equivalent';
5. have an original Social Security card;
6. have 'no outstanding obligations to the DMV, NYC PVB, or NYC TLC';

7.   'file a notarized Child Support Certification form';
8.   'complete a NYS DMV certified defensive driving class no
     more than 6 months before filing the application';
9.   'complete the TLC driver application and have the form . .
     . notarized . . .'; and
10. 'purchase 3 money orders totaling $219.'

The procedure was surprisingly straightforward: I appeared at
the TLC office one afternoon, with a manila folder stuffed with
forms, photographs, identification cards, and other paperwork,
and walked out forty-five minutes later with what is called a hack
license. Then Mini Auntie organized a doctor's examination at Beth
Israel (I told her it was required by my next job, which *she* assumed
was in the financial services industry), and Abdul Karim hooked
me up with his friend for the requisite eighty-hour driving course
at the cumbersomely named H.A.N.A.C./ NYS Federation of
Taxi Drivers Academy in Long Island City. The course was tough
going.

For two weeks, I woke at the crack of dawn, showered, shaved,
and changed, grabbed a blueberry bagel and coffee at the corner
bodega, took the 2 to Times Square, and then the W to Long
Island City. Fifteen minutes by car on clear roads, it was a grueling
hour, hour-and-a-half commute at rush hour to H.A.N.A.C./NYS
Federation of Taxi Drivers Academy. Known to us cabbies as
Hunuck, the building, like most of the architecture in Long Island
City, is uninspired and functional. The classroom was neat and spare
but reeked of sweat, anxiety, and by day's end, mysterious foreign
foods. Classes began at eight-thirty and continued till five-thirty,
and if you were late, you'd have to make up lost time.

There were nineteen of us, none of whom was Pakistani (although
I learned that South Asians comprised a third of the New York
cabbie population, distributed almost equally among Pakistanis,
Bangladeshis, and Indians). A bony Indian from Patna, a wide-eyed
Bangladeshi, a square-faced Egyptian, and a small, intense Xingjiangi

fellow sat up front, taking abundant notes, while the self-designated backbenchers—an Albanian, a Haitian, and a Sikh—mostly glowered. They had that look in their eyes that said, *I break you in two*. The rest hailed from the Dark Continent: there was a Kenyan nightwatchman, a Beninese busboy, and a convivial Congolese tribesman named Kojo with whom I became lunch buddies. Over sandwiches and soda, he regaled me with riveting tales of his barefoot and bloody escape from the copper-rich province of Kivu during a routine spasm of violence.

The whole Hunuck experience recalled freshman orientation, without the balloons and handouts, pizza parties, barbecues, and otherwise nurturing environment. Our instructor, the sole Caucasian in our midst, introduced himself as Gator. Bald, slack-jawed, six feet something, and an A-hole, Gator was known to pitch an eraser at you if you fell asleep, or were not paying attention, or sometimes if you couldn't string together a sentence in the Queen's English. 'Listen up, knuckleheads,' he'd say every morning, 'we got a shitload to do, so I ain't repeatin' myself, 'n' I ain't teachin' ESL.'

Over the course of a fortnight, we covered much ground, from traffic laws to the topography of each borough, including each hotel, hospital, highway extension, and dead end. Lectures were typically punctuated by off-color anecdotes from what could have only been personal experience: 'There are still crack whores in Bushwick who'll give you a blowjob for *five smackers*!' At such junctures, the frontbenchers inevitably asked, 'But will it be on the exam, please?' Gator might have been a proper asshole, but the Gator Method seemed to work: only one of us failed (and everybody called everybody else knucklehead by the end).

On the last day, we said our farewells with genuine feeling, though nobody really kept in touch, but on 9/11 we frantically dug up each other's numbers, scrawled on the backs of receipts and folded scraps of notebook paper, and called to exchange disyllabic assurances and expressions of disbelief: 'You all right, man?' 'Yeah, I'm okay, you all right?' 'Yeah, I'm okay but is screwed up.' 'Yeah, screwed up.' 'You hear about anybody?' Only the Albanian and the Beninese busboy were unaccounted for. They might have returned to their homelands, or changed houses or numbers. We never knew.

Kojo and I remained friendly and took the TLC taxi test together at eight in the morning of an auspicious day, August 14th, 2001, Pakistan Day. A hundred or so hopeful cabbies milled about outside the center on Queens Boulevard, red-eyed, excited, pacing while chain-smoking Newports—everybody with the same fears and aspirations, the same information pulsing in their heads. Kojo, dressed in a metallic green suit and wafting cologne, quizzed me as we stood outside. At half past eight, we hugged each other and filed inside. Under the vigilant gaze of the five proctors, we were handed numbers that corresponded to seats in the hall. Soon afterward the Master Cabbie arrived, a small gray man with a weak voice, and went over the format of the three-part exam: in the English section the MC played an audiotape of street addresses that we were to match on our booklets; the map-reading section involved matching street addresses to our individual handout maps; and finally, the tertiary portion was SAT-style, multiple choice, with questions that included the following:

Which of the following is false?

A. Madison Square Park is located at 25th Street and Fifth Avenue.
B. Times Square is so named because there is a big clock on the tower.
C. Wall Street is so named because there used to be a wall there to keep the Indians out.
D. Manhattan College is not located in Manhattan.
E. Long Island University is located on Long Island.

Throgs Neck Bridge crosses

A. Jamaica Bay
B. Westchester Bay

C. The East River
D. The Harlem River
E. Newtown Creek

Another name for Willowbrook Parkway is

A. Malcolm X Boulevard
B. Jackie Robinson Parkway
C. Dr. Martin Luther King Junior Expressway
D. H. Rap Brown Drive
E. Master Fard Mohammed Parkway

Although the test was challenging, Kojo and I finished on time and passed with flying colors, getting only two questions wrong between us. We hugged and high-fived outside as if we had just won the green card lottery. Kojo's palms were sweaty, and he seemed to glow with a halo of joy. 'You need calling card?' he asked.

'Huh?' I replied.

'You call yo fada,' he said. 'I call mine's. Fadas be proud.'

When I smiled and shook my head, he sprinted to a nearby phone booth, holding his pockets to keep the change from jangling. I watched him dial excitedly, massage his shapely bald head as he waited for the line to go through, and yelp into the receiver like a child when he heard the voice on the other end.

I pulled out a smoke, lit it, and inhaled deeply.

The day after the night at Jake's, I stayed in bed, insensible and inert, but when the phone rang later that afternoon, I moved slightly, stretching my stubby legs and straightening my hairless toes, and when the answering machine switched on, I turned over on my stomach and buried my head under the pillow but could still hear AC's voice. 'Rise and shine, chum,' he began in a rasp that suggested that he hadn't slept or had just woken. 'You know, you shouldn't pick fights. You have neither the physique nor the talent.' After a sigh, he continued, 'I'm, ah, sorry about what happened . . . I should've seen it coming . . . but didn't, or didn't want to . . . and there I was, like some kind of moron, caught between aggressor and victim, arbitrating with brute force, like an animal . . .' Blowing smoke into the mouthpiece, he added, 'Let me tell you this much: when push comes to shove, we're all the same. When somebody hits you, you hit back.' There was a long contemplative pause, followed by the characteristic sound of chewing. He had probably been chewing things over for a while. 'Anyway,' he added, 'I'm calling to tell you that I'm headed to the Shaman's and would like you to come along. Do you think you can secure your, ah, conveyance?'

Rolling out of bed half-dressed and half-asleep, I reached for the receiver, but prudence dictated delaying the discussion. The Shaman Run, an expedition deep into the recesses of Connecticut, was a wacky, misguided project, born, perhaps, of AC's recent anxieties and crusader kick. Besides, taking Abdul Karim's cab would have been irresponsible of me. I would have to come up with an excuse, something plausible yet airtight, but my head was cloudy, and I needed to be fully conscious and caffeinated before calling AC back. In the interim, I performed my waking rituals—drinking a half gallon of cold water, urinating, smoking by the window, sipping a mug of muddy Lipton—and checked the other messages on the machine.

Somebody from the 'boutique research house' where I had interviewed several weeks ago had called, and a terse electronic voice informed me that my credit rating would be adversely affected if I did not pay up immediately. Ma, in a voice stretched over thousands of miles, time zones, static, exhorted me to have multivitamins daily, say my prayers, and make reservations on PIA, the national carrier, for the winter. As always she also relayed the news: 'Things are tense here, beta—there is talk of some Afghanistan campaign-shampaign. I don't know what it means for us, but it is not good. Don't worry. Musharraf is going to make a speech any day. Take care of yourself,

Shehzad, say your prayers, and remember, you are my life. Khuda-hafiz.' About to call her back, I remembered that I had cut long distance (and made a mental note to buy a calling card).

Jimbo had phoned four times and left two messages. In the first he sounded rip-roaring drunk and sang the fragment of a song that went *I said no no no no baby, please don't cry . . . 'cause all the leaves come down*, but in the next he soberly reminded me that I had to accompany him to his father's in half an hour, a monthly event I had been roped into soon after we became friends. I had subsequently become an integral part of the ceremony. Left to their devices, Jimbo and 'Old Man Khan' typically yelled at each other from across the table or, at best, dined in silence. I enjoyed dinner at the Khan residence, the company, the food, and the attention of Amo, Jimbo's hot kid sister. 'Din-din dude,' he said, 'same bat time, same bat channel.'

'Shit,' I said, smacking my head. I was late. And you do not want to keep Old Man Khan waiting. In twelve minutes flat, I showered, changed, and donned my Superman T-shirt, a pair of jeans, and lizard-skin cowboy boots. Then, surprisingly, having time to kill, I cracked open a Corona, lit another cigarette, and turned on the TV. A sullen meteorologist on New York One announced that the weather would remain warm and overcast, 'temperatures in the mid-seventies with a fifty percent chance of rain after midnight.'

When the news followed, I had the urge to flip, tune out, watch Telemundo. Since I had cut cable, however, I had to contend with network programming: talking heads and reality shows and advertising. Instead, I switched the TV off, grabbed a jacket, patted myself down for wallet, cigarettes, and keys, and headed out.

At the Moroccan's newsstand down the street, I found myself leafing through dailies and weeklies when I should have been in and out with the calling card. It was compelling reading: a columnist for the *Post* wrote, 'The response to this unimaginable 21st-century Pearl Harbor should be simple and swift—kill the bastards . . . As for the cities or countries that host these worms, bomb them to basketball courts.' In *Time* I came across a piece entitled 'The Case of Rage and Retribution' that began: 'For once let's have no "grief counselors" standing by with banal consolations . . . no fatuous rhetoric about "healing" . . . What we need is a unified, unifying Pearl Harbor sort of purple American fury—a ruthless indignation that doesn't leak away in a week or two, wandering into Prozac-induced forgetfulness . . . or into corruptly thoughtful relativism—'

The exercise was interrupted by the Moroccan, who emerged from the booth, asking, 'What happen?'

A voluble, inquisitive guy, he wore round professor's glasses, a perpetual five o'clock shadow, and a checkered button-down every day. He allowed me credit if I left home without my wallet and took the liberty of reporting whether Pakistan had figured in the headlines. In recent weeks, there was much reporting to do. Consequently, I attempted to be quick, repeating his query, 'What happened?'

'I,' he replied.

'I?'

'Your I?'

'My I?'

'Is busted.'

'Oh!' I blurted, tracing the ring of soreness with my fingertips. It was a simple question and begged a simple answer, but I found myself lying. 'I fell,' I said. 'It's fine . . . it's healing.'

'You falling down,' he asked, or told me, I couldn't quite tell, but his voice betrayed palpable concern, perhaps the concern one Muslim has for another. Sucking his teeth, he scrutinized my face, waiting for me to add something, but I pursed my lips, maintaining a poker face. I was in no mood to solicit sympathy or assign fault. As my VP would say, *You gotta roll with the punches.* Purchasing the newspaper of record, and the latest edition of *Big Butt*, I marched off, duly forgetting the calling card in all the excitement.

Leaning on the derelict scaffolding outside my apartment building, I awaited Jimbo, shielding myself from the world with the open newspaper, with one eye on the street, the way private dicks posed in the movies. At precisely seven-thirty, a behemoth schlepped heavily toward me in hand-stitched moccasins, listening, as it were, to his own theme music. There was no mistaking Jimbo. We hugged, high-fived; he complimented me on my shiner. As we started toward the 72nd Street subway stop, he absently inquired, 'What news, dude?' I told him that there was a chance of rain tonight, realizing we did not have an umbrella between us.

FOUR

Old Man Khan lived in a neat narrow two-story, three-bedroom row house on Woodland, a street lined with solid leafy oaks not more than a ten-minute walk from the PATH station in downtown Jersey City. Jersey City was like Manhattan gone awry. I always found this strange, not only because they are separated by the same river but because of their proximate and parallel histories. Old Man Khan would tell you that like Manhattan, Jersey City was settled by Indians (the Lenni Lenape) and colonized by the Dutch, as if he had been around then. He derived this weird sense of pride from having lived in Jersey City for twenty-five years. In fact, after politely refusing his offer many times, one precious Sunday afternoon I found myself in the Jersey City Museum—situated in the historic Van Vorst district—alongside Jimbo and Amo, shepherded by the patriarch. It was an underwhelming experience at best and a peculiarly stubborn memory. I gave Jimbo crap about it whenever I got the chance. The three of us shuffled around the cramped rooms like schoolchildren who need to pee, gaping at maladroit sketches of local historic figures such as Burgermeester Reyniersz Puaw and Paulus Hook and lithographs of Jersey City through the ages in sepia—beginning with the first settlement at Communipaw or what's now Liberty State Park (but was, till the seventies, quite literally a dump). We learned that other settlements followed adjacently, suspicious of each other, often at daggers drawn. In the early nineteenth century, they were, I imagine, forcibly incorporated into the unimaginatively named town. There was a brief Golden Age of Jersey City, when the town had a certain role in regional commerce, but Jersey City was where the railroads ended, and toward the end of the Great Railroad Era, it fell into decline. It hadn't been a pretty place to begin with. Then it became ugly.

Since Jersey City is about as close to Ellis Island as Manhattan—you can see the Statue of Liberty's backside from Liberty State Park—waves of immigrants washed ashore. Till about World War II, they were mostly German, Italian, Irish. Subsequently they were Filipinos, Indians, Cubans. At one point of the tour, a recorded female voice informed us that Jersey City is one of the most diverse towns in the States: 'Like parts of California, Caucasians are a minority, or less than a third of the population, outnumbered by African-Americans and Hispanics.' Old Man Khan would tell you that during his watch, the city had also become one of the largest American hubs of Arabs and Muslims. These communities, like their antecedents perhaps, remained largely insular, sequestered, grating against each other. From the thirty-year tenure of the infamous Mayor 'Hanky Panky' Hague (who harped about 'darkies' and outed commies) in the first half of the century, to the reign of the murderous Dotbusters (the gang who stalked and killed Asians with clubs and boots and pipes) well into the eighties, Jersey City has been defined by a decidedly troubled bustle.

You could feel it walking down some streets: people didn't avert their eyes or nod when you walked past but often stared, either tacitly claiming you as their own or dismissing you as the Other. You couldn't be sure if it was the ingredients or the pot. The skyscrapers downtown were erected in the seventies and looked it: you didn't see any stucco or stonework, only steel and darkened windows. At night, the buildings seemed to brood. And despite the gentrification of Jersey City through the Great Bull Run, there were boarded-up storefronts in the side streets, closed movie theaters, bodegas with iron grills. Except for a Duane Reade and a McDonald's, there weren't many familiar signs.

We walked fast because we were running late, and when Jimbo was running late, he would stick his head out and teeter on his toes, compelled, it would seem, by a formidable gust. Usually he would point out the ramshackle mosque implicated in the first World Trade Center bombing, as if it were part of a walking tour, like the Jackie Robinson statue or the 'world famous Colgate Clock.' The mosque—which appeared about as sinister as a walk-up dance studio or a karate dojo—had been stoned back in the day, and for months its windows remained cracked. Before the calamity, Old Man Khan would attend the mosque for Friday prayer, pubescent Jimbo in tow.

But Jimbo had not said much during the hour-long commute, save *yeah, whatever*, as I reviewed, for my own benefit mostly, the Girl from Ipanema episode, the incident at Jake's, the exchange with the Moroccan, and most urgently, the developing Shaman Run. 'Don't you think,' I continued, 'it's unfair of AC to ask me to drive the cab to Connecticut? It may mean a lot to him, but it would be reckless of me. I mean, what if something was to happen, like we get pulled over, or have an accident?'

Jimbo grunted in response. It was as if he were orbiting another planet. *Gee*, I thought, *thanks*. He spoke up only when I asked, 'What am I supposed to tell your father about my eye?'

'You got mugged, dude.'

When I reminded him that Giuliani had largely purged the city of muggers, Jimbo said, 'He don't know that.' Apparently the last time Old Man Khan had been in the city was during the tenure of Mayor Dinkins, as part of the construction crew that culled the wreckage from the first attack on the World Trade Center.

As we turned onto Woodland, we walked passed the suburban artifacts that always seemed odd to me as a denizen of Manhattan, or Karachi, for that matter: barbecue sets, bicycles, tricycles, plastic slides, lawn furniture, a hammock, a gnome. There weren't any such items outside the Khan residence, but the tapered patch of grass where Old Man Khan spent his summer evenings had recently been

shorn, the tiger lilies and gardenias watered, and the small hedge
expertly manicured. On tiptoe, you could peer into the spare Khan
drawing room through parted curtains and iron bars. A pea green
sofa and a tall shelf housing a TV and VCR were the only furniture
pieces of note. The floor was covered by wall-to-wall pine shag,
and the walls were bare but for a wide-angle picture of the Kaaba
surrounded by specks of pilgrims.

Pausing to collect himself before the door, Jimbo mumbled,
'Dude, don't like mention the Duck or nothin'.'

'You know I'd never do that, yaar.'

AC would. AC was also persona non grata in the Khan household.
Not only had he shown up four Wild Turkeys into the evening one
night, but over dinner had announced that Jimbo had been going
out with the Duck for years. He also called legendary leader Khan
Abdul Ghaffar Khan, the Pathan Gandhi, a pansy. AC and Old
Man Khan reportedly came close to blows.

Slapping me on the back, Jimbo said, 'You're a good man, Charlie
Brown.'

Suspecting something afoot, I asked, 'What *is* going on with the
Duck?'

'Nothin' dude, nothin'.'

'Bull. Something's not right. It's obvious. If you don't tell me, I'll
start howling.'

'Okay, okay, simmer down, dude. I'll tell ya: the Duck popped
the question.'

'Whoa!' I exclaimed. 'Congrats, yaar!'

'*Shush!*'

'When was this? What did you say? Why didn't you tell me?'

'Like a month ago,' he said, biting his lip. 'I told her, gimme some
time to think about it, so I thought about it, but when I asked Old
Man Khan, he shot it down, like fuggettaboutit!'

'So?' It seemed that I could only manage either monosyllabic
exclamations or exasperated queries when I should've uttered some
appropriate words of support or consolation.

'So nothin', dude,' he said, ringing the buzzer. 'Gotta go in.'

We made our way down the wainscoted hallway wafting the heady aroma of fried onions and garlic, passed the door on the right that led up to the Khans' tenants—Eddie and Myla Davis, a smart young African-American couple—and down, to the basement, which housed a broken bamboo furniture set, Jimbo's Ping-Pong table, and miscellaneous Pakistani memorabilia. On the left-hand side, there was a superfluous door that was always kept locked and led to the 'living room' and 'study,' although the living room and study were not more than a stretch running parallel to the hallway, divided by an ornate walnut screen. The place was simple, even humble, but from the way Old Man Khan held himself in supreme equipoise, gripping the arms of the leatherette armchair as if it were a throne, you could be sure that he believed his home was his castle.

A bald, fair, barrel-chested man with arching eyebrows, fierce blue eyes, and a bulbous nose set in a corrugated face, Old Man Khan had the bearing of a bull and, except for his clipped white beard, reminded me of a textbook picture of Mussolini. Jimbo told me that he passed for Italian in Bensonhurst, Greek in Astoria, Russian in Brighton, Jewish on the Upper West Side (or the old Lower East Side) and was always told that he did not look Pakistani, which of course meant nothing. Any Pakistani could tell you that the population of the sixth-largest country in the world ranges from black, kinky-haired Makranis on the southern coast to blond, blue-eyed descendants of Alexander's armies in the snow-streaked valleys of the north. Unlike most Pakistani men, or Mussolini for that matter, Old Man Khan would usually be found wearing a tight little apron over a wifebeater, a faded, singed fuchsia thing that read KISS THE COOK in white letters across the front.

When we entered, he growled. 'I have not seen you in a long time, Jamshed beta.' The month before, Jimbo had canceled our visit without explanation. I guessed it had to do with the Duck. 'Sorry I'm late, Baba jan,' Jimbo replied, kissing his father on the forehead. 'The trains ain't runnin' right.' Not only were trains still running irregularly, but the detour through 34th Street had taken longer than the usual Chambers Street route. Chambers Street was rubble.

Jimbo circled around the breakfast table to Amo, who had been standing by the stove, beaming, held her by the waist, and kissed her on the forehead: 'Hi, hot stuff.' Amo rolled her eyes before glancing over at me. She had a thing for me. When we had entered, she did a sort of half wave, like, *hi, you*, before coyly averting her narrow, beryline eyes. Each feature on her face was arranged with great precision. She was reminiscent of Vivien Leigh—an eighteen-year-old Vivien Leigh in hijab, blue jeans, and red and white Puma sneakers.

In family photographs, however, Amo had been a chubby kid, wholly unremarkable (not unlike her mother), who had only recently metamorphosed into a swan. Consequently, she was still getting used to her body, as if she had just been bought an expensive new dress. A few weeks into her freshman year at Rutgers (where she was studying to be an actuary, of all things), she donned a hijab. I did not know why she did it. I did not particularly care for it. When she noticed my bruise, she had covered her open mouth, but I had shrugged and coolly grinned, like I was a tough guy, and these things happen to tough guys.

It was my turn to pay my respects to the Pathan patriarch. Raising my hand to my forehead, I approached him and said, 'Salam, Khan Sahab.'

Waving his arms in the air, he cried, 'What happened, beta?'

'I got mugged,' I blurted.

Leaning forward, Old Man Khan crushed his fingers in two veiny fists and said, 'You went down fighting, did you?'

'Of course,' I replied, lying baldly, blushing.

'That is my boy!' he exclaimed, running his heavy, calloused hands over my head. I could not help loving the old man in spite of his temper and idiosyncrasies and peculiar attachment to Jersey City. He was genuine, affectionate, like a father should be. 'Now tell me,' he said. 'How is your mother?'

Old Man Khan always asked me about Ma, as if they were old friends from back home, even though they had never met. Although he might have imagined her to be like his late wife, from what I could gather, the two were nothing alike. Referred to only as Begum, Mrs. Khan had been short and dark, the eldest of a brood of seven. After their houses had been burned down by a Hindu mob in India, her parents escaped to Pakistan in '47, only to spend years in the wilderness of early Karachi, residing in makeshift housing outside the city with no running water or electricity. Eventually her father managed to secure some clerical position with the government and modest accommodation in the middle-class neighborhood of Paposh Nagar. Despite their circumstances, her father made sure Begum received a 'first-class education.'

Even though Old Man Khan hailed from a part of the country where women were not generally encouraged to attend school, he took great pride in his late wife's academic accomplishments. Ironically, Begum may not have amounted to much without the Pathan. As Old Man Khan told it, she dropped out of Inter to take care of her siblings when her mother was diagnosed with ovarian cancer. The two met in the emergency room of the Seventh-Day Adventist Hospital, the night he had checked in for a knife wound to the gut—suffered during a dustup with the 'Chinese ruffians of Saddar'—and the night she had brought her mother in to die. They fell desperately in love. Except Begum could not simply leave her siblings or 'marry below her station.' Consequently for years they maintained a secret affair, 'through the thick and the thin,' warding off suitors and other tribulations while meeting weekly at Hill Park.

When circumstances finally permitted, they decided to immigrate to America. They upped and left in the summer of '72. Old Man Khan took the first job a ruffian could attain—in an Irish-owned construction outfit—and supported Begum through a bachelor's and a master's in psychology. She bore him two children on maternity leave from Hudson County Community College, where she taught till 1989, when, like her mother before her, she succumbed to cancer. 'I don't know why God did not take me,' Old Man Khan once said to me. 'But who am I to question Him?'

'My mother is well,' I replied, remembering that I had forgotten to call her back. 'She was asking after you.'

'You will give her my salam,' Old Man Khan instructed.

'Yes, sir.'

Then in a tone meant for recalcitrant children, he boomed, 'Why are you all around standing like this? Sit down! Dinner is served.'

We squeezed around the table before the feast that Old Man Khan had prepared (because he maintained modern women should not cook) and Amo had quickly laid out. There was saffron-spiced lamb biryani, chicken karahi with tomatoes, cilantro and green peppers, bite-sized shami kababs, and an earthenware pot of daal garnished with fried onions and garlic. As usual, I was informed that everything was halal, and as always, Old Man Khan proclaimed, *In the name of God, the Beneficent and Merciful*, before digging in. Before he could reach for the chicken, however, Amo said, 'Baba jan, you know you can't have any of that.'

'I made it, beti,' he replied.

'Y'know you've got to watch your cholesterol, and the karahi is like swimming in ghee!' Glistening with clarified butter, the chicken was killer. 'You can only have the daal and biryani.'

'When my time comes, beti, God will take me.'

'Yeah and then what will happen to me?'

'Acha, acha,' Old Man Khan muttered, browbeaten, 'I will do as you say.'

As we ate, we heard the muffled thumps of the Davises walking about above and the occasional but palpable screech of chairs across their parquet floor. 'Jamshed Lala,' Amo began, 'd'you know Myla just had a baby? They named him Anthony, and he's like one of those Cabbage Patch Kids. You gotta see him.' Hunched over a heaping plate of biryani, Jimbo grunted. '*You* should have a baby.' I couldn't tell if Amo was messing with her brother. 'Jamshed Lala,' Amo repeated, craning to get his attention, 'when do I get a nephew?'

With his big head bowed, Jimbo muttered, 'Gotta get hitched first, sweety.' Just then Old Man Khan looked up fiercely, his bushy white eyebrows meeting in a tight knot on his broad furrowed forehead.

'Then get married,' Amo chirped. 'You're the right age and everything. You just, like, need to find the right girl—'

'Aamna khanum,' Old Man Khan growled, 'eat your food.'

'Baba jan,' Amo said, 'sometimes you're such a killjoy.'

In an attempt to change the subject, Old Man Khan turned toward me and asked, 'How is the hotshot banker?'

All eyes were suddenly on me, and for an instant I considered what reaction my turn as a cabbie would bring. 'Well,' I began, 'actually, I'm kind of on sabbatical, Khan Sahab. I thought it was time for a change,' I continued, 'for something better.'

My disclosure met with a general consensus of silence, as if the Family Khan had at last discovered that I was a fraud, a failure. Old Man Khan's eyes narrowed as if processing the information word by word. Then he proclaimed, 'Bravo!'

Jimbo looked up, like *What the?*

'My only regret in life,' Old Man Khan continued, 'is that I didn't have the courage to change my profession. It was too late for me . . . but, ma'shallah, I have lived a full life in America. I have raised a family. I will not cry crocodile's tears.'

'You mean you won't *cry over spilled milk?*' Amo interjected.

Old Man Khan looked at her quizzically. 'Why would I cry about the spilling of the milk?'

'*Any*-way, they say that college grads today change jobs like five point six times, on average.'

Sitting opposite me, Jimbo made a funny face, probably because he had had more than five point six jobs since graduation—more like nine or ten—none to his father's satisfaction. Admittedly, Old Man Khan was a difficult man to please. Once upon a time he had had elaborate plans for Jimbo, managing somehow to get him into

P.S. 6 where, he would remind you, *Kramer vs. Kramer* was shot (though he'd never seen the movie). Every morning at seven little Jimbo would board the PATH, change trains, sometimes take a bus, hauling a backpack and an Indiana Jones lunchbox that alternately yielded peanut-butter-and-jelly and shami-kabab-and-butter sandwiches. Within a year he made it into the Gifted and Talented class and school band, requiring him to haul a tuba. After Begum's death, however, Jimbo fell in with the 'bad crowd' in junior high and once, while 'tagging' a train, was even arrested. Old Man Khan had decided then that Jimbo was a bad seed. He remained one ever since. The two years he spent at CUNY, Jimbo took courses that sounded like mumbo jumbo to Old Man Khan: ear training, music theory, acoustics engineering, mastering, multitrack recording. Jimbo told me that his father once said, 'Fifteen years I worked for you, and you are going to play bongo drums?' Ironically, Jimbo attributed his innate musical sense to listening to his old man hammering nails into joists and rafters.

Since careers and plans were fraught issues, I asked Old Man Khan about gardening. If you cared to listen, Old Man Khan could and would hold forth on plant husbandry methods that he claimed to have pioneered over the years:

1. Crushed ground coffee sprinkled in topsoil helps plants grow better.
2. Crushed cayenne pepper works as a pesticide.
3. Cinnamon halts disease.
4. Milk can be used to clean plants (because it possesses the requisite acidity).

'Only yesterday,' Old Man Khan gushed, 'I ordered a very specialized plant that is inavailable in all the United States of America! Can you believe it? Something that is inavailable here!'

'What is it called, Khan Sahab?'

'In China it is called *mudan*. *Mu* means male and *dan* means red.

Together it means 'the plant that can reproduce by sucker and seed.' They also call it *Hua Wang*, 'King of Flowers.' In English it is only called tree peony. Peony! Everything is lost in the translation.'

'Why is it so special?'

'It is like an orchid. It is beautiful and incommon.'

'Uncommon,' Amo interjected.

'You know, Shehzad beta,' he said, squinting philosophically, 'you feel like you are doing God's work, making Heaven on earth. This has always been my jihad.'

I nodded vigorously, as if I understood exactly what he was trying to say, but didn't quite get it. It didn't jell with the modern connotation of jihad that had entered discourse with a bang: waging war against errant Muslims and non-Muslims alike. 'You have to be productive in life,' he continued. 'You have to struggle against yourself.' Old Man Khan reminded me that the term translates to 'struggle,' particularly the struggle within: to remain moral and charitable, acquire knowledge, and so on.

While I mulled what my jihad should be, Amo passed the dish of biryani. 'You must try it,' she insisted. 'It's Begum's recipe.' Although stuffed, I took the casserole because Amo had such delicate wrists, I was afraid they would snap right off. 'It's not delicious,' I said, shoving a spoonful in my mouth. 'It's out of this world.' Amo beamed again. She had a winning smile.

During dinner, I caught her stealing glances at me. In turn, I smiled tightly, politely, pulling my chin in to hide the lump in my throat. There was no doubt that Amo was beautiful, vivacious, a firecracker in hijab, but she was off limits, not only because she was my pal's sister but because she was Old Man Khan's daughter. If something untoward happened, he would make boti out of me.

Besides, I figured, Amo and I were not on the same page anyway. The hijab weirded me out. Donning the thing was a matter of interpretation, faulty interpretation; Ma, a paragon of virtue and grace and sensibility, never wore one.

Like most Muslims, I read the Koran once circa age ten and, like some, had combed through it afterward. There were issues in the Holy Book that were indisputable, like eating pork, but the directives concerning liquor could easily be interpreted either way. You should not, for instance, pray when hammered. As for the hijab, the Koran mentions that women should cover their 'ornaments,' and any way you look at it, that means breasts and beyond. Men are exempt because they do not possess ornaments.

Moreover, unlike Amo, I did not care to wear my identity on my sleeve.

∾

When Old Man Khan withdrew to the bedroom after dinner to say his prayers, and Jimbo and Amo cleared the table, I snuck out for a smoke on the way to the restroom. There are few pleasures in life comparable to smoking after a Pakistani meal. Indeed, it was a rare event, like sitting at a proper table with a fork and a knife and a folded napkin; but the best smoke I had had in years did not follow a Pakistani meal but a traditional American one: after spending Thanksgivings with Mini Auntie and the Khans, my gay friend Lawrence né Larry had invited me to Omaha to a real American turkey dinner, complete with stuffing, cranberry sauce, and a drunken uncle swinging elbows, knocking down bottles and chairs. As Thanksgiving was around the corner again, Lawrence had informed me that he would be 'delighted' to have me once again. Last time his mother had said, 'He's so well-mannered.' 'Maybe,' she mused, 'it's because he's *Mooslim*.' Those were the days.

Jimbo joined me halfway into my Rothman, and together we watched the massive violet cloud that hung above us. After some time he asked, 'Whaddya think?'

'Don't think it'll rain, yaar, at least not right now.'

'That ain't what I'm talkin' about, dude.'

'Oh. Sorry. You mean, about the Duck situation.'

'Wake up 'n' smell the chai!'

Don't ask me, I thought. *I don't know nothing.* AC was the go-to guy for advice and instruction. I was a village idiot. 'I don't know, I mean, it's not like the end of the world,' I said, feebly parroting AC's words of wisdom to me. 'He'll eventually come around, right?'

'Negative.'

'Of course, he will, yaar. You're his only son. Give him time.'

'Too late, dude. Duck's on the warpath, throwin' fits, givin' ultimatums. She asked me before, and I kept tellin' her, just wait, gimme time, I'm going to talk it over with the old man, you know, get his blessings an' all, but he never did, and she can't wait no more. She's five years older an' wants to make babies 'cause her ovaries are dyin' or dryin' up or somethin'.'

'Right. Okay. So I guess you have to figure some things out. I mean, maybe you should think of it as an exercise, in terms of absolutes, Old Man Khan versus the Duck: who can you do without? It's a rhetorical exercise, because your father's your father—'

Jimbo sighed. 'I kinda love her, dude . . .'

My cigarette had burned to the filter, but I kept sucking on it for inspiration. 'Then tell him,' I managed to say.

Just then Amo's voice rang like an alarm through the corridor: '*Jam-shed La-la! Sheh-zad La-la!*' Handing me a pod of cardamom for my breath, Jimbo stomped deliberately inside, muttering, 'Gotta go in.' Popping the pod in my mouth, I crushed the cigarette under my heel and followed.

They were in the living room—Old Man Khan leaning forward on the sofa, Amo curled by his feet like a Siamese—watching the ten o'clock news with the volume turned way up. The news was all bad. There were reports that the tap water might be poisoned, that anthrax permeated the air; reports of strange occurrences just outside our field of vision or the purview of our consciousness; sightings of dark men with dirty bombs and devices in their shoes. Planes appeared and disappeared over the horizon. Our nerves already frayed, we were told to report suspicious activities, to be vigilant.

Above all, death recurred on TV, in vivid color, charred bodies among concrete ruins, like pornography.

'*Allah rehem karay*,' proclaimed Old Man Khan. God have mercy on us all. Apparently Rumsfeld had announced a major offensive against the Taliban. It would be a good war, a just war. 'Is it right?' Old Man Khan cried. His face had turned beet red. 'Can anybody tell me?' Reaching for the remote, Amo turned the TV off. 'I don't understand, Aamna khanum. Why bomb? Why break? Why destroy?'

Although I had no particular sympathy for the Afghans—they had been shooting themselves in the foot for the last thirty years— Old Man Khan was as much a citizen of Jersey as a Pathan, which commentators were reporting 'is the broad ethnic umbrella covering a portion of northern Pakistan *and* most of Afghanistan.' Old Man Khan sympathized with his people even if they contributed to the Taliban. But it wasn't that he was simply torn between here and there; I think he was cut up about watching the edifices he had built with his own hands being razed again and again. 'We should plant seeds in the mountains, grow flowers. Imagine, beta, trees everywhere and orchards, gardens . . . What do you think?' he asked nobody in particular, holding his chest. 'What do you think?'

'Baba jan,' Amo pleaded, 'you've got to chill out. It's not worth it. You're gonna get another heart attack.'

As Old Man Khan took deep yogic breaths, I gave Jimbo a look that said *this probably isn't the best time for a chat about the Duck situation,* and he looked back as if to say *hey, no shit.* Then I excused myself to make a phone call and called AC from the wall phone in the kitchen. 'Hello? You there? Okay, well, anyway, we're on for the Shaman Run. Connecticut, or bust.' In Jersey that night, I had figured out my jihad. 'But there's no way I get the cab before tomorrow night. All right, yaar, gotta go. Ciao, for now.'

When I returned, I found the three sitting on the divan, Old Man Khan in the middle, flanked by his children, as if posing for a family portrait. Old Man Khan was smoking one of those short filterless cigarillos that smelled wonderful, like a night out in Lisbon or something, but tasted like pure crap. Peeling himself off the sunken seat, Jimbo said, 'Gotta jet.'

'But you haven't even had dessert yet, Jamshed Lala,' Amo interjected.

'Next time, doll face.'

'Okay, just like wait a second.' Running into the kitchen, she returned with a Tupperware container of sweet carrot halvah that she placed in my hands. 'This is for you.'

'Thought you didn't cook.'

'This is dessert.'

'Well, um, thank you, Amo, for your hospitality.'

'You're very welcome, Shehzad Lala.'

After Jimbo kissed his father and sister, I salamed Old Man Khan and patted Amo on the back, who raised her shoulder in appreciation. As we were walking out, Old Man Khan yelled out, 'I am looking forward to seeing you again next month, Jamshed beta.'

Jimbo turned around and smiled.

Outside, he started talking, as if addressing his conscience: 'But like when the old man gets angry or choked up or whatever, he starts holdin' his heart and his face turns red, and he starts breathin' like a warthog. It happened a couple of times. It's crazy scary. He says it's nothin', he pretends he's still tough but he ain't, and I don't want to make him suffer. He's already suffered a lot, y'know?'

'I know, yaar,' I replied, 'I know.'

We walked up Woodland in silence, smelling of fried onions and tired cigarillos.

FIVE

I drove my first car at age five. It was a sky-blue convertible rounded in the front like a Corvette. It had a stick-on fuel gauge and speedometer and a yellow biscuit-box-sized dashboard that opened out. The steering wheel was also functional, but the car wasn't equipped with a chassis, pedals, or any sort of bottom. It moved by way of ambulation—environmentally friendly but not particularly energy efficient. Not that it mattered: I was all vim then. I zipped around in it, navigating the byways of our living room, kitchen, and backyard, blowing raspberries. Apparently, I was attached to the car for 'six long months.' Ma said she even remembered me having dinner in it while watching TV, drive-in-style.

I didn't drive again till my teenage years, when suddenly my legs stretched disproportionately faster than my arms and torso. When Ma determined that my feet could touch the clutch, accelerator, and brake, she said, 'We're going for a ride, Daddy Long Legs.' So one afternoon in the summer of '94 we drove to the deserted road past Clifton Beach in our second-hand purple Daihatsu Charade, impelled by the doctrine of necessity: Ma needed me to do groceries, collect my father's pension checks, and deposit the electric and phone bills. 'You're the man of the house,' she said, and this role required me to operate the levers of manhood.

After a few false starts, several skid marks, and a break during which I was treated to a pep talk and a newspaper cone of spiced peanuts, I got the hang of it. The trick, I learned, was lifting your foot off the clutch while pressing the gas and vice versa. 'And,' Ma instructed, 'keep your eyes open. Always check your mirrors. You have to always know what is going on around you.' As per the directions, I kept my eyes on the road, avoiding potholes, dodging the errant cyclist, and slowing down before speed bumps, but later, feeling confident, I did manage to wave to a family of lost picnickers and glimpse the sunset over the frothy gray sea.

Ma was a patient teacher because she was taught in the same way by another, her late husband, '*Inna lillaihay wa inna illahay rajayune.*' She was also a hard taskmaster. Announcing, 'Now, for your test,' she directed me home to Saddar via Gizri, one of the busiest intersections this side of the megalopolis. Karachi traffic, I was to learn, requires skill and testosterone. I had neither. Consequently, the drive back was harrowing. The nightly caravan of trucks traveling from the port to the interior swept me to Submarine Chowk, and at Submarine Chowk it happened: in an attempt to brake in bumper-to-bumper traffic, I accelerated, hitting the Honda in front of me.

I remember it being very hot. We had the windows down because the air conditioner had malfunctioned years ago—which worked fine with the sea breeze blowing in at the beach, but not in city traffic, and certainly not during the accident. Ma's beige chiffon sari clung to her body, and my shirt was dark with sweat. My right leg shook uncontrollably. I didn't know what to do: I was underage, in the wrong, and without a license. Ma, putting her hand on my knee, said, 'Sit here,' and with that she opened the car door and slammed it behind her.

The driver of the Honda Civic, a stout man with a magician's beard, was already outside, gesticulating wildly. Other people, mostly men, had gotten out of their cars, forming a raucous circle around the two. It was a real scene, and in the headlights Ma cut a pose like a fifties' film actress with her long black hair tied up in a bun, her sari wrapped tightly around her hips, and her kohl-lined eyes flashing, but she was no damsel in distress: with one fist on her waist, she wagged a finger at the man, who, not knowing what hit him, didn't get a word in edgewise. 'And one more thing,' I heard Ma say. 'Your beard needs cutting!' The magician waddled back away.

When Ma got back in, I leaned over and planted a kiss on her sweaty cheek. She was my hero. Looking at me squarely in the eye, she said, 'This is your first and last accident.' Then slapping her thigh, she announced, 'Let's go, beta,' as if her work here were done.

∾

The episode recurred in my mind the evening of the frenetic, fateful Shaman Run. By the time I had taken the number 7 into Jackson Heights, riding in the first carriage to watch the tracks widen ahead, acquired the keys and cab from Abdul Karim—who received me at his walk-up in a royal blue bath robe and matching sponge slippers and delicately inquired why I was wearing sunglasses—and driven back into town with a passenger who, I correctly predicted, needed a ride downtown, though not to the Village but just outside the Nolita, it was after eight. Across town in Hell's Kitchen, AC had been waiting for me since seven. Meanwhile, Jimbo had asked to be collected from the Duck's place in SoHo, an unanticipated detour that complicated an already complicated expedition. The smart thing would have been to take Houston to West Broadway, pick up Jimbo, then take Ninth Avenue to AC's because, as any cabbie can tell you, the lights on Ninth open up all the way through at thirty-four miles per hour, but Houston was backed up, so I decided to cut through Alphabet City and fetch AC first because I figured Jimbo could wait and AC was already stewing like a pot of nihari. He would have to stew some more. The streets were helter-skelter, cars weaving in, swerving out, cutting each other off, caravans of buses lurching past like rampaging elephants. Drivers honked, cussed, raised fists and fingers, and there were cops everywhere: in patrol cars, on horseback, and in twos and threes on the street. It was as if everybody were escaping some epic catastrophe: tidal wave, airborne toxic event, Godzilla. I suspected it had something to do with the vaguely dire announcement on the news concerning the area bridges and tunnels, but instead of an exodus, everybody seemed to be going round and round.

When I finally reached Madison, the road cleared. Rolling down the windows, I cranked up WPLJ, Power 95, and bobbed to the rousing beat of a great old Doobies number. I flew past the carpet shops in the thirties, the hotels in the forties, in seven minutes flat, and for those seven minutes, I was fast and free like an errant atom. At such junctures—and they were not infrequent—being a cabbie was joy. It beat sitting head down in a cubicle for sixteen-hour stretches, staring at a screen. Cruising into the city on I-95 at night, for instance, or from Hoboken, across the George Washington, was thrilling each and every goddamn time. It was like discovering Manhattan anew. Each turn promised something else. You would see crazy fistfights in Yonkers, crazy wedding parties in Chinatown. You would meet the great celebrities of our age, raise your thumb to that naked cowboy guitarist in Times Square. There was, however, a consensus among us that one of the best parts of the job was that the most beautiful women in the world would chase after you in stilettos and states of dishabille at four, five in the morning. They would enter your place of business, leg first, handbag dangling, and make conversation. Some were known to bare flushed breasts for no reason whatsoever; others had bared their souls.

Although the job had its perks, few would agree that being a cabbie in turn-of-the-century New York City was a peachy proposition. One had to navigate drunks, druggies, potholes, labyrinthine detours, speed traps, ticket traps, summons abuses. The cops, for instance, did this thing on 42nd: if you tried taking a left from Third Avenue on a green light, you got a ticket for *failure to yield to pedestrians*, but if you allowed them to pass, you would receive a summons for running a red. And you paid for tickets, gas, and the $120-per-shift leasing fee from your own pocket; you got no Social Security, pension, paid vacation, or health insurance, even though you risked life and limb every night. Robberies were common, robbery-related fatalities not uncommon. During my brief and wondrous tenure, two livery cab drivers were knifed. In 2000 eleven died.

The night of the Shaman Run, I had my first near-death experience: in an attempt to confirm the meteorologists' insistence on rain, I slowed to survey the low, hanging sky, when a figure scampered into the middle of the street as if chasing a line drive or death wish. Slamming the brake, I yelled something like JESUS H. CHRIST ALAIY SALAM! The cab screeched, then skidded, then stopped. With one hand stuck in his trouser pocket, the other hand shielding his eyes, a familiar character in a boxy suit swooned before me, tie slung over his shoulder. When I got out to curse the jackass, he strode over, opened a door, and sprawled onto the backseat. 'Greenwich Street,' he commanded as if nothing had happened. 'And step on it, sport.'

There was something about his extraordinary, cavalier manner, something in the pitch of his voice and Jersey brogue, that placed him. It was my VP. Although inevitable, it was the first time something like this had happened to me since my incarnation as a cabbie. There was no way I was going to give him the satisfaction of knowing that I had come down in the world. In a made-up foreign accent, somewhere between Bengali and Swahili, I said, 'I don go!'

'You go!' he yelled through the scratched Plexiglas partition.

'I off duty!'

'Well, you know what?' he said, crossing his legs. 'So am I. And you know what I'm going to do? I'm going to kick back, relax, and smoke a cigar.'

Throwing up my hands in the air, I cried, 'No ciggy! No ciggy!'

Producing a fat one, which was promptly dropped below, he barked, 'Go to hell!' As he grunted and fumbled and kicked the back of my seat, I wondered, *What the hell am I going to do with this guy?* My first impulse was to deposit him along Manhattan Alley and let him fare for himself among the Hondurans in wifebeaters huddled on stairs and stoops. 'Okay,' I mumbled under my breath, slamming the accelerator, 'I go to hell.'

One night not so long after I arrived in the States, I had accompanied AC to Manhattan Alley on an 'errand,' only to find myself twiddling my thumbs on the sidewalk when he disappeared into a tenement for a 'pit stop.' As I paced the trash-strewn sidewalks, dodging rats the size of kittens, I caught the attention of a squat gangbanger, hanging back on the stoop with his crew, picking the dirt beneath his fingernails with a butterfly knife. 'Yo, homeboy,' he had called out, 'you wanna tattoo?' As his posse let out whoops of laughter like a pack of undernourished hyenas, I remember trembling, wondering: *Am I a home boy?* I began to whistle because Ma told me to whistle when I was afraid, a questionable strategy; then AC emerged like Hercules after the Twelve Labors, hollering, *¡Familias Latinas! ¡Tranquilo, tranquilo!*

When I glanced at my VP again, however, slumped against the backseat, peering outside through dark, swollen eyes, I realized I did not feel particularly vindictive toward him. The imperative did not jell with my jihad. Besides, there was no time for a tour of the Upper Upper West Side. So I swung around, lowered the windows for cross-ventilation, and turned up the evening jazz set on National Public Radio. In turn, my VP kicked back, closed his eyes, enjoying, it would seem, Dizzy Gillespie tearing shit up.

We reached AC's close to nine. Pulling up in front of his building, I checked on my passenger—who looked up, then down, as if his head were fixed on a hinge—then made for the cluster of phone booths across the street. Getting through to AC was a production at the best of times. One needed a pocketful of quarters and heroic patience because he screened calls to avoid his landlord, creditors, and drug dealers, not to mention acolytes, ex-girlfriends, present girlfriends, and anybody else who wanted a piece of him. You would have to call him once, hang up, call him again in exactly seven seconds—counting one Mississippi, two Mississippi, and so on—hang up again, and then, if he was home, he would call back. If not, you would be left chilling in a phone booth like an idiot.

There was a period when, having borrowed fifteen hundred dollars from a loan shark in Spanish Harlem—a character suitably known as The Grasshopper—AC stopped taking calls altogether.

He had his front door replaced with a solid iron fixture that he'd salvaged from a bankrupt halal butchery in Coney and equipped with several old-fashioned scroll-end slide bolts and a contraption known as a mortise lock, an invention, he breathlessly informed us, attributed to the nephew of Eli Whitney, the man behind 'the renaissance in pre–Civil War Southern agriculture.' During the fraught Days of The Grasshopper, he had also carpeted the floors twice over and soundproofed the entrance walls with blankets and egg cartons so you could not hear him inside. Mail and flyers and rolled newspapers would be scattered on his doormat as if he were on permanent vacation. The only way to contact him then was to follow the elaborate instructions he had dispatched to us by post, which involved a pulley, a garden gnome, and a bowling pin tethered to a string off the fire escape in the alley out back. In the dead of night, we would climb up the ladder and enter his apartment through the window like Ali Baba's Two Straggling Thieves.

Inside the inner sanctum, you learned that AC's childhood mythology had been informed in part by dog-eared copies of bildungsromans such as *Tom Sawyer*. And *How to Be a Detective* rested prominently on his desk alongside translations of the *Babur-Nama*, the first modern memoir, and Ibn Khaldun's *Muqaddimah*, the first treatise on anthropology, sociology, and economics. AC would tell you that he had reorganized his collection according to personal relevance: 'Should Dante take precedence over Ghalib,' he had asked rhetorically, 'just by virtue of his name? That would be ridiculous, chum.' *The Anarchist Cookbook*—a *How to Be a Detective* for grown-ups—was often consulted after a few drinks. As a result, we had all smoked dried banana-peel residue, an experience that left a bad taste for days. We had, however, balked at the prospect of attempting the hallucinogen that can be manufactured from boiling, drying, and crushing toad skins into powder with mortar and pestle.

Bracing for another screed on punctuality, I dialed, waited, and dialed again, but when he finally called back, AC simply told me to meet him in the 'alley in five.' Then it began to drizzle, just like that, with no warning, no fanfare, heralded only by a faint breeze and a diffuse smell of urine. Crossing the street, I took cover under the awning of a nearby newsstand. A few yards away I noticed my VP plant his hand on the trunk of the cab and retch ferociously. A man in overalls, heaving a stack of newspapers, yelled, 'You okay there, fella?' My VP waved, smiled, vomited again.

In the alley around back, a familiar, jaunty tune carried over the pitter-patter of rain. Cocking my head to one side, I heard, '...shows 'em pearly whites,' something, something, 'out of sight.' Four floors above, I watched AC emerge from an open window, climb onto the fire escape, coattails flapping, beer in hand, and clamber down like Batman, before dropping seven, maybe eight feet, and landing on a mound of garbage bags without spilling a drop of Sierra Nevada Pale Ale. It was, by any measure, an impressive performance. Standing up, he brushed rust flakes off his lapel, ran his hand through his hair, and bounded toward me like a mountain cat, clenching his big square jaw. He appeared ballistic, like he was going to kick some ass, but before he could, I briefed him on the developing VP crisis.

'So let me get this straight, chum,' AC said. 'The fellow who fired you? He's in the cab? Right now?

'Yeah.'

'And he just retched?'

'On the road. Not inside, thank God—'

'Indeed,' AC muttered. 'How considerate.'

'Look, yaar, he's totally wasted—'

'Well,' he said, 'we'll, ah, have to knock some sense into him, won't we?'

Then AC took a step closer. I could count the brittle curled hairs in his nose. I thought he was going to knock some sense into me as well. Instead, he picked the sunglasses off my nose with the delicate precision of an ophthalmologist and placed them in his kerchief pocket. 'Echymosis,' he stated.

'Sorry?'

'Discoloration of skin caused by internal bleeding, dry blood.'

'Sounds like a disease.'

Producing an unlabelled yellow vial from his secret armpit pouch—a traveling first-aid kit that included nips, poppers, 'smelling salts,' chocolate-covered ants, and whatnot—he clasped my temple and dabbed a sticky, astringent balm under my eye, which he massaged gently with the flat of his thumb. It felt good. After replacing my shades, he popped the vial back into the pouch and marched forth. 'Well, c'mon!' he called. 'We're late, chum! At this rate we won't make it to the Shaman's by late next week.' As we made our way out of the alley, we passed the pool of chewed bits of sausage and watery red onions that my VP had spewed out. 'Charming,' AC remarked, pinching his mustache. 'Mixed media on, ah, asphalt.'

In the car, AC threatened to lock my VP in the trunk until he gave me my job back. 'Please don't, yaar,' I pleaded. 'At least let him come to.' In that effort, AC slapped him with the back of his hand. Mercifully, my VP did not stir, and if he had any sense of self-preservation, if he knew what was good for him, he would remain dead to the world, because AC was in a dangerous mood. 'Look,' I argued, 'if he isn't conscious of making the decision, then it's no good, right?' Agreeing in principle, AC could not quite check the imperatives of justice: blindfolding my VP with a polka-dot handkerchief, he bound his hands with his own Hermès tie, 'so that, ah, his hands remain tied.'

During the ride, AC, always the sleuth, also guessed at my VP's extracurricular activities. 'You picked him up where?' he asked. 'Fifty-third? The cheeky bastard's been to Flash Dancers, getting lap dances and his face mashed by great big mammary glands and rubbery aureoles.' There was not much evidence for the hypothesis until AC pulled two wads of cash from either trouser pocket. 'He makes what, three hundred grand a year? Well, he's carrying, ah, point one percent of his salary on him. In singles.' Slipping the moolah into his own jacket, he declared, 'Consider this a tax, dickhead.'

At precisely ten o' clock, I found parking on Sullivan and, from my vantage, could see the lights on at the Duck's. We hadn't seen her much that summer but once upon a time we'd visited her weekly, bearing gifts, bouquets, bottles of Chianti and Brunello, and knickknacks for the house: Klimt-print coasters, a fancy corkscrew, a Dustbuster. Kissing her on both cheeks, AC would say, 'Accept these insufficient tokens of our, ah, affection.' And maybe they were, but how else do you really reciprocate such consummate hospitality? We would also invite her over and once even threw an elaborate dinner party on a sailboat in her honor, complete with printed invitations and menus on ivory paper. The Duck, however, was not an eager guest herself. If she arrived at all, she would make quiet conversation with somebody she knew, strictly mano a mano, and after some time wink or make a secret gesture at Jimbo, because he would jump up, make up some paltry excuse, then lead her out.

Maybe we weren't such good hosts, or were bad guests, or perhaps our novelty had worn thin, because we had been invited less and less to the Duck's in the preceding few months. It had to do, in part, with Jimbo—every relationship has its natural ups and downs—but we liked to believe that we had an independent relationship with her. AC even said, 'The best thing about you, Jimbo, is your girlfriend. If you two ever break up, I'm not only, ah, taking her side but taking her, period.' Although he didn't mean it—or I didn't think he did—he said it often enough. Of course AC never admitted that he might have contributed to the cooling off of our relationship. At a midsummer soirée, he had mounted the Duck's best friend in the bathroom, and the best friend's fiancé—the fey, tan, mole-faced rockstar whom we all know—held the Duck unfairly responsible for the tryst.

Nevertheless we still harbored great plans with the Duck, plans we had discussed several times when everybody else had left and we had her to ourselves. We talked about a road trip out West, across America, a pilgrimage, really, to Las Vegas. 'Wouldn't that be something, boys?' she'd said. Sitting on a bergère chair, sipping ice wine for breakfast, I imagined the journey: there would be Main

Streets and motels and postcard vistas on the way, the singing of show tunes, chatty nights in small-town Comfort Inns, and finally the dazzling city of glass rising in the desert like a mirage. It might have all been fanciful conversation, but it didn't really matter anymore. Who then could have anticipated that it would soon not be possible for three brown men to drive across America in a rented car, even with a blond in tow?

'What the hell are you waiting for, chum?' AC yelled. 'I swear to God that blow has knocked a screw loose in your head.'

'Aren't we, um, going to say hello to the Duck?'

AC swept his broad forehead with his free hand as if to sweep an errant thought. '*No*. We're here to *summon* Jimbo. This is *not* a social call. This *is* an exercise in touch and go. You follow?'

Nodding toward my VP, I said, 'Okay, okay, but what do we do with this guy?' As he lay prone across the backseat, a silver glob of drool dribbled down his cheek. 'We can't just leave him.'

AC sighed. 'You want to say hello to the Duck? Then go say hello. But don't exchange kisses and formal pleasantries and notes on the inclement weather. I'm warning you: if you're not back in six minutes flat, I *will* shanghai this cab and dump your VP in the Hudson.'

'Okay, yaar, okay. I get it. I get it.'

When I opened the car door, AC grabbed me by the shoulder. 'One more thing,' he said. 'Convey my, ah, love to the Duck.'

Jumping out, I sprinted inside the gray building, which I had once overheard being described by a tenant as neo-Bauhaus. The lobby was deserted but was usually populated by a marvelous set whose vocation involved a strict regime of walking their dogs and dining at Cipriani's. At the reception, I introduced myself to the doorman, a portly Bulgar defined by mutton chops and a lazy eye. Picking up the receiver, he looked me up and down with his good eye as he dialed, glancing at his watch as if to suggest that *this is no time for men like you to visit here*. 'Another one down here,' he announced with Eastern European bluntness. 'Yes, miss, yes, miss, that the one, miss.' Turning to me, he instructed, 'You get your friend.'

As I rode the elevator up to the penthouse, my ears, as usual, popped. Although I heard strident voices when the doors slid open, I missed the back-and-forth, save the following emphatic pronouncement: *'You're drunk, Jimbo! You're always drunk!'* When I turned the corner, I found Jimbo, wobbly and watery-eyed, and he wordlessly tumbled into my arms. 'Easy on, big fella,' I grunted, falling against the wall. Somehow I managed to guide him into the elevator and prop him against one side, cheek against the wall. He mumbled some mumbo jumbo that I could not readily decipher, though the gist was obvious. Assisting him the best I could, I walked him through the lobby to the cab. 'I'll make things right, yaar,' I whispered.

When AC jumped out to help, I told him, 'Give me a minute,' and was already jogging back in when he yelled after me. The doorman stumbled off his stool, waving me down, crying 'Hai You! Hai You!' but he was also too slow. Jamming the elevator on the fifth floor with a horizontally placed pack of cigarettes, I strode determinedly to the Duck's, though I was not sure what impelled me or what I was going to say or do. I just needed to see her.

She stood in the doorway, wrist on hip, arm on frame, in plush cherry red slippers and a knee-length lavender nightgown. She wore a tired smile and, save a cursory application of Chapstick, no makeup; and though she would typically have her gold locks in a bagel-shaped bun, that night her hair was damp and loose like she had just stepped out of the shower. 'Hiya, Chuck.'

'Hiya, Dora!' I said, kissing her on either cheek, taking in the wheat-germ freshness of her shampoo.

'Why on earth are you wearing shades?' she asked. Then exclaimed, 'Oh my God!' when I took them off to reveal my shiner. Brushing my bruise with creamy fingertips, as if to make sure it was real, she asked, 'What happened?'

'It's nothing, really.' I figured that I could not or maybe did not have to lie, but later I thought maybe I should have. 'We got into a scuffle. It was a misunderstanding, I don't know. These guys, they thought we were talking about blowing up something, or something . . .'

Crinkling her pug nose, the Duck asked, 'Why would they think that?'

'I don't quite know.'

Not knowing where to look, we stood in the cold corridor, smiling vaguely at each other's feet. The Duck slipped one foot out of her slipper, scratched her ankle, and said, 'Well, it's wonderful to see you, Chuck, but what're you doing here?'

'Just thought I'd say hello?'

'Oh,' she said with a tender laugh. 'You're darling.'

As she shifted on her feet, I could glimpse into her apartment. Save for a big blank trademark Rothko on the facing wall (which I had attempted to make sense of for several years), everything inside—the furniture, drapes, carpeting, ceiling—was in earth tones. It was a warm, inviting scene. Lyman, however, a permanent fixture, was nowhere in sight, but at that instant I felt the urge to pat him, have him lick my hand. I found myself saying, 'Isn't it too late for goodbyes?'

'What does that mean?' the Duck asked, cradling her elbows in her hands. I shrugged. Then she said, 'The last few weeks have been rough for all of us—'

'I just kind of wanted to know what happened here tonight.'

'Why?'

'I don't know,' I replied. 'Because we're friends?'

'Well, okay, Chuck, if you really want to know: your friend barged in drunk as a sailor, and I baby-sat him for a while, but it's late, and I'm tired, and I shouldn't be explaining myself to him again and again and again. It's time he explain himself to me, but instead he babbles. Do you know he's been calling at four in the morning? I listen for a while but then put the receiver on the pillow. I mean, I love Jimbo to death—you know that—but this can't go on. You're his friend. Get him on the wagon or something—'

'This isn't about Jimbo's drinking.'

'Look,' she said, the skin tightening across her face, 'you're a good guy, you really are, but what's happening between us is none of your business!'

'Just give him some time, Dora.'

'I'm not doing this right now—'

'You're his world!'

'Then he needs to stand up for me!'

Just then the Bulgar rolled down the hall, huffing and puffing and red in the face. 'I run, miss,' he panted, resting his hands on his thighs, 'but he run faster.' The Duck glanced at me, then at him, and for a moment I thought, *That's it, it's over*, I would be escorted unceremoniously out of the building by the irascible Bulgar. That would have been that. Except the Duck said, 'It's okay, Georgi. There's been a misunderstanding.'

Georgi did not care for the disclosure. Before turning to leave, he solemnly shook his head as if he had been insulted, had been told, *All Bulgars are bastards, Georgi*. When he was out of earshot, the Duck, smiling, said, 'You've caused a stir. You boys always do.'

'I'm sorry, Dora, I'm sorry. I'm out of line—'

'No, I'm sorry, dear—'

'I should get going.'

'Well, *it is* getting late,' she said. 'I'm sure I'll see you around. Kiss, kiss. Ciao bella.'

'Ciao, ciao,' I said, but as I turned away, I thought I heard the Duck mumble, 'I don't get you guys . . .'

There was something in the tenor of the phrase, in the way she said *you guys*, that got me hot and bothered. It might have been the offhand suggestion that we eluded her despite all the time we had spent together or that we had somehow mutated overnight. Although I felt no different, I had this feeling that the Duck wasn't the same. The few times we had happened to run into her, it was as if she had become more normal, more like us, like everybody else, contending with her own neuroses and anxieties, searching for something meaningful, something real. Someday soon she would find love again and find herself, take salsa classes, go bungee-jumping, move to Europe. And someday we might cross paths again, wave across a room, perhaps even exchange kisses and pleasantries.

Turning around, I asked, 'What don't you get?'

'Huh?' came the reply through the crack in the door.

'I said, what don't you get?'

'You really want to know?'

'Yes, I do.'

Pulling the door open with a purposeful tug, she persisted, 'Right now?'

I nodded again. 'Yes,' I said, 'I do.'

'Okay, Chuck. Here goes. I don't get how you guys are always boozing it up and everything but, like, aren't supposed to. Jimbo's father doesn't know his son drinks. He certainly doesn't know that we've been dating for years. That's crazy to me, just crazy. I mean, you guys are like one way here, like hardcore, homeboys, whatever, but when you guys go home, you become different, all proper and conservative. You have to decide what you're about—'

'Whoa, whoa, whoa! Easy on, Dora!' My mouth was dry, and I felt sweaty and dizzy. 'You're what, like thirty-one? Have you decided what you're all about yet? Why is it so strange that our behavior is, um, defined by certain contexts? Do you snort coke in front of your parents? I mean, what's this really all about?'

'I'm not going to listen to your childish speech!'

'Fine,' I said, putting my shades on and turning my back. 'Don't.'

'Wait!' she cried, 'don't walk away,' but I kept walking, and then the elevator doors closed on us.

❧

We could have turned back. We should have turned back. We had had an inauspicious start and were no closer to Connecticut than when we left four hours earlier. After the events of the night, I had a bad feeling about the expedition, a kind of numinous unease. Most people are unaware that cabbies belong to a particularly superstitious demographic; every cabbie believes that he (and the odd she) is protected from the whimsical vicissitudes of city streets by God or gods, by some system or talisman. The perceptive passenger would notice a rabbit's foot, a pair of hairy dice, a heavy Haitian amulet swinging from the rearview mirror to ward off the evil eye, or the hand of Fatima, a statuette of the Virgin fixed on the dashboard or the Grim Reaper of Santa Muerte, stickers of the Sikh prophet Guru Nanak or the Hindu monkey god Hanuman on the inside of a door. After 9/11, Muslim cabbies bore American flags. Although I did not subscribe to portents or voodoo and had not been committed to the directives of Allah in any meaningful way, I wished I had something, anything to hold on to then.

Pressing on, we rattled by parked cars, shuttered shops, green orbs refracted through wisps of steam rising from open manholes. Just before the rain began coming down in sheets, a crisp gust scattered newspapers and plastic bags. Outside the meatpacking district, a lone prostitute holding down a precariously perched orange wig blew me a kiss. When I nodded in gentlemanly acknowledgment, AC said, 'You're not having much luck with women tonight.'

'Why would you say that?'

'That was a tranny, chum.'

'You would know.'

If Lady Luck had not been smiling at me, she had bitch-slapped Jimbo. Tipped over, he rested his large head in AC's lap as AC ran his fingers through his dreadlocks, consoling him with a variation of the platypus and dodo homily. It did not seem to make any discernible impression on him because he continued to murmur inaudibly like a toddler too exhausted to bawl. Watching him in the rearview, I felt horrid, like I had let him down. I couldn't make things right. I wasn't sure why I even tried.

AC had started singing raucous bhangra numbers for our heartsick friend's benefit—*Saday naal ravo gay to aish karo gay / Zindagi kay saray mazay cash karo gay*—when he suddenly yelled, 'Five-O at twelve o' clock!'

As advertised, there was a roadblock up ahead: two patrol cars facing each other at a slight angle, a couple of cops in raincoats waving us down. As a cabbie, I derived comfort from police presence, especially at night, because the crazies came out at night. That night, however, *we* were the crazies: we had a hostage situation in the backseat. Curled up against the door, my VP remained cuffed and blindfolded, and though he hadn't stirred again, he whimpered as if to remind us of his presence. The last thing we needed that night was a brush with the law.

'Quick, yaar!' I yelled, slowing down. 'Untie that guy!' Reaching over, AC unraveled the tie and hung it around his neck like a scarf, but when he whisked the handkerchief off, my VP awakened with a start, rubbing his eyes and wiping his mouth with the retail $225 Hermès. Turning to AC, he asked, 'Who the *fuck* are you?'

'The bouncer from Flash Dancers, numnuts,' AC replied. 'We caught you groping Belinda.'

'Belinda?'

'In the VIP room. Remember?'

The VP's eyes widened. 'What?'

'Let me put it in, ah, vernacular: you're in deep shit, chum.'

Pointing timidly at Jimbo (who, in turn, studied him with one open eye), he asked, 'And who's he?'

'You groped him as well! Now shut up! And sit tight! One peep out of you, and I swear I'll hand you over to New York's finest, and you know they don't take kindly to sex offenders.'

When I stopped, a beefy middle-aged cop swaggered toward the cab, flashlight in hand. He had the mien of a Marine, and his name tag read BROPHY. Leaning out, I asked, 'Is there a problem, officer?'

'Yeah,' he drawled. 'For starters, why're you wearing shades, friend?' Cops always busted balls. That was their job. It would be weird if they were like, *Isn't it a nice night, sir? The moon's out, and you can see the North Star, and oh, there's Orion's belt.*

'What? Oh. These? They're, um, prescription. I broke my last pair.'

'Why isn't your meter running?'

'What?'

'Your "off duty" sign's on.'

'Oh.'

'You speak English, right?'

'Yes, sir, officer.'

'We took a wrong turn back there,' AC yelled from inside the cab. 'And our cabbie—being fair and morally upright, a, ah, man of genuine character—switched the meter off so as not to overcharge us. Rest assured, officer, we'll tip him accordingly.'

Officer Brophy regarded the scene in the back and lingered for a few moments. In the rearview mirror, I could see Jimbo propped up, head tilted back as if he were nursing a nosebleed, one eye half-open, and AC smiling widely, appearing somewhat derelict if not quite sinister. As the muscles on Brophy's face tightened, he muttered something into his radio. 'Step out of the vehicle,' he instructed.

I had no idea what triggered his concern—and frankly, I never may—but at the time the following thought hit me: *We're a bunch of brown men in a car, the night of heightened security in the city.* We looked appropriately unshaven, unkempt, possibly unwholesome. I could have been silly or paranoid, but it was the first time I had felt this way: uneasy, guilty, criminal. I hesitated for an instant, trying to think of something to say, something conciliatory or funny, but I couldn't—perhaps because I figured that I was developing a talent for putting my foot in my mouth. So I simply, silently opened the door.

'Let me see your license.'

When I produced the relevant document, Brophy examined it closely, comparing my laminated passport-sized photo to my face.

I smiled and squinted, shielding my eyes from the rain.

'Where're you headed?'

'Um, Greenwich Street.'

By now, another cop had appeared by the other side of the cab, a Hispanic sporting a crew cut and straight mustache. Again AC intervened: 'I've got a couple of bankers in the back,' he yelled. 'We were out celebrating a two-hundred-million Euro-bond offering at a strip club. You can't blame us. There's so little to celebrate these days.'

Brophy processed the information slowly, as if AC had just gushed a verse of Urdu poetry. Removing his hand from the hilt, he sighed. 'You know you shouldn't be driving around at night with shades.'

'Yes sir, officer. I'm sorry.'

Swatting the license in my open hand, Brophy and the other cop turned to walk back, but just as I sat back down, drenched and relieved, my VP cried, 'Hey! Wait! I don't know these guys!' The cops stopped in their tracks, looked at each other, and then turned to look back at us. As they wearily plodded back in the downpour, I heard a resounding *thwack*, followed by an *oomph* in the back, and from the corner of my eye, caught my VP hunched, handling what I imagined were his family jewels. Slapping him on the back, AC whispered, 'You try that again, chum, and you won't be able to produce progeny.' My VP grunted weakly.

When the cops glanced inside, AC raised an invisible glass to his lips and took several generous swigs while pointing to the crumpled figure beside him, suggesting a state of obvious and utter inebriation. I sat immobile but shitting bricks because in that instant I knew that anything could have happened. I murmured a prayer, an appeal to the Beneficent and Merciful, and perhaps divine intervention worked: eager to avoid the rain, to get back to their coffee and doughnuts, or just to shoot the shit, the two walked away for the second time that night.

'This happen to you before?' AC asked. I shook my head. 'First time?' I nodded. 'Let's get out of here.' As we drove past the squad cars, AC beat on the partition like it was a tabla, '*Fuck tha po-lice comin' straight from the underground / Young nigga got it bad cuz I'm brown . . .*'

Jimbo, stirred from his stupor, chimed in: '*I'm not the other color, so police think / They have the authority to kill a minority*—'

Interrupting, my VP asked, '*Who are you guys?*'

'Call us Metrostanis, chum,' AC chortled. 'Cheers! Skål! Adab!'

Although AC seemed to be entertaining himself, I had had enough fun for the evening. If the encounter with the Duck had left me saddened and stung, the brief encounter with the authorities had shaken me up. And I felt reckless for taking unnecessary liberties with the cab on what was, at the end of the day, a lark. I had already decided to take my VP where he wanted to go: back to work. On 9/11, he and his colleagues had been evacuated to the building built like a fortress, less than a mile north, so they could continue conducting the business of business.

As AC jounced like a robot to one of Jimbo's remixed tapes, I sped the ten odd blocks toward our final stop in the city without saying a word. It seemed of all the cantons in one of the largest cities in the world, we kept circling back to the periphery of disaster. Stopping curbside by the giant red umbrella, I announced, 'No more joy ride.'

My VP looked up with the face he would make when an Excel sheet didn't add up or, as he would say, *iterate*. 'Why?'

'Because, ah, all good things come to an end,' replied AC, reaching for the door handle and nudging him out.

'But—'

'Here,' AC said, pressing something into his palm. 'Here's a pill.' AC was known to administer benzodiazepines and barbiturates like Tic Tacs. He had an ample supply because he ordered generic varieties in bulk from Pakistan, where drugs were something like one-tenth the dollar value. 'And don't forget to drink a lot of water. Good luck. And Godspeed!'

'But—'

'But what, chum?'

With his shoelaces untied and his moist hair stuck to his forehead, my VP had the air of a child abandoned by his parents at summer camp. 'Why am I here?' he asked, as if posing a question about the nature of being.

'You give this address,' I replied.

'I did?' he replied quizzically. 'But I got fired today.'

'You poor bastard,' AC said without missing a beat. 'I suppose that's poetic justice, chum.'

In a final act of charity, he pulled out a wad of cash from his jacket pocket. 'Here's two hundred and fifty bucks. Go find yourself a cab.'

The last time we had been in Westbrook, Connecticut, it had been on a perfect, moonlit midsummer night for a Fourth of July barbecue. The Shaman must have had two, three hundred people over but was nowhere to be seen himself. There was the whiff of smoking meat and mesquite and mosquito repellent in the air, and suddenly the fireworks began with a volley of color like a rainbow in the dark. For a few minutes everybody stood still, oohing and aahing and staring at the sky. Then a horsey blonde in a neon-orange boob tube, who could have been the Shaman's girlfriend, directed us to the bar at the far end of the lawn. The bar was manned by a paunchy Pakistani Christian who introduced himself as Ron and religiously plied us with the choicest liquor for the remainder of the evening as if it were a matter of *jus soli* or national duty.

It was an eventful night. We all got lucky. A tall, kimono-clad mulatta with cat eyes and a delicate chin waltzed up to me and pulled me to the dance floor, insisting in a breathy whisper on teaching me the 'forbidden dance.' We made a spectacle of ourselves, gyrating and grinding to the classics of early nineties techno. Then, under steaming silver dishes and assorted cutlery, I would see fireworks again. When we returned to the bar, sweaty and flushed, our clothes speckled with grass, Ron slid us shots of a concoction garnished with slivers of cayenne pepper and sugarcane that he called the Karachi Special. Although the tonic revived me, my partner, dizzy and weak-kneed, dozed on a lawn chaise like a Wyeth. In the interim, Jimbo had been chatting with a taut, tanned, long-necked, middle-aged southern Californian, cultish about dharma yoga. 'Know anything about it?' she asked. When Jimbo uttered an innocuous 'um,' she excitedly mistook it for 'Om,' and soon afterward led him to some low bushes. He would emerge sixteen minutes later—we were keeping time—sporting an agreeable grin and an open fly.

AC met two girls from Georgia, with whom he had a threesome in the toolshed. As evidence, he would pick a wood shaving out of his ass. His adventures, however, had only begun. A heavyset girl with a fringe of red hair would follow AC back to the city afterward, where they would wind up on the fire escape of his building, smoking authentic charas from Pakistan's northern badlands, shooting the breeze and making out. While they were at it, they lost their clothes to the river breeze—he, his shirt, she, her skirt—attracting the attention of the horrified tenants of the adjacent building, who called the police on them. When the cops showed up, however, and banged on the door, AC and his paramour slid down the fire escape and scampered to the corner bodega. New York's finest managed to catch up with them, but when asked whether they were 'the two humpin' up on the sixth floor,' they denied all knowledge, 'like Adam and Eve before God.' When a cop asked, 'Then where's your top, wiseguy?,' AC solemnly replied, 'We were playing a couple of hands of strip poker, officer. Surely we haven't broken the law?' The cops persisted. 'It's actually an annual ritual. We, ah, celebrate Independence Day in this manner. After all, this is the land of the free, home of the brave.' The authorities relented.

But before all these theatrics transpired, we spotted the Shaman by the garage entrance beside his tall shadow, sporting an off-white linen jacket, a cream T-shirt, and baggy trousers. Prematurely bald, his few strands of hair were combed back, and his liquid eyes gleamed like nuggets of gold. He held an unlit Sobranie Black Russian, though he didn't smoke, and a long cocktail glass fitted with an umbrella, though he was an avowed teetotaller. You could never figure him out. 'You guys have a good time?' he asked. *Great fucking party, yaar!* we said. *Bohaut maza aya!* We hugged him drunkenly, sentimentally, and expressed further gratitude. The Shaman seemed very pleased and informed us that such rocking soirées would become a regular feature at his place. We had not seen him since.

∾

When we arrived, it was raining with the consistency of tap water. Turning into Elm Street, we could make out the outline of the Shaman's slanted, triangle-shaped house. When we pulled up to the curb, AC looked at me, his face momentarily lit by lightning, then at Jimbo, before getting out. Jimbo and I looked at each other, unsure what we were supposed to do, so we sat for some time, watching the wiper slither across the windshield, the red rain in the car lights. Then I decided to follow. Sprinting up the front lawn, I was lashed and nearly slipped on the incline as a clod of earth gave way under my foot. It would have been a fine way to end the evening: sprawled spread-eagle with a fractured toe in Connecticut. There was no sign of AC, or the Shaman for that matter, on the porch: the lights above the entrance were switched off, the door was locked, and I couldn't peer through the bay windows because the blinds were down. Of course, it was after two in the morning and if home, the Shaman would have been fast asleep—as we should have been.

Presently I heard a dull clamor around the corner, and when I peered into the darkness, I thought I saw a large, raccoon-sized animal burrowing into an opening into the side of the house. It was kind of spooky. Then something grazed my neck, as brittle as a new toothbrush. Crying like a girl, I turned around to find Jimbo looming over me. 'Boo, hoo,' he mumbled solemnly.

'Stop screwing around!' the raccoon shouted. It was unmistakably AC.

'What the hell are you doing, yaar?' I shouted back.

'Breaking and entering, chum!'

'Did you try the doorbell?'

'Yeah,' he yelled, 'car's not in the garage . . . he's not in.'

When I squinted to see what was going on, it seemed he had been swallowed headfirst by the house. A minute later his disembodied face, partly obscured by a wet confusion of hair, appeared in the window. Opening the door, he stood before us with his trousers rolled up to his ankles and soiled at the knees, instructing us to find the lights. I switched on a standard-issue bachelor halogen. The space was bare save a black, faux-leather couch facing a nineteen-inch TV. Apparently the Shaman adhered to the tried-and-tested minimalist aesthetic. The cover of the underrated flick *The Mighty Quinn* was wedged in the crevice of the couch near an empty bottle of Gatorade. An onyx vase and a framed photo, presumably of his parents, adorned the fireplace. They appeared to keep vigil, Father Shaman in a skullcap and hennaed beard, Mother Shaman featuring a tight headscarf and downy mustache. 'Dudes are hard corps,' remarked Jimbo. At the other end of the room, a modern kitchen with polished aluminum surfaces spilled into a dining area, minus chairs and table. The Shaman must have recently done groceries because soup cans, cola bottles, and pasta boxes, as well as cartons of Chinese takeout, were strewn across the counters. Near the sink, a knife jutted out of a variegated melon.

'Why's it so goddamn cold?' AC asked nobody in particular.

A faint electric whir could be heard over the sound of rain on the roof. 'Air-conditioning's on,' I observed. 'I'll find the thermostat.'

'And open the windows, chum,' he yelled after me. 'It's oppressive in here.'

The thermostat was located in the pantry by the kitchen. The needle was shy of fifty degrees. The system groaned when I shut it down. It was weird. As I turned to join the others, I noticed something weirder. Instead of cereal boxes and mineral water and canned soup, the shelves were stocked with rows of cigarette cartons. There were local, garden-variety Marlboros and Camels and Parliaments, as well as an extensive collection of exotics: Gauloises, Gitanes, Ducados, Caballeros, du Maurier, Davidoffs, Dunhills, Rothmans, John Player Specials, Sobranie Black Russians. 'What the hell,' I muttered to myself. It didn't make any sense at first. Eager to disclose my discovery, I emerged from the pantry like Moses from Mount Sinai, only to find Jimbo propped against a wall in the dining area, staring into space. I don't think he noticed I was there. 'Everything all right, yaar?' I asked. Then AC called from upstairs: 'You guys coming or what?'

We marched up to the second floor. There was enough space for the average family of four, plus floppy-eared Labrador. The smell of dirty socks and stale deodorant hung in the air of the smallest room. A heap of clothes lay on an office chair, a pair of buckled suede shoes and a shopping bag lay next to the closet, and a row of shiny suits, bright shirts, and printed ties hung neatly inside. A ragged pink duvet was rolled into a ball on the twin-sized mattress on the floor as if the occupant planned a laundry run. The other rooms were carpeted wall-to-wall in steel gray and wholly unfurnished, save a selection of random artifacts: a phone charger, a field hockey trophy and a battery-powered yo-yo. We noticed that there were no garbage cans anywhere. Wrappers, receipts, crumpled tissue paper lay in small heaps in corners. In the bathroom, we found a six-year-old IKEA catalog, and books that were must-reads in some circles: *Liar's Poker* and *The Art of War*. For good measure, we parted the goldfish-themed shower curtain and checked the bathtub, where we found a coil of dried hair on the drain cover.

After completing our survey of the premises, we collected dumbly on the landing. 'Can anybody tell me what we're doing here?' I asked. Teetering on the railing, Jimbo slid off and dumbly escaped downstairs. I felt horrible for him. 'Can *you* tell me what the hell we're doing here?' I repeated myself. Concentrating on his mud-stained two-toned rattlesnake-skin boots, AC said nothing. I couldn't tell if he was tired or plotting his next move. It didn't matter. Either way, I was pissed. The night, from my vantage, had been a proper fiasco.

'Did you know,' I began, 'the Shaman runs some sort of cigarette operation out of the pantry? I bet he's out running cigarettes out of the trunk of his Merc right now.' AC noisily scratched his nape in response. 'Or maybe our man got lucky tonight,' I fumed. 'Maybe the sheikh shtick works out and he stays the weekend out in Long Island with some hottie. Who knows? Who cares? I don't even know this guy, and neither do you. I know this much, though: you're on some stupid trip. This isn't about the Shaman. This is about you.'

Storming down, I joined Jimbo. I figured he needed us more than the Shaman. Sprawled on the couch, staring at a corner of the ceiling, one arm dangling, Jimbo nursed his wounds with an application of booze: a nip of Goldschläger, a memento, no doubt, from AC's pouch, rested on his ample teat. Settling beside him, I hit him softly in the ribs, a stab at reassurance, at commiseration. 'Don't worry,' I said. 'It'll work out, yaar . . . Things always work out . . . You know what? If you want, I'll talk to Old Man Khan. You know he'll listen to me.' It was probably too late for uninspired bromides. He probably wasn't even listening. He just lay lifelessly, breathing loudly. 'Say something, yaar,' I said. 'Say anything. How're you doing? How're you feeling?'

'Shitty shitty bang bang.'

Taking the nip from him, I took a poisonous swig. The saccharine liqueur burned down my esophagus. 'Have you thought about getting on the wagon,' I asked, 'or is it off the wagon?' but before he could reply, AC appeared from upstairs, holding fistfuls of paper like a homeless man who has salvaged yesterday's newspaper from the garbage. In an even, by-the-way tenor, he pronounced, 'So I, ah, found a bunch of receipts, and guess what?'

'Not now, yaar,' I said.

'Just listen to me for a minute—'

'No,' I cried. '*You* listen to *me*! This is not the time!'

AC stepped menacingly close to me, growling, 'I'll lick you, chum!'

Not sure whether he was serious, I got up and moved closer as well. It didn't matter. My blood was up. 'I'd like to see you try,' I growled back.

'Well, I can!'

'You can't—'

'Easy on,' Jimbo interjected.

'*Can!*'

'*Can't*—'

'PIPE DOWN, DUDES!'

Jimbo's cracked rasp startled us. I suspect it startled Jimbo as well. In any event, it worked. Chastened, AC and I drifted to separate corners of the room, checking our nails for dirt, our pockets for lint. Then we watched our friend hoist himself off the couch with the dexterity of a grounded bush elephant, steady himself on the arm of the couch, and drag himself to the music system as if it were the last thing he had to do before he keeled over. When an old Tiffany hit filled the room, he winced. "'Best of the friggin' Eighties,'" he mumbled, reading the CD cover. 'Go figure.' Reaching into his track pants, he produced one of his signature post-disco, proto-house, neo-soul mixed cassettes, which he dropped into the player with aplomb, and returning to the couch, he closed his eyes and sighed to a remixed rendition of the song that went *where troubles melt like lemon drops* . . .

'Make face and suck up,' he instructed. 'I'm gonna lie here, gonna listen to some tunes. I ain't going nowhere tonight.'

Left to our own devices, AC and I stretched, feigned yawns; then I proceeded to the kitchen to pour myself a glass of water. Before I could retire, however, I heard noises outside: a clang, the sound of footsteps, a voice calling out over the rain. Chucking the receipts in the air like confetti, AC made for the door like a child hearing telltale sounds of parents returning home after a dinner. I followed.

At the end of the driveway, near my parked cab, there stood a man holding a yellow umbrella, waving wildly, as if signaling an airplane, and before I could figure out what was going on, I saw a smallish dog—a terrier or Chihuahua—dart from the garage to the fellow. Taken aback by AC's prompt appearance and wild-eyed concern, the man yelled, 'Sorry, I'm real sorry . . . he must have seen a cat or opossum, or something.' Standing in the middle of the lawn, hands on his hips, AC boomed, 'You might, ah, consider putting Buster on a leash.'

Leaving AC in the rain, attending to the neighborhood leashing protocol, I returned inside. It was time to call it a night. I dimmed the lights, caressed Jimbo's big head, and put away the Goldschläger, but before I made it up the stairs, AC returned, drenched, tracking dirt. 'Why's it so oppressive in here?' he asked nobody in particular.

In a conciliatory gesture, I went around opening all the windows as if it were daybreak. The sound of the falling rain and the smell of wet soil filled the room; a breeze rustled the blinds and scattered the crumpled receipts on the floor, the empty boxes of Chinese in the kitchen. Then I trudged upstairs, unrolled the Shaman's sheets, as he must have done every night, and fell asleep.

Grayness filtered through the blinds when I woke. I tried my damnedest to go back to sleep but kept getting roused by the onset of a childhood nightmare featuring creepy crawlies slithering over me—caterpillars, roaches, bugs with forty eyes. When I finally shook them off, I began imagining the Shaman pulling himself out of bed to the call of the alarm, scratching his ass, shuffling to the bathroom, dreamily reading *Liar's Poker* before shaving and showering and heading out to pursue the American Dream, cigarette cartons tucked under his arm. It was weird being in his lair, inhaling his funky smells, privy, in a way, to his routine, humdrum state of mind.

The exercise of conjuring the Shaman was cut short by Jimbo who ambled in, announcing, 'I wanna Mongolian mustache, dude, like 'em upside-down crescents, but my hair, it don't grow that way. Wonder what'd happen if I rubbed Rogaine under my nose—'

'Have you slept, yaar?'

'Negative.'

'You need to sleep. You're not making any sense.'

Leaning against the doorframe, Jimbo said, 'Yeah, okay but I just wanna know one thing, Chuck, just one thing, then I'm crashin'.'

'What's that?'

'Last time I remember, I was chillin' like a villain. I had me a girl, couple a hot gigs, stuff in the pipeline that was going to bring da house down. Sho 'nuff, there was plenty of stuff that was wack—me and my old man for one but we ain't jelled since the sixth grade, so I ain't countin' that, and yeah, I detoxed only to retox—but that ain't what I'm talkin' about. I'm talkin' about how I woke up one day, and I ain't in Kansas no more. I'm in crap city. All of a sudden I got to be up to snuff on ovaries, an' the old man's comin' down on me like a ton a brick, an' now I'm, like, in Connecticut. I lived all my life in this country an' I've never been to friggin' Connecticut.' Pausing to take a breath, he asked, 'What's with that, dude?'

Getting out of bed, I grabbed Jimbo by the arm and sat him down. Taking off his hand-stitched moccasins, I replied, 'It's not so bad, yaar. It's quiet here. There's no traffic, no sirens. And this is a really comfortable mattress. I think it's got lumbar support. You'll sleep like a baby.' Rearranging the sheets, I put him to bed, whispering, 'Don't let the bed bugs bite.' Turning on his side, Jimbo spooned the down pillow and began snoring instantaneously. It was as if he had been somnambulating.

In the bathroom next door, I found myself studying my unshaven face in the toothpaste-stained mirror while urinating, noting that my bruise had acquired the hue and texture of an unripe eggplant. I searched the shelves and cabinets in vain for a razor before resigning myself to Ewok chic. Shedding my clothes, I parted the curtain and, for some reason, picked up the coil of hair on the drain and carefully deposited it on the glass shelf inside the cabinet. I showered quickly under the anemic spray, and afterwards, dabbed the Shaman's deodorant under my pits, but in the interest of hygiene, decided against using his electric toothbrush. Besides, I thought, *I'll be home soon enough.* Before heading out, I flipped the toilet seat and ritualistically replaced the coil of hair on the drain. It seemed like the right, responsible thing to do.

Downstairs I found AC was watching porn in his underwear and boots as if tuned in to breaking news. A can of Milwaukee's Best was balanced artfully on his soft boozer's gut while he had an arm around a family pack of Ranch-flavored Doritos. When I walked in, he inquired, 'Have you, ah, seen such a large orifice?'

Transfixed and repulsed at the same time, I replied, 'Um, no, can't say I have.'

'It actually recalls the time I had sex on the fire escape with this really big girl.'

Plopping down next to him, I asked, 'What is this?'

Putting a damp arm around my shoulder, he said, 'A selection from the Shaman collection: *Dirty Debutantes*. It's conceptually novel in the century-old history of celluloid pornography: real women having real sex. Mark my words: this will spawn a revolution spanning the media, if it hasn't already. Why would anybody watch women with silicone tatties faking orgasms when you've got the real deal?'

The camera panned out as the subject, a meaty redhead with tiny pointed breasts, yelped when a piglike man with thick glasses mounted her from behind. 'How about we check the news, yaar?'

'Do you think sociocultural factors inform the, ah, groans women emit during intercourse? You would think the grunt is primal and instinctive, but anecdotal evidence suggests that women from different nations don't groan in the same way. For instance, French women do *oohs*, Iranis *auwnh*. Latins go *aiey*. Or to take a Marxist, or technically a post-Marxist perspective, I'd, ah, wager that British aristocracy—wives of earls, barons, and dukes—groan differently from their cockney compatriots.'

'Maybe there'll be something about Musharraf's speech.'

'What about women from our part of the world?' he persisted. 'Do they go *hai*?'

'Don't you want to know what's happening?'

'*No*. Actually, I don't,' AC replied. 'I'm sick of the news, chum. I'll be happy if I never watch CNN again.' Switching the TV off, he rearranged his crotch. 'Nobody knows what's going on, but everybody's busy parceling myths and prejudice as analysis and reportage. Suddenly everybody's become an expert on different varieties of turbans in the world.' AC paused to sip his beer and then began talking to himself. 'All I want to know is why I can't get off on garden-variety porn these days. Nothing less than lactating women and midgets with strap-ons works.'

We considered the issue silently for some time while listening to the sound of crickets outside and taking in the hearty smell of fertilizer wafting through the open bay windows. Across the street, the browning leaves of poplar trees fluttered in the breeze. Sitting there, I had the sensation of sitting amiably in a glass house. Then without warning, AC produced the yellow vial again, unscrewed it, and dabbed a glob of balm on my bruise. 'There,' he officiously pronounced, 'it's improving.'

'Thanks, AC.'

'You're most welcome, Chuck. Actually, I've been playing doctor all evening. I administered some bromazepam not too long ago. It should knock our friend out for a few hours.'

'Why did you do that?'

'Jimbo wasn't doing so well. In point of fact, he was going apeshit. I sat him down during his more lucid spells, and there were a couple, counseling him on the Duck situation.'

'And?'

'He listened, made strange noises, but mark my words, chum: whatever happens, he'll be okay. He's a champ . . . I'm the big fat pussy . . . That's why I fight.'

As I considered said dichotomy—champ versus big fat pussy— AC asked me if I wanted something to eat. I did. I was famished. Offering to make pasta, some vodka penne, he waddled to the kitchen, cigarette in mouth, and went about doctoring some bottled tomato sauce that he found in the pantry. Pots clanged, water boiled, oil hissed, boxes were torn open.

The household sounds, quotidian activities, were comforting. The Shaman was probably not privy to them. I imagined him returning home, kicking off his shoes, and turning on *Jeopardy* before calling for takeout, Chinese or Dominoes. In the interim, he might kick back, listening to *The Best of the Eighties*: Hartman's 'I Can Dream About You,' Dream Academy's 'Life in a Northern Town.' After dinner he might head into the city in his 500 SEL, sunroof open, music blaring. At the rooftop bar of the Peninsula Hotel, he might position himself on a barstool and hit on women, employing the worn conceit of an Arab sheikh. When it would work, he would check into a room and make love, never appreciating that the dynamic of a one-night stand does not lend itself to feeling. But there was always *Dirty Debutantes*.

'Is it about ready?' I yelled.

'Just about,' AC yelled back.

With time to kill, I switched on the TV to a local news channel and caught a story pertaining to a compatriot: '*Twenty-four-year-old Ansar Mahmood, a Pakistan-born permanent resident, asked a passer-by to photograph him against the Hudson. A guard at a nearby post called the police because the shot included a water treatment plant. Although the FBI found that Mahmood had no terrorist objectives, an investigation revealed he had assisted some friends who had overstayed their visas, making him guilty of harboring illegal immigrants . . .*'

Just then I noticed AC standing by the stairs in a checkered apron, wiping a dripping plate with a washcloth, staring at the TV.

'*. . . Mahmood is being held today at the Federal Detention Facility in Batavia. He is fighting deportation. He was, quite simply, in the wrong place at the wrong time—*'

'Turn it off!' AC yelled. 'Turn it off, chum! I told you I'm sick of the fucking news!' I immediately switched the TV off. Returning to the kitchen, AC asked, 'What's your status?'

Following him, I asked, 'What do you mean?'

'Your *visa* status?'

'Oh! Um. I'm not sure. I'm not an illegal alien, if that's what you mean. I was on an H-1B visa, the work visa but . . . but now . . . I actually don't know.'

I recalled that the good folks at the Immigration and Naturalization Service allowed some time between jobs—in the ballpark of sixty or ninety days—but I had already been out of a job for over two months. Consequently, there was a distinct possibility that I was what was known as *out of status*. Standing there, I was hit with the quick violence of a one-two combination: not only was I in possible legal limbo—or worse, in criminal violation of some INS code—but because of me, my friends might be in jeopardy.

'Well, shit, chum,' AC declared. 'It's about time you check.'

As AC plated the pasta, I said, 'I'm sorry about last night.'

'No,' AC replied, noisily scratching his Adam's apple, 'I'm sorry.'

We silently swallowed the penne down with Coke.

SEVEN

We decided to leave when Jimbo woke, but when we checked in on him three, four hours later, he was lying on his side like a beached whale, snoring and wheezing, it would seem, peacefully. Then we parted ways, as if we'd made a tacit agreement to stay out of each other's hair for some time, an arrangement that allowed me to leisurely sip Goldschläger from a teacup while listening to 'We Don't Have to Take Our Clothes Off (To Have a Good Time)' and other classics of the epoch. In the meantime, AC rummaged upstairs, downstairs, outside, quietly, diligently, single-mindedly, keeping discarded receipts, muffled phone calls, and other research concerning the ongoing Shaman Project to himself. Out of idle curiosity, I had quietly been to the basement myself to find stacked cartons of cigarettes. It would seem that the Shaman had singlehandedly cornered the exotic cigarette market in Connecticut.

After some time, I turned the TV on, and ten minutes into whatever I was watching—an episode of a reality show in which characters are voluntarily abandoned on a tropical island—I switched the channel to the presidential address, either a repeat telecast or a live event. I had the urge to flip, tune out, but before I could, the president had already begun,

> Mr. Speaker, Mr. President Pro Tempore, members of Congress, and fellow Americans: In the normal course of events, Presidents come to this chamber to report on the state of the Union. Tonight, no such report is needed. It has already been delivered by the American people. We have seen it in the courage of passengers,

who rushed terrorists to save others on the ground, passengers like
an exceptional man named Todd Beamer. And would you please
help me to welcome his wife, Lisa Beamer, here tonight. We have
seen the state of our Union in the endurance of rescuers, working
past exhaustion. We have seen the unfurling of flags, the lighting
of candles, the giving of blood, the saying of prayers in English,
Hebrew, and Arabic. We have seen the decency of a loving and
giving people who have made the grief of strangers their own. My
fellow citizens, for the last nine days, the entire world has seen
for itself the state of our Union and it is strong. Tonight we are a
country awakened to danger and called to defend freedom. Our
grief has turned to anger, and anger to resolution. Whether we
bring our enemies to justice, or bring justice to our enemies, justice
will be done.

The applause that followed was loud and sustained, like white noise, like rain. Stirred by the words, I too had the urge to applaud; *Thank God for the Union!*, I thought, *and that justice will be done!* My sense of grief, however, had not quite turned to anger, and anger had certainly not turned to the stuff of resolution.

After my father died, I learned that when tragedy strikes, you can either open up or shut down. My mother opened up and was not herself for some time. I shut down, and it worked for me. I shut down again on the day of September the eleventh.

Every New Yorker has a 9/11 story, and every New Yorker has a need to repeat it, to pathologically revisit the tragedy, until the tragedy becomes but a story. Mine goes like this. The morning had been bright and clear, but I had been dull and running late for an interview. I am not a morning person, and I had nicked myself shaving and the blood would not coagulate, possibly because I had treated the cut with tiny squares of double-ply toilet paper and an application of Corona, a home remedy pioneered by none other than AC. I would have taken the subway because attempting to hail a cab on Columbus at half past eight in the morning is like trying to get a reservation at that sushi joint in Tribeca at half past eight in the evening, but I happened upon a vacant gypsy cab, who agreed to take me when I flashed a crisp twenty. As I headed down the Avenue of the Americas, scanning my résumé, recalling the subtle mechanics of discounted cash flow analysis and the terms for the two plain-vanilla financings that had defined my career as a banker, I thought I heard something on the radio about a plane hitting Rockefeller Center. Many outrageous stories would circulate that day. Fiction would collide against fact. Preachers would pound the pulpit, promulgating acts of God. When I asked the driver to turn up the volume, he hollered 'That'll be extra,' so I let it go. I had more urgent issues to contend with.

Nearer midtown the traffic thickened. At 50th there was gridlock. At such times, the city got to you. Everyday, straightforward things like getting from point A to point B became epic struggles. 'It's like "playing chess with the Devil,"' AC liked to say. After several moments of characteristic indecision, I jumped out outside St. Pat's Cathedral, crossed over to the statue of Atlas in a loincloth, sprinted past the flower beds dividing the esplanade, and skirted the ice rink, noting in passing that the Rock remained unscathed. I breathlessly announced myself in the lobby. It was seven after nine. I was late. The managing director would be predictably livid. Cursing myself all the way up, I braced for the angry reception, for fireworks, except that there were no palpable signs of life on the fifty-sixth floor: no secretary, analyst, intern, or managing director. At first I thought my ears had popped because I could not hear the routine sounds of office bustle: ringing phones, gurgling coffee machines, photocopiers grinding out paper. It was eerie, odd, a bank holiday or Judgment Day. There was really nothing to do but wait. Glancing at the Hudson through the bay windows, hands professionally clasped, I mulled the future.

A wheezy sob finally broke the deathly silence. At first I tried
to ignore it, but when the noise persisted in muffled bursts, I was
compelled by curiosity to follow it to the end of the corridor. Peering
around the corner, I found ten, fifteen people gathered before a
window facing south. A fiftysomething lady was among them,
holding her heart with one hand, cupping her mouth with the other.
Handing her the folded toilet paper that I had kept in my pocket in
case my scab came loose, I pressed through to the smudged glass.
I stood there for a long time, dazed and a little dizzy. I would have
remained there for longer had the building not been evacuated, and
though I found myself on the street afterward, safe and sound, in
brilliant sunshine, I remained in a daze for weeks.

∽

At the Shaman's, however, I began to sob unexpectedly and
ridiculously. Closing my eyes, I repeated the Koranic mantra Ma
would repeat after my father died—'*Inna lillaihay wa inna illahay
rajayune*', or, 'We come from God and return to God'—as the
presidential address continued in the background:

> And on behalf of the American people, I thank the world for its
> outpouring of support. America will never forget the sounds of our
> National Anthem playing at Buckingham Palace, on the streets of
> Paris, and at Berlin's Brandenburg Gate. We will not forget South
> Korean children gathering to pray outside our embassy in Seoul,
> or the prayers of sympathy offered at a mosque in Cairo. We will
> not forget moments of silence and days of mourning in Australia
> and Africa and Latin America. Nor will we forget the citizens of
> 80 other nations who died with our own: dozens of Pakistanis;
> more than 130 Israelis; more than 250 citizens of India; men and
> women from El Salvador, Iran, Mexico and Japan; and hundreds
> of British citizens . . .

At that instant, I thought I heard AC's metronomic breathing behind me, but when I turned around, there was nobody there. 'Hello?' I called out. Getting up, I checked the kitchen, the pantry, stuck my head in the stairwell, and for good measure opened the front door to survey the porch, the lawn, the length of Elm Street. There wasn't anybody outside and no cars on the road, but the lights were on in the neighboring houses, and you could see the blue flicker of TV screens reflected in the windowpanes. Returning inside, I found AC standing in the middle of the room, watching the address like a zombie.

I also want to speak tonight directly to Muslims throughout the world. We respect your faith. It's practiced freely by many millions of Americans, and by millions more in countries that America counts as friends. Its teachings are good and peaceful, and those who commit evil in the name of Allah blaspheme the name of Allah. The terrorists are traitors to their own faith, trying, in effect, to hijack Islam itself. The enemy of America is not our many Muslim friends; it is not our many Arab friends. Our enemy is a radical network of terrorists, and every government that supports them.

'Islam's not good and peaceful, chum,' AC protested. 'It's a violent, bastard religion, as violent as, say, Christianity, Judaism, Hinduism, whatever. Man's been killing and maiming in the name of God since the dawn of time.'

'Why does it matter to you?'

'What do you mean? I'm a self-respecting Muslim atheist, just like any, ah, nonpracticing Christian, secular Jew, or carnivorous Hindu—'

Our response involves far more than instant retaliation and isolated strikes. Americans should not expect one battle, but a lengthy campaign, unlike any other we have ever seen. It may include dramatic strikes, visible on TV, and covert operations, secret even in success. We will starve terrorists of funding, turn them one against another, drive them from place to place, until there is no refuge or no rest. And we will pursue nations that provide aid or safe haven to terrorism. Every nation, in every region, now has a decision to make. Either you are with us, or you are with the terrorists.

'Eye for an eye, baby! The heirs of the fucking Enlightenment, and our response is, ah, biblical. How d'ya like dem apples? When push comes to shove, chum, we're all animals, every last one of us. Someone hits you, and you hit back. That's the law of the jungle. That's human nature.'

'Can I ask you something?'

'Ask me anything!'

'Why do you want to become an American?'

'C'mon, chum!' AC snapped, turning the TV volume down. 'I don't have to see eye to eye with this bastard! Hail Emma Goldman! Hail Chomsky! Hail Zinn! Hail Mary! *Yo, I thought this country was based upon freedom of speech / Freedom of press, freedom of your own religion / To make your own decision, now that's baloney / Cause if I gotta play by your rules, I'm bein' phony—*'

The riff was interrupted by the sound of a car pulling up outside. An engine churned to a stop; a door opened and shut. AC and I exchanged bemused, expectant looks with raised eyebrows, stiff necks. We both figured that it was the Shaman because that's the way he was: random. You could imagine the Shaman entering bearing a lopsided grin, unconcerned that we were ensconced in his living room, that AC was frolicking in his tighty whities, or I was sipping Goldschläger from a teacup. He would have just been happy as hell to see us.

Except something was not right. We heard unfamiliar, orotund voices and the deliberate, lockstep click of heels on the sidewalk. We followed the footsteps across the lawn with our eyes, up the steps, to the front door. There was a heavy knock-knock-knock, *knock*, more admonition than announcement. 'Are you expecting anybody?' AC inquired, just to make sure.

'Nope,' I replied.

'Well,' he said, folding his arms like a djinn. 'Let's see who's dropped by for happy hour.'

Two clean-cut men—one young, one not so young—stood in the porch like totems. From a distance, they might have appeared to be a pair of proselytizing brothers, more Church of Latter-day Saints than Jehovah's Witnesses. They cut stiff, polite poses, wore cotton shirts, dark suits, broad filigreed ties, and black shoes. Up close, however, it was obvious that they weren't men of God. The elder, arguably middle-aged guy wore a combed crown of dirty blond hair and a dubious expression. 'Mr. Shaw?' he asked.

'*What?*' I blurted. '*Oh*, oh no. You mean the Shaman, I mean, Mohammed, Mohammed Shah. He's not in.'

Fixing me with small cornflower eyes, he asked, 'Are you family, sir?'

'What? No, no. We're actually just friends of his—'

'I'm Agent Trig,' he said by way of introduction and, gesturing vaguely to his colleague, added, 'and that's Agent Holt.' Holt scratched his head. Towheaded and floppy-eared, he was not much older than us. 'We're from the FBI,' Trig reported and, after a pause, clarified, 'The Federal Bureau of Investigation.' Flashing a badge, he said, 'Do you mind if we come in?'

'Sure,' I shrugged, playing it cool, as if the good folks from the FBI were regular cocktail guests, but I was jelly. In my mind, I tried tallying the number of possible reasons that could have brought the Federal Bureau of Investigation to our door that night. I couldn't. There were too many.

Trig trudged in, wiped his feet on the doormat, and glanced around in the circumspect manner characteristic of a trained German shepherd, acknowledging AC's presence and state of dishabille with a nod. 'Whose cab is parked outside, gentlemen?'

'What's this about, officer?' AC asked.

'Mine,' I replied. 'Actually,' I added, 'technically, it's not really mine. I just lease it and drive it on shifts—'

'What happened to your eye, son?'

'Oh. I, um, got mugged. A few nights ago. Monday, or actually, it was Tuesday—'

'Did you file a police report?'

'No, sir. It was late, real late.' Trig wanted more so I found myself saying, 'I didn't want to get the police involved,' before biting my tongue.

'Why not? The authorities are here to serve you, son—unless you've got something to hide.'

'Hide? What would I have to hide?'

Trig searched my face for some indication of evasion or deceit, but he did not have to look hard because his accusatory gaze made me feel guilty, criminal, and I must have looked it. 'Where's Mr. Mo-hammid Shaw?' he asked.

'What's this about?' AC persisted, and again the query did not register. I noticed a cold hard glint in his narrowing eyes, and for an instant I wondered whether AC was more dangerous drunk or sober. At that juncture, however, it was an academic issue. At that juncture, it was imperative that AC shut his face. Instead, AC blurted in Punjabi, '*Ay ki bakvass eh?*'

Enunciating, Trig repeated, 'Where. Is. Mr. Mo-hammid Shaw?'

'He,' I began, 'I don't exactly know where he is—'

'What are you gentlemen doing here?'

'Well, we hadn't heard from Mohammed for some time, so we thought we'd just, you know, check up on him.'

'Does anybody else live here with him?'

'I don't think so, officer . . . no.'

'You mind if we look around?'

'Do you have a search warrant?' AC interjected. Arms crossed, hairy legs astride, world on shoulders, he stood like Atlas in a loincloth, daring to be trifled with. It was a pigheaded pose, a misguided, arguably American strategy. 'I know my rights,' he testily continued, 'and I'm sure you are cognizant of the concept of *habeas corpus ad subjiciendum* that's virtually enshrined in our Constitution—the, ah, *American Constitution*. Article one, section nine, clause two. "The Privilege of the Writ of habeas corpus shall not be suspended, unless when in cases of rebellion or invasion the public safety may require it." So even though you've briskly, and I must say, rather rudely, ignored my queries, I'm going to ask you again: *What. Is. This. About?* '

Trig blinked rapidly, processing the rodomontade, while Holt, who had been by the door all this time, stiff and erect, one hand on belt, began fidgeting. I could tell he had not been in such a situation before. Neither had we. Turning his head slowly toward AC, then his body, Trig addressed him in a decidedly measured tone: 'We received an anonymous tip last night that there's been some . . . suspicious activity. We were told that a cab—a New York City yellow cab—has been standing outside all night, and these days we take these things seriously. So if you've got nothing to hide, I'd strongly urge you to cooperate with us. This *is* a matter of public safety.'

'Yes, yes,' I said, 'we're ready to cooperate.'

'Where are you gentlemen from?'

'With all due respect, officer, that's none of your goddamn business,' AC interjected.

'You need to relax!'

'I'll tell you what I'm going to do, chum,' AC began. 'I'm going to light an American Spirit, put my legs up on this couch, and scratch my groin with, ah, bestial abandon. The pursuit of happiness is my constitutional right. I'm going to exercise it right now. *Ki samjha, chitay?*' As AC proceeded to deliver, I noticed his hand tremble lighting the cigarette. Then all hell broke loose.

The sequence of each discrete incident that led to our arrest remains somewhat fuzzy, partly because it all happened so fast, partly because the adrenaline coursing through my head blinded me, but whatever happened, happened with the momentum of inevitability. When Trig demanded to see identification, AC showed him the birdie, and then I think Jimbo thundered down the stairwell, bellowing 'BANZAI,' as if startled by a nightmare. Although we knew Jimbo to be a gentle giant, Jimbo is a large man, the sort you may not want trailing you in a dark alley. And who knows, maybe Holt felt as if he were in a dark alley. I think he was the first to draw, and for the first time in my life, I found myself staring into the nozzle of a gun. Instead of raising my arms, however, I instinctively cowered. I remember holding my head between my hands. I remember Trig instructed us to *sit-the-fuck-down* and *shut-the-fuck-up*. I remember Jimbo muttering, 'We're cool, we're cool.'

When we squeezed uncomfortably next to each other on the couch, necks stretched, knees clamped, one of us sat on the remote, triggering the volume control.

> *After all that has just passed, all the lives taken, and all the possibilities and hopes that died with them, it is natural to wonder if America's future is one of fear. Some speak of an age of terror. I know there are struggles ahead, and dangers to face. But this country will define our times, not be defined by them. As long as the United States of America is determined and strong, this will not be an age of terror; this will be an age of liberty, here and across the world.*

For a moment, the agents, like us, listened. Then Holt barked, 'YOU NEED TO TURN THAT OFF RIGHT NOW.' We complied immediately, guiltily.

EIGHT

The night was pleasant and the poplars were still, but there was great activity on Elm Street. People had come out on their porches in ones and twos, in striped pajamas and robes to gawk at the spectacle: in the coruscating lights of four squad cars and an unmarked sedan arranged around a yellow cab, a congregation of a dozen or so cops talked among themselves in low voices and into radios as a couple of suits paraded by with three disheveled, swarthy men in handcuffs. Although there were no reporters or cameras, there was an air of theatricality to the mise-en-scène. The local cops might have been extras in the grand scheme of things, but they had arrived in numbers in a show of force. They were on edge but played their parts, posing stiffly with brave, brittle faces. And I was broken, depleted, more cipher than actor, but kept thinking *don't trip, don't break a leg, walk with your head up high, like you've done nothing wrong*, but couldn't, and it didn't really matter, because no matter what I did, I couldn't change the way I was perceived.

From the corner of my eye, I caught a woman silhouetted in a doorway pick up a child and whisk him inside as if to shield him from the grim vicissitudes of the world. You could imagine the child asking unusually probing questions for a five- or six-year-old when being tucked in bed that night, touching geopolitics, and who knows, notions of collective identity. The next-door neighbor, an elderly lady with pink curlers in her hair, covered her mouth as I passed by. In better times, she might have been yawning. You could imagine what she'd say to reporters if asked: *I saw them going in, coming out, and they seemed okay—you know, not from around here—but okay, but who knows anything about anybody else, especially these days.* The man with the dog was stationed at the top of the cul-de-sac, hand on hip, pooch muzzling the air.

A cop announced over a bullhorn, 'Show's over, folks. Go home. There's nothin' to be worried about.' Then I was shoved into the sedan, hooded, and sandwiched between two bodies, presumably Agents Holt and Trig, but I couldn't be sure. I was sure that I wasn't nestled among friends. Jimbo and AC had been behind me out the door, but I realized I had lost track of them in all the hoopla.

We drove fast, taking several quick turns, and before long were gunning down some highway, honking, swerving, overtaking cars. The interior smelled of wet cigarettes and Old Spice, a heady, insidious aroma that permeated my hood and settled into my consciousness. I had to open my mouth to breathe, close my eyes to think. As I hurtled through the dark, a voice in my head kept saying *just relax, stay calm, this isn't happening,* but the smell and chafing cuffs reminded me *this is happening, this is for real.* About a half hour into the drive, full-on nausea threatened. When a wad of phlegm shot up my esophagus, I cleared my throat and asked, 'Would you mind stopping? I'm afraid I might vomit . . .'

There was a beat, an exchange of looks perhaps. The guy to my left said, 'You gotta be kiddin'!' It wasn't Holt or Trig. Shrill and out of breath, the speaker sounded small and dumpy, like Mickey Rooney.

'No, sir,' I replied, my stomach churning audibly. 'I'm not kidding. I wouldn't kid about something like this . . . not right now.' Somebody up front lowered a window, and we began to slow down. A voice warned, 'Don't do anything stupid,' which could only have meant: do not attempt to break free and scamper, hooded and hands bound, across the highway.

When we stopped, I was grabbed by the arm like a recalcitrant child and yanked out onto the curb. A couple of cars sped noisily and dangerously by. We weren't at or outside a rest stop. The air was cooler and fragrant with grass and wet earth. Swallowing mouthfuls, I felt better. Then I was led a few steps away from the vehicle and instructed to retch: 'Go ahead. Do it. Do it here! Barf, buddy, barf!'

As instructed, I attempted several times, but performance anxiety, or something like it, stifled the urge. Had I not been cuffed, I might have gagged myself. Turning to my handler, I shrugged, saying, 'It's not, um, coming out—'

'You're messin' with me,' yelled Rooney. 'I knew it,' he added, 'I knew it,' almost to himself. Yanking me back inside, he announced, 'He didn't puke! Can you believe that shit?' Turning to me, he cried, 'You even squirm now, and I swear you gonna regret it. You hear me?'

I nodded but needed to piss.

❧

Two, maybe three hours later, we arrived somewhere. We could have been in Boston, or Albany, or Mars, PA, for that matter, though when I thought about it, I had heard a scratchy voice over the CB say something like *Passaic*, then somebody else say *no, MDC*. I didn't think twice about it at the time, but we would later learn that the worst abuses in the American prison system after 9/11 took place at MDC, the Metropolitan Detention Center. According to later, possibly hyperbolic headlines, MDC was 'America's Own Abu Ghraib'.

At the time, I was only sure that we weren't upstate, as there were intimations of a city in the background mewl of traffic and in the breeze that carried the whiff of garbage and the tincture of smog. I could imagine being surrounded by buildings, by great facades of stone, and it was mildly and momentarily reassuring.

Then I was briskly led through a series of heavy gates, down a musty flight of stairs, and deposited in a cold room on a metal chair that was fixed to the ground. A door slammed shut, and I was alone. The night assumed the tenor of a childhood nightmare: my hood was fastened tight, the darkness was severe, complete; sweat trickled down my side; I needed to go, but there was nothing to do but squirm. I wondered if Jimbo and AC were nearby, in adjacent cells, also squirming and wet under the armpits, and the thought of camaraderie comforted. *Stop sweating, chum,* I chastened myself, *we're in this together. We've done nothing wrong. We've got nothing to worry about. This is obviously a mistake. You'll get your phone call. Everybody gets a phone call—*

Just then the door swung open, and footsteps marched in. 'What were you doin' at Mo-hammid Shaw's?' It was Rooney, and he was in my face.

'Look,' I began, crossing and uncrossing my legs as my bladder pushed against my insides, 'there's been some kind of mistake—'

'Let's get things straight, buddy. The name of the game is: We Ask the Questions, You Answer Them. All right? All right!'

'All right, all right,' I repeated. 'I just want to know what's going on.'

'You want to know what's goin' on? You're in big fucking trouble. That's what's goin' on. We're holding you under the Material Witness Statute. Know what that is? That means that you're a material witness to a crime—'

'What crime?' I blurted. He was obviously fishing.

'What crime? What crime?' he repeated, his disembodied voice now before me, now behind me, now whispering in my ear. 'How about breaking and entering?'

'*What?*'

'How about cigarette running?'

Shit, I thought. 'Cigarettes?' I said. 'What cigarettes?' I would fail the polygraph.

'Lemme ask you something: How d'you feel about what happened on September eleventh?'

'What—'

'Did it make you happy?'

'This is ridiculous. I want to make my phone call. I know my rights.'

'You aren't American!' he fired back. 'You got no fucking rights.'

Pausing, he allowed me to process the assertion. The logic was strangely unassailable. I had never thought of it that way and had no reason to. 'And you got no time,' Rooney was saying. 'We just checked with the INS. Your visa's expiring, buddy—the what's it—H-1B? You'll be illegal in a week.' *Shit*, I thought. 'So you cooperate with us, or we can lock you away for a long time—no phone call, no lawyer, no nothing. And if you're lucky, someday we'll put you on a plane—a one-way ticket back to Bumfuckistan. We can and will deport you. We can and will deport your pals.' *Shit, shit, shit*, I thought. 'So let's start again. Why were you at Shaw's?'

'Mohammed's a friend of ours,' I began weakly. 'We hadn't heard from him for a couple of weeks, so we decided to drive up from the city, from New York, from Manhattan, to check on him, and because he wasn't there, we just hung around and—'

'When was the last time you spoke to him?'

'I guess I haven't spoken to him since July, July fourth.'

'What kinda friend are you?'

'What? Oh. Well, I know Mohammed through AC, I mean Ali, Ali Chaudhry.'

'You messin' with me, aren't you? I told you not to mess with me, buddy.'

'I'm not messing with anybody—'

'Listen,' Rooney said conspiratorially. 'You admit that your pals were involved in terrorist activities, and we'll go easy on you. We'll plead for leniency. Don't protect your friends, because they aren't gonna protect you. All right, all right?'

'Terrorist activities?'

'What were you guys planning at Shaw's? Don't bullshit me because we've already busted into your pal Aly's apartment over in the city. We found books, books in Arabic, and bomb-making manuals. So do yourself a favor and cooperate.'

'Bomb-making manuals?' I repeated incredulously. 'I don't know what you're talking about.'

'You speak English, don't you? What fucking part didn't you understand? You understand that you're in deep shit, right? You understand that if you cooperate, we'll go easy on you?'

'I think you're mistaken—'

'I'm not asking you what you think, buddy. I'm asking you what you know. There's a big difference—'

'But I don't know anything about—'

'You know what? I'm done with this fucking guy,' declared Rooney. 'Lock 'em up. Throw away the key.'

After a quick conference of murmurs, I was grabbed by either arm, lifted up, and led out. *Wait*, I should've said, *let me explain myself*, or something else, anything else—who I am, what I do—but I just shuffled along blindly and dumbly, angling my head to one side for fear of walking into a wall.

In another room, I was uncuffed by the guards, then commanded to strip. They must have watched as I reached around my waist, unbuttoned my shirt, kicked off my lizard-skins one by one, and then unraveled my belt and slipped off my jeans like a pantomime getting into a tub of hot water. 'Take off everything, sand nigger,' they instructed. I repeated the creative slur in my mind as I stood before them in sagging black polyester-blend socks, my limp head dangling between my thighs. 'He's cut, he's cut,' they cried, clapping or slapping fives.

Clad in a cold, coarse, loose body suit that zipped up from the crotch, and fitted with flip-flops that were two sizes too big on my feet, I was led by the arm down a series of interconnected corridors. When the hood was whisked off my head like a magician's handkerchief, I found myself in a cell. The door shut emphatically behind me.

Sliding against the wall, I shrank into a corner, dragged down by gravity and fatigue and the weight of my bladder. In my mind, I measured the confines of my predicament with my soles. About eight by eight feet, the cell featured a metal cot, a tawny, seatless toilet, and swimming-pool-green walls. Paint flaked across the granite blocks where other prisoners had rested their backs before me: thieves, thugs, pimps, pedophiles, rapists, murderers. Like them, I considered how fate had conspired to put me away, and for the first time anger welled within me. If AC really was a terrorist, I thought, why hadn't he enlisted me in the cause?

'Fuck the police,' I said out loud, pleased with the concision with which the phrase conveyed my sentiment. *'Fuck the police comin' straight from the underground / Young nigga got it bad cuz I'm brown ...'* Although I'd been listening to N.W.A. since I was a teenager, it was the first time I understood where they were coming from. The anthem's resonance was no longer mere novelty or a boyish sense of affinity with the hood; no, it put things in perspective.

But anger requires stamina, and I had none. It took Herculean effort just to drag myself to the toilet, which, to my horror, was backed up. My fractured reflection floated on the muddy surface, and below it, shreds of the *Sun* flailed in slow motion like seaweed. Struck, I just stood there, dizzily hovering above myself. I appeared criminal: my hair had congealed in thick clumps, and a film of beard covered my jaw like a growth of moss. For a moment, I considered dunking my head, but the urge passed and I urinated. Cascading over the rim, the overflow spread on the floor in an expanding puddle, the color but not the consistency of maple syrup. Then collapsing on the cot, I passed out.

NINE

When I woke, it was bright, and I was numb, and for an instant I thought I was dead, but then the stench of cold urine filled my nostrils, and feeling returned to my body like an ache. There was no way to tell what time it was since the quality of light was unchanged, but I wasn't rested, and my mouth was dry and tasted like shit. Shutting my eyes, I watched chimerical shapes shift in the electric darkness.

After my father's death, I would shut my eyes, sometimes in broad daylight, sometimes in bed at night, and imagine traveling at the speed of light, past planets and brightly lit stars and galaxies whirling in slow motion on an invisible axis. There would be high adventure, an urgent mission to save mankind, a chase by aliens, close encounters with meteor storms, requiring routine feats of dexterity and great presence of mind. Tossing in bed, I would issue muffled orders, make beeping sounds and sounds of things blowing up. My imaginary flights would stir restlessness and inevitably make me thirsty and want to pee, but I'd hold it in because I didn't want to upset Ma.

At some juncture, however, I'd find her hovering above me in her red caftan with a halo of hallway light around her head. Of course, I'd pretend to sleep, attempt evasive maneuvers, but it would be too late. 'What were you doing, baby?' she'd ask, sitting down beside me. Inspired from the sci-fi serial on Pakistan Television, the story usually but not always involved the Cylons—evil robots who *speak like this*—and Baltar, the bald overlord *who always sits on a high chair.* Together they would launch a sneak attack on Planet Earth, and even though I was young and inexperienced, I was good and brave and fighting back.

Running her fingers through my hair, Ma would listen with mild amusement, and after I was done, she would say something like 'Listen, baby, space is very, very far away. You and me can't worry about things so far away. We have to worry about right now, and tomorrow. You have school tomorrow. You have to do well in school. You are the man of the family. This is more responsibility than saving the universe.'

My universe had diminished: after my father died, we moved from our house off Tariq Road to a two-and-a-half-bedroom apartment in an apartment block off Bandar Road, on the other side of town. We no longer had a garden, no place to make mud men or loaf or play cricket; instead, there was a common concrete yard downstairs where teenagers often scuffled, and there was the street. I had no friends in the neighborhood, and it took almost an hour to get to and from school by van. When things changed, they seemed to change for the worse. But I made do.

There was also a tragedy of a different scale. We had spent almost a month packing our lives into cardboard boxes and steel trunks, and it took us another month to unpack. I'd insisted on doing my room myself: the clothes in my closet, the books on my bookshelf, my dinky car collection, toy soldier battalion, Mechano set, Chinese checkers board, karram board, two teddy bears—fat Chumpat Rai and slight and hairy Mr. Butt—and the cereal-box-toilet-paper-roll-and-Styrofoam model of Battlestar Galactica, which was about as large as me. It had taken six weeks to construct, paint, and perfect, through the funeral, mourning rituals, and condolence visits. When I opened the carton marked fragile and this side up, I discovered it had been irreparably damaged in the move, somehow crushed by an unabridged edition of *Grimm's Fairy Tales.* Legs folded, I sat quietly on the floor of my new room among brown paper and open boxes contemplating what was and had been. It was a sign to move on.

Sensing the gravity of the situation, Ma went to town and within a fortnight presented me with a second-hand, garbage-can-size replica of R2-D2 and a functioning, battery-operated lightsaber. Although the items might have been from a different galaxy, a different war, and I had moved on, to other exercises of the imagination, it was a winning gesture. There were always consolations then.

As I lapsed in and out of consciousness, reconciling where I had been and where I was—two worlds separated, as it were, by light-years—the door banged open. Two guards entered—one black, one white, one with a goatee, one with an Afro—bearing chains like gifts from the Magi. Swatting the back of my head, the white guy cried, 'You pissed yourself, pencil-dick! I'm gonna make you pay for my kickers!' It seemed routine, the invective, the casual violence, the way things are, the way things are going to be: doors would open, doors would close, and I would be smacked around, molested, hauled back and forth between cells and interrogation sessions. The black guy pinned me with a knee. 'You like that?' he inquired. 'Get the fuck up!' Shackled, I could barely move, much less put one foot in front of another. Consequently, I was dragged down one corridor and then another, slipping and scraping against the linoleum.

I found myself in a small, well-lit, windowless room furnished with two chairs on either side of a desk. In a corner of the ceiling I could observe my diminutive reflection in a translucent orb. 'Sit your ass down,' the goateed guard instructed (and grabbing a handful of hair, reminded me that he'd see me soon). As per his instructions, I sat glued to the seat, braced for the worst: hamstringing, kneecapping, garrotting, shock therapy, Chinese water torture. In a changed America, it seemed anything could happen. I could abide the cursing and spitting and casual violence, but the threat of systematic brutality stirred a profound sense of panic, so when the interrogator shambled in, I found myself trembling.

A manila folder was placed between us in a gesture that suggested that we had convened to discuss its contents, though the two sheaves of yellow legal and folded fax didn't appear to be particularly incriminating. Beyond my immigration record, they couldn't have had much more on me than my height, weight, color of eyes, and distinguishing characteristics, but I could imagine Rooney penning a damning missive in red pen, with the words *uncooperative* and *obvious terrorist leanings* double-underlined. Presumably, it was the interrogator's job to dot the *i*'s and cross the *t*'s.

The graying, fiftysomething grizzly bear of a man crossed his arms, took a deep breath—something between a wheeze and a whistle—and peered at me from under unruly eyebrows that met at the middle of his brow. 'You wanna start talking?' My mouth was dry, my saliva warm, viscous. 'About what, sir, exactly?' I asked. The interrogation that followed could be read like some warped catechism:

Grizzly: You a terrorist?
Chuck: No, sir.
Grizzly: You a Moslem?
Chuck: Yes, sir.
Grizzly: So you read the Ko-Ran?
Chuck: I've read it.
Grizzly: And pray five times a day to Al-La?'
Chuck: No, sir. I pray several times a year, on special occasions like Eid.
Grizzly: You keep the Ram-a-Dan?
Chuck: Yes, sir, I usually keep about half, sometimes more but mostly less—
Grizzly: D'you eat pork?
Chuck: No sir.
Grizzly: Drink?
Chuck: Liquor? Yes, sir.
Grizzly: Won't Al-La get mad?

Chuck: I don't think it's all that important to Him, sir, you
          know, whether I drink or not.
Grizzly: (Interrogator scratches cleft of his chin.) What's
          important to Him then?
Chuck: (Subject scratches himself as well. The suit makes him
          itch.) Well, I suppose . . . that I'm good . . . to people.

Grizzly searched my face for an unnervingly long time with sunken blue eyes ringed with freckles. 'What's your story, kid?' The timbre of his voice did not suggest empathy or curiosity but invited exposition. Unsure whether the question demanded exposition or some sort of map of my sociopolitical coordinates, I found myself saying, 'I was born in Karachi, in Pakistan, in 1981.' It seemed natural to begin at the beginning. 'My father died when I was five and a half.' I paused. 'It was tough,' I added, but what more could I have said? That we ate meat twice a week? Saved on toothpaste by brushing with salt? Preserved toothbrushes to polish my school shoes? I wasn't going to talk about the move, the Battlestar Galactica tragedy. I certainly was not going to tell him that I missed my father desperately but it pained me to recall him.

'We got by,' I continued, dehydrated and a little delirious. 'Ma always told me: you've got to work really, really hard. And I did. Ever since I can remember, I've been a pretty good student. I suppose the single guiding motivation of my life has been to impress Ma. I never rebelled as a teenager, never shaved my head or came home at dawn, whatever. Instead my mother and I cooked together, we watched movies, went on drives. Of course, once in a while I went to have ice cream with friends, with cousins, I played cricket, but you could say I was kind of straightlaced. I read a lot, anything I could get my hands on, *Reader's Digest*, *Moby-Dick*, Archie. I got ten A's in my O-levels and when I turned seventeen, I secured a scholarship to study lit, English literature, at NYU that met almost eighty percent of my needs . . .'

Although I was babbling, Grizzly had not interrupted once. 'Hold on, son,' he finally said. 'So you're telling me you're a literature student?'

'No, sir,' I replied, 'not anymore.'

'Then?'

'I graduated last year and became an investment banker.'

'So you're a banker?'

'Not anymore, sir. I was fired, in July.'

'And now?'

'I'm a cabbie.'

'Let me get this straight: you were like some Wall Street banker, and now you're a *cabbie?*'

'Yes, sir.'

'That's one hell of a career change.'

'Yes, sir, but you've got to do what you've got to do. It's not that bad. I like driving.'

Grizzly began massaging his eyelids. 'All right, this is what I'm going to do. I'm gonna get you a glass of water. In the meantime, I want you to help me out here. I'm trying to understand why Muslims terrorize. I want you to think about this issue, and then tell me what you think.'

As a Muslim, he figured, I would have special insight into the phenomenon—knowledge of the relevant fatwa or some verse in the Koran—just like a black man, any black man, should be privy to black-on-black violence or the allure of a forty-ounce. But like everybody, I figured the hijackers were a bunch of crazy Saudi bastards. Although Grizzly might have agreed, my analysis was admittedly cursory.

But I couldn't think straight. I had a headache, a hard, precise pain like a pair of tongs clamped on my temple. Consequently, when he returned, I was less prepared than when he left. Placing a paper cup on the table, he sat down and folded his arms again. 'So where were we?' Raising the cup to my lips with both hands as if it were a chalice

of sacramental wine, I gulped the contents in one go. The water was
cold and sweet and tasted like freedom. 'I'm not sure,' I said.

Frowning, Grizzly said, 'Wrong answer.'

'Okay, sorry. I think you asked why do terrorists terrorize?'
Closing my eyes, I attempted to channel AC, channel history. 'Well,'
I began, 'I guess you could trace it back to when it all started. That's
one way of going about it.'

Grizzly shrugged.

'As far as I understand, Islam, historically speaking, was not
associated with terrorism. It was like associated with empire—the
Ottomans, the Mughals in Pakistan, in India, the Safavids next door.
I guess the first terrorist of the twentieth century was that Serbian
guy who kicked off World War I by assassinating the archduke,
I don't know. Anyway, the whole Palestinian-Jewish thing began
afterwards. The Jews were the terrorists before 1948, then it was
the Palestinians. They weren't blowing themselves up though. The
Japanese started that, and I suppose suicide bombing was pioneered
much later, in the eighties, by Hindus, the Tamil Tigers. Muslims
are like Johnny-come-latelies. We, I mean, Muslims, only picked
up on it recently—'

Grizzly: Okay, okay, why don't you just stick to the Islamic
           religion?
Chuck: Okay.
Grizzly: I want to know does the Koran sanction terrorism?
Chuck: I've read it. I'm no terrorist.
Grizzly: Then why do Moslems use it to justify terrorism?
Chuck: It's all a matter of interpretation, isn't it? I mean take
           the Bible. It's interpreted differently by, like,
           Unitarians and Mormons, Lutherans, Pentecostals—
Grizzly: Okay—
Chuck: Eric Rudolph, Mother Teresa, Jerry Falwell, the
           Lord's Liberation Army—

Grizzly: I said *okay*! Look. All I want to know is why the hell
          did they have to blow up the Twin Towers?
Chuck: Your guess, sir, is as good as mine.
Grizzly: Can't you put yourself in their shoes?
Chuck: No, can you?
Grizzly: Okay, just take it easy, boy, just take it easy.

Hunched over the table, Grizzly scrawled something into the folder—two or three sentences in ballpoint cursive—muttering to himself as he wrote, like a poet reworking a sentence by utterance. *Boy's excitable. Spoke about childhood, history. Defended Islamic religion, terrorism.* I didn't really mean to but didn't mean to apologize for myself either.

When he was finished penning the profile, he got up and left without uttering a word. The guards followed after. They smacked me around, dragged me back to my cell. It was bright as day inside, and bleak as hell.

∾

There is no meaningful way to convey the abjectness of prison life. You review the events that led to your incarceration again and again and again. You dwell on permutations that could have led you to another place, a better place, home. You calculate the probability that the door will open. You imagine defying gravity, walking upside down, flying. You count anything, everything—the blocks in the wall, the marks sketched across the blocks, the metal teeth in the zipper of your suit, the lines across your clammy palms—comparing the latest tally to your last count to make sure you're sane before you realize that keeping count of the unchangeable is a telltale sign of madness.

In rare moments of clarity, I considered a strict regime of push-ups, stomach crunches, jumping jacks. I considered God, prayer, jihad, but mostly I considered sustenance—hot dog, chicken wing, cherry tomato—small meals, nothing fancy; a slice of Wonder Bread would have been manna. When lunch or dinner finally arrived—lentil-like gruel and a piece of round, hard bread served on a plastic tray—it tasted like old oatmeal and Styrofoam and made me even hungrier. Prison is like that; no consolations, no catharsis. You might hold your head in your hands, pound your fists, sob like a baby, but the floor will remain wet, the toilet backed up, and your cell will continue to stink like a chicken run. And just when you think you've figured the routine, things change.

At some juncture, the black guard entered, cuffed and hooded me, and led me out by the elbow in a hurry. For all I knew, he might have been taking me to the shooting range out back where they would read me my last rites and execute me before a firing squad, no dying request, no nothing. Instead I found myself in a locker room and in an open locker, found my blue jeans, six dollars, Abdul Karim's car keys, and wallet in the pockets, but no cigarettes; my polyester shirt was folded on the top shelf; my jacket hung from a peg below; my lizard-skins lay beneath. For the first time in days, maybe weeks, I felt joy. I was ready to be taken wherever, whenever, shooting range, hell. I was going to part with my boots again. After changing, I waited for direction, for a sign; then there was a knock on the door.

It was Grizzly, hands in pockets, legs astride, manila folder tucked under his arm. Marching, he ordered, 'Let's go.' Trailing by a few paces, I followed him past offices staffed with diligent corrections officers in gray uniforms, armed with holstered pistols. Ominous signs along the way read METROPOLITAN DETENTION CENTER. Unlike the gritty, brick borough precincts, the building seemed to be a recent construction, featuring tiled corridors and slick fixtures. There were cameras everywhere, monitoring my every step, gesture, move.

When we reached the cavernous lobby, Grizzly proclaimed, 'You're outta here.'

'I beg your pardon?' I blurted.

'I made some calls, tracked down your returns, your transcript. Your story checks out.'

'You're sure I'm not a terrorist?'

A flicker of something like amusement crossed Grizzly's forehead. Then, looming over me he said, 'I've stuck my neck out for you.'

'Thank you, sir, thank you for granting me—'

'You're welcome,' he growled. 'Now don't screw it up.'

As he turned to leave, he added, 'There's one more thing: your visa runs out in five days. You've got five days to leave the country. We'll be watching.'

'Wait!' I cried as he walked away. 'What?'

'You heard me.'

'Hey!' I yelled. 'And what about my friends?'

In the background, the security personnel stationed at the metal detector by the main entrance tensed.

'I'm not dealing with them—'

'Yeah, well, I'm not leaving without them.'

'Don't be a pinhead!' Grizzly yelled back. 'Go home, boy!'

In the scrutiny of at least six closed-circuit cameras, I considered my options—principled stand versus strategic retreat—and opted for the latter. It was not much of a choice really. I walked out, walked fast without looking back. The Brooklyn-Queens Expressway rattled above. The Sunset Park station was not far away. It would be a twenty-minute ride into town, half an hour to Mini Auntie's.

TEN

Once at Tja! my sommelier friend Roger had informed me that a black man has to adhere to a tacit code 'right here, right now, today, in the twenty-first century U S of A.' It was late, and he was several drinks into the evening and kept talking while I sat wordlessly beside him in a booth, hands folded, eyes glazed. The lights had come on and then, by popular demand, had been turned off again, but in the brief interlude, you could see the stains on the upholstery and the browning crust of water damage across a portion of the roof above us.

'It's not about glass ceilings and that kind of intangible shit. It's an everyday thing. You know I can't make quick body movements in public? My presence threatens people. When a big white guy moves quickly, people laugh, but when a big black guy moves quickly, they take cover: mothers fear for their children, I've seen cops reach for their batons. And I work chi-chi restaurants. I dress well, speak English in grammatically defensible sentences, hey, I even speak French, *j'ai pas d'accent, tu sais?* But I could be talking about a six-hundred-dollar bottle of wine, like, I don't know, a '95 Château Margaux, and I look into the eyes of these people, and I know they're thinking, you got no business telling me about no Lestonnac family and no Pavillon Rouge! Know what I'm sayin'?'

Although I had knowingly nodded, Roger's heartfelt spiel did not make sense to me then. You could have attributed his earnest indignation to misunderstandings, miscommunication, misplaced sensitivity, his third martini, a rough day at work. After all, how do you peer into somebody's heart or head? It wasn't that I was a Pollyanna, but I had no functional appreciation for prejudice, because I had never faced any. Besides, it was noisy, and I had had other concerns that night.

There was a girl perched on a distant barstool, unattached or unattended, not quite beckoning but not quite cool to my furtive, admiring glances, and though I considered approaching her, when push came to shove, I found I could not summon the playboy inside. Entropy, as usual, had me by the cojones. And other dramas were unfolding then. The Duck had Jimbo pinned in a corner—I couldn't tell if they were smooching or squabbling from my vantage—and on the other side of the room, AC had picked a fight with a Scandinavian who was taking advantage of a swooning Japanese girl in fishnet stockings. 'Pick on somebody your size,' AC boomed, 'you Viking son of a bitch!' Then, when the lights came on, Roger announced, 'Closing time, man, it's closing time.'

In prison, I finally got it. I understood that just like three black men were gangbangers, and three Jews a conspiracy, three Muslims had become a sleeper cell. And later, much later, the pendulum would swing back, and everybody would celebrate progress, the storied tradition of accommodation, on TV talk shows and posters in middle schools. There would be ceremonies, public apologies, cardboard displays. In the interim, however, I threatened order, threatened civilization. In the interim, I too had to adhere to an unwritten code.

∽

On the subway ride from prison, I looked away when people looked at me. An ancient Chinese couple in matching embroidered Mao suits watched me unflinchingly and, it would seem, unforgivingly. Two seats over a hipster mother nursed a baby in a sling while glancing sideways from time to time. A group of Hispanic teenagers equipped with rucksacks huddled by the door, joking, making eyes. And in the far corner, a waifish man sporting a streaked crew cut eyed me while tugging the stud in his ear. It was a free country: he was free to stare; I was free to cringe. I scratched my temple, studied the floor, pretended to commit to memory the banner advertising cures for erectile dysfunction. I was conscious of the way I looked, behaved, the way I anxiously scratched my nose, my ear. When they announced 'Please report any suspicious activity or behavior' over the speakers, I closed my eyes like a child attempting to render himself invisible. When a hand grabbed me by the shoulder then, I almost cried bloody murder.

'*Take it easy, man!*'

Swinging above me by the handrail, his crisp white shirt, as always, opened to his navel, Legionnaire Jon was peering down at me with bug eyes.

'Sorry,' I blurted. 'I'm a little jumpy. You know, lot on my mind, not enough sleep—'

'No problemo, old friend. I know how it is: too much coffee or too much coke, but it's best to keep your nose clean these days. Otherwise,' he said, making a fist, 'the city will close in on you like a vise.'

'Yeah—'

'You know, back in the old legionnaire days, I was sent to Kisangani, and when I arrived I could tell that something was out of whack. There was a real estate boom going on and the *sapeurs* were raging, but people were trickling out—back to the bush, or Brazzaville, wherever—and those who couldn't or wouldn't were wasted on *khat* and *mokoyo* . . .'

Jon trailed off, staring into the blur behind me. He seemed different from his behind-the-bar persona, a little smaller, a little louder. 'Anyway, what are you doing in these parts? You don't have to say. Let me guess? You have a bird here. I know your kind: stealthy, deadly.'

'Something like that—'

'You know they just discovered that alkaloids use the same neural mechanisms as love? Both fire up this area of the brain called the caudate nucleus,' he kibitzed, pointing in the vicinity of his nape. 'Is that wild or is that wild?'

'Pretty wild,' I offered, but before he could update me on other developments in clinical research, I said, 'Man, I missed you last time at Tja!'

'Oh yeah?'

'Yeah, it wasn't quite the same.'

'Thanks, old friend,' he said smilingly. 'Well, since we go back, I'll share some news with you, but keep it on the down low. I'm heading south for the winter. I've some chinks saved up, and I'm thinking of putting them in this lot in Playa Brava. You know the Playa? Of course you do. It's warm there, and there's the smell of salt on the breeze, and women in the water, like mermaids—'

All of a sudden the lights went out in the car. The train lurched and slowed, skidding on the rails. A nervous clamor rose about us. The teenagers whooped, the infant began to howl. Then we ground to a complete standstill. There were bursts of static over the PA system that sounded like the cries of the conductor being devoured by a swarm of killer bees. A voice implored, 'Somebody do something, for God's sake.' It was a weird moment, at once typical and vaguely apocalyptic; for all we knew, the sky might have fallen, and sitting there in the dark, you could imagine the Hudson turning red. I began to whistle softly.

When the lights came back on—no more than ten, fifteen seconds later—the Chinese couple was locked in a wordless, expressionless embrace. They disengaged unconsciously, as if the episode had been a dream they had woken from, and returned their respective hands to their respective knees. In the meantime, the hipster mother was hunched over, head bowed, arms gathered around her child. Then a miniature pink fist poked out of the veil of tresses, waving angrily in the air. Unlike everybody else, the baby was not unsettled by the drama: as soon as the child was suckled, the wailing ceased.

All this time Jon had been crouching next to me, eyes agog, palm planted on the floor. Standing up, he dusted his hands, and I'm sure I

heard him mutter something like *not coming back*. As the train jerked
ahead, he rearranged his feet for balance and grabbed the overhead
railing. I was going to say something about the weirdness, but Jon
was lost in thought as we were pulling up to the Pacific Street stop.
Apparently we'd been stranded just a few yards from civilization.
Turning to me, Jon announced, 'This is where I get off. It was good
to see you, old friend.'

'And you.'

We shook hands officiously, and though his palm was clammy,
his grip was firm. 'Look me up in the Playa.' As he exited, he did a
two-finger half-salute and cried, 'Drinks on me, as always . . .' The
others left with him: the Chinese couple, the blonde with the baby,
and the raucous teenagers. Only the character with the crew cut
remained, sequestered in the corner, staring baldly, but as more
passengers entered, I lost him.

The mood and demographic changed as we neared Manhattan.
There were people chatting and chirping and nodding to music.
It was nice to be in a packed car, in a crowd, and in earshot of
conversations concerning the weather, *the best spiced tripe in town*
and *that New Yorker piece on geological wear and tear*. The guy next
to me pointed out a Poetry in Motion poster to his girlfriend. 'Can't
see it from here,' she said. 'What does it say?'

Craning his neck, he read the following verses haltingly: 'You
ask me about that country whose details now escape me, I don't
remember its geography, nothing of its history. And should I visit it
in memory, it would be as I would a past lover, After years, for a night,
no longer restless with passion, with no fear of regret. I have reached
that age . . . when one visits the heart merely as a courtesy.'

∾

The words remained with me as I disembarked at Union Square
and resonated quietly in my head as I meandered through the station.

Before switching lines, I bought a remainder copy of the Sunday *Times* with the last three dollars in my pocket. The weight of the paper tucked under my arm somehow felt good, felt right. There is indeed solace in ritual. But then as the train pulled up to the platform, I thought I caught a glimpse of the guy with the crew cut trailing me. Either he was gay or a tail. They said they would be watching.

ELEVEN

The Upper East Side was familiar, familial territory. It was here I had first ventured after spending six days in and out of a suitcase and a bright, bare, windowless dorm room near Astor Place. Either I had arrived too early or my roommate, Big Jack, had been late, but I had found the room so horribly oppressive that I had decided to return to Karachi on the returning Sunday night flight that had brought me to New York via Manchester. Lying on the plastic-wrapped mattress, using an undeclared mango for a headrest, I counted the hours. I figured I had one hundred and forty nine to kill, less an estimated fifteen minutes, the time it would take me to pack my belongings, an inventory that included a rug (which, Ma averred, could also serve as a prayer mat), an unnecessary stainless steel lota, three pairs of wash 'n' wear pajamas, and a lifetime supply of Chili Chips, jammed somehow into a single suitcase. The suitcase had been my father's and was produced from storage after a thorough dusting and presented to me by Ma as some coming-of-age guerdon. Decidedly Old School and Old World in its construction and capacity, it featured leather flaps and beige trimmings, and one of its many pockets yielded a box of blue matches with gold tips and a glazed pen impressed with my father's name. There was some story there but I didn't know it. I didn't know anything about anything.

The enigma of arrival was compounded by the fact that the New World was so unexpectedly new. Before I arrived, America had become terra cognita as I had been educated by classics such as *Coming to America*, *Crocodile Dundee*, and *Ghostbusters*, and by American programming on PTV that included the *A-Team* and *Manimal.* And of course, I had listened to tunes on bootleg cassettes by the likes of Boss and the King of Pop. But you learn that everyday, commonplace things operate differently than you would expect, according to a whimsical set of laws, a rarefied ethos. Not only do you drive on the other side of the road, but sockets are slits, not hole-shaped, and taps turn open counterclockwise. You learn to deploy quarters into washers, dryers, public telephones, vending machines. You discover Twinkies at five in the morning, when you're disoriented by jet lag and there is a clawing emptiness in your belly and your soul. In the violent throes of cabin fever, teary and at wit's end, I found myself clutching ripped tags that read,

WARNING: THE REMOVAL OF THIS TAG IS ILLEGAL.
VIOLATORS WILL BE PROSECUTED TO THE
FULL EXTENT OF THE LAW

Hopping off the mattress, fingers outstretched, teeth clenched, I took three deliberate steps back, as if that were the right thing to do:

IF YOU'VE MISTAKENLY RIPPED THIS TAG TAKE
THREE STEPS BACK

For a full minute, I dizzily scanned the room for other dire warnings, pools of quicksand. The world had stopped making sense. I needed to talk to somebody, anybody, a mandarin, Ma. I needed to hear platitudes, cooing words of reassurance. It occurred to me then that Ma had dispatched a palm-sized diary in which she had painstakingly catalogued the numbers of her friends and friends' friends in America.

With a sense of urgency, I searched for the thing in my clothes, in the pockets of the suitcase, and once located, I scurried out, found a public phone down the hall, popped in a quarter, and dialed the first number. The phone rang for a long time, and when the answering machine switched on, I followed the explicit instructions.

Just as I was about to hang up, a gravelly voice interrupted me: 'Ah. Hullo?'

'Hello, hello?'

'Yes?'

'May I speak to Mini Auntie, please?'

'No, you can't.'

'I can't?'

'She isn't here.'

'She isn't?'

'That's correct.'

'*Oh!*' It would be fair to characterize the tone of my voice as hysterical. '*No!*'

'No need to get excited, chum. I can have her call you back. She *will* eventually return.'

'Yes, yes,' I stuttered. 'Thank you,' I added, 'thank you very much,' but before I could hang up, the voice asked, 'Who are you?'

Introducing myself, I mentioned that Ma and Mini Auntie attended the Convent of Jesus and Mary as classmates, and that I had just arrived from Karachi, *in Pakistan.*

There was a pause, the sound of chewing. 'So, ah, what do you make of the US of A?'

'It's strange,' I blurted, 'very strange . . . because it's so familiar . . . but it isn't at all . . . I've realized I don't know anything . . . about anything . . . I think I did but don't—'

'Listen chum, I'll tell you a little story. When I was a lad of, ah, five I made the mistake of telling my father of my fear of the dark. My father, an old-fashioned patriarch, made me march around our house alone at night. I yelled and protested, but he packed me off with a swift kick to the butt. It took me close to eternity to cover the rolling grounds, but I did it, and guess what, chum? That night I lost my fear of the dark.'

There was another pause, punctuated by the sound of ice cubes and a gulp. 'Upon arriving in the city, I decided to get completely lost, so I walked the five boroughs, the fifteen bridges. I've been to the Cloisters, Fort Wadsworth, Mount Loretto in Staten Island, the abandoned DeKalb Avenue platform. Once I landed up in this place called Bushwick. Make a note, chum—you don't want to go there. Crack epidemic, high homicide rate. Anyway, what I mean to convey is that after a time, I knew this city like I, ah, know myself. You'll find your way around. Everybody does.'

The voice, its timbre, the monologue, apologue, comforted. I made appreciative noises. As advised, I would walk the streets later that day till my feet were sore. I would return to my room, full of the world.

'Listen, I've got to go,' the voice was saying. 'I'm sure I'll see you one of these days. I'll tell Mini to call you back.'

That Sunday I was invited to Mini Auntie's for dinner, where I would meet one Ali Chaudhry in the flesh for the first time. This Sunday I was going to tell Mini Auntie that her brother was in jail.

∾

When the door opened, I expected to relate the news to Mini Auntie immediately. I had rehearsed what I would say as I walked the length of East 86th, staring at the sidewalk—*Something bad has happened . . . I think you should sit down . . . Please just listen to me*—and continued rehearsing while I loitered outside the wall of Carl Schurz Park, peering inside. The trees twittered and trilled with night birds, and through the thicket, I could make out the grove of purple pansies, a tidy patch of serenity in the dark. Just beyond, a stairwell wound up to the promenade along the East River, where we often strolled. On nice summer evenings, there would be others out, parents pushing strollers, trailed by pattering infants, pointing out a tugboat effortlessly pulling a massive barge. The park would be closed at night, but you could scale the wall, scamper across the grass, and then clamber over the balustrade to sit, smoke some weed, and watch the sky and skyline shimmer in the water below. And if you squinted after a hit, you would have the sensation of teetering on the edge of the world and being privy to what's beyond.

But Mini Auntie wasn't at the door. A gentleman in a pinstripe suit and a cerise cravat let me in. 'Welcome, young man,' he intoned in a tenor that suggested he was the master of ceremonies. Later I would learn that he was known as Haq. 'You must be the mystery guest!' he continued. 'You must be Late Latif! Ha! Well, don't worry, you've arrived in time. Mini hasn't served dinner yet, and we've been imbibing since, well, half past eight. What's your poison? Let me guess, you're a gin and tonic man. Ha! I can tell from the cut of your jib. But before we raid the bar, we must have a sober chat about what you do and your plans for the future. I take a great interest in our young generation.'

'I, sir . . . have been a banker—'

'No less than a master of the universe!' he proclaimed, slapping me on the back. 'Mergers and acquisitions! Aggressive growth! Buy low, sell high! Ha! Come, come! Let's drink to that!'

The gentleman climbed the narrow carpeted stairwell sideways, avuncularly proffering his free hand. At the entrance to the spacious drawing room, he announced, 'We are honored tonight to host the who's who.' Fifteen or twenty people stood conversing in groups inside. They seemed, at a glance, well spoken and well dressed: the men in dark blazers, the women in ankle-length shalwars, skirts, and pleated trousers. An elderly American couple stood in the midst, nodding to some dulcet-voiced ghazal singer, and in a corner, a tubby character in a Nehru jacket stuffed hors d'oeuvres into his mouth from the small silver trays that were lazily making the rounds. Mini Auntie had arranged striking bouquets of chrysanthemums around the room in flamingo-shaped vases that created the salubrious ambience of a garden party. She, however, was nowhere to be seen.

'What is your good name?' Haq inquired. 'Whose son are you?' Although neither reply seemed to register, it did not seem to matter because when he ushered me in, he announced, 'Do you know who this is? This is Bano's son! The Pakistani J.P. Morgan!'

A few heads turned to smile in acknowledgment. Suddenly I became conscious of my criminal appearance, of the odor of caked sweat wafting from my body. Stiffening, I tugged at the ends of my collar and brushed the stray hairs from my forehead with a flick of the hand. It was too late to dart into the nearby bathroom to clean myself up, perhaps even shave with a discarded razor and cocoa butter as I had once before, because just then a fair, smallish lady raised a beckoning arm. 'Ha!' exclaimed my voluble host with a gentle shove. 'Somebody was bound to know you, young man. You know Niggo?'

It turned out that Niggo, like Mini Auntie, was also Ma's classmate from Convent days. Ma seemed to be connected by degrees to everybody in Pakistan because of Our Lord and Savior. After graduating from Convent, Niggo had become the wife of a big besuited man whom she pointed out behind some foliage. A federal minister in Musharraf's cabinet, he was en route to Washington, D.C., for consultations with the State Department. 'I'm just tagging along,' Niggo said. 'But tell me about your mother. How is she? Where is she?'

'She's well,' I said, lying, 'very well, very happy.'

'You know, you look just like her. Your mother was stunning. She had these typically classical features: delicately curved mouth and big almond eyes—eyes, mind you, that stopped boys dead in their tracks. And such a good student, she was! Always first in class. I remember we were always copying her homework. I think we all secretly wanted to be her. We thought she was perfect. We thought she would—'

Locking her fingers and smiling, Niggo stopped short of whatever she was about to say. I didn't like the way she spoke about Ma in the past tense, the tragic subjunctive. I noticed the edges of Niggo's mouth were wrinkled and that her round visage was basted with foundation. Ma remained stunning. As I stared past Niggo at a tray of sashimi, an argument erupted between her husband and Haq. Apparently, Musharraf had finally addressed the nation.

'Many on the left and right,' the former was saying, 'have been maintaining that we should have held out, bargained, what have you, but Musharraf has joined the coalition at considerable personal and national risk. Mark my words: Al-Qaeda will never forgive him. Al-Qaeda will never forgive us.'

'But how can you defend a dictator?' Haq cried. 'That's the problem with you Pakistanis—'

'And what are you, my friend?'

'Address the question, sir! You are not addressing the question!'

'Okay. I will. Do you remember the state of our country two years ago? The PM—the democratically elected PM, I might remind you—went after every institution that challenged his . . . his absolutism. He deposed the president *and* the army chief. Then he sent thugs to raid the supreme court. They climbed up the walls and clamored for justice! Journalists were yanked out of their beds at night and imprisoned. And you will remember, my good friend, that just before he was forced out, he was set to pass legislation that would make him the Commander of the Faithful! Imagine that! The man who would be king!'

'Yes but he wasn't a dictator, sir, as Mugabe and Pinochet—'

'When a democrat behaves like a dictator and vice versa, the difference between the two becomes semantic. Quite frankly, it doesn't matter to me whether President Musharraf is a dictator or a democrat, whether he's left- or right-handed, colors his hair or is kind to small animals. What matters is whether he's able to deliver a few fundamental things: honest governance—Musharraf is not corrupt at all; law and order—barring exogenous shocks, there's been peace in the country; and economic development. There's macroeconomic stability and development in a country that had all but two weeks of reserves left. We were two weeks away from hyperinflation, two weeks from hell . . .'

'You, sir, gloss over freedom! If there's an elixir to life, it is freedom! Freedom is the bedrock on which civilization was founded! Whither freedom—'

'You're a self-proclaimed political scientist, friend. You should know political enfranchisement follows economic enfranchisement. People want food on their table. You can't eat freedom—'

Niggo's husband was cut short by a stern voice that rang like a ghazal singer hitting a high note: *That's enough, gentlemen!* Standing at the top of the stairs with her small hands resting on her wide hips, Mini Auntie wore a sequined pistachio chemise and her hair in a loose bun. 'Dinner is served,' she announced. 'Please leave your politics in the drawing room,' she added. 'Only small talk is permitted downstairs.'

As she turned to descend, I leaped after her but was cut off by Haq, who palmed off a glass of gin and tonic to me as he toasted '*Liberté, egalité, fraternité!*' and, it would seem, himself. Taking a perfunctory sip, I excused myself and made a beeline across the room. Following the exquisite aroma of fried onions down the stairs, I found Mini Auntie in the kitchen surrounded by several ladies, stirring an industrial capacity pot with one hand and fidgeting with the microwave with the other. 'Oho,' she fretted, 'the chapatis are too dry. These chapatis from Little India always turn out too dry.'

One of the ladies—a busty divorcée who was a regular household fixture—said, 'I have them made fresh, Mini. I have got a man who comes in once a week who cooks—'

'Will you do me a favor,' Mini Auntie asked her, 'and put in another batch? The guests are coming down, and I've to attend to the baghaar.'

The thought of the oily, garlicky patina over a hot glob of lentils made me dizzy. I could have had the whole pot to myself, like Amitabh in that classic Bollywood flick. Dinner, however, would have to wait. 'Mini Auntie?'

Continuing to stir furiously, she exclaimed, 'Well, well, well! 'Where've you been, child? Your mother's been worried sick about you. And where's that good-for-nothing brother of mine? Or maybe I shouldn't ask. Don't think I don't know about all the naughtiness you boys get up to.'

'I've something to tell you—'

Turning to get a good look at me, she cried, 'Hai, hai, hai! You look like a mangy puppy, child! I want you to go to the bathroom this instant and wash up. And don't use the hand towels. Use the bath towel.'

'But Mini Auntie—'

'No buts, child! We don't sit at the dinner table in this state. Chop, chop!'

The women observed me pityingly as I limped out of the kitchen, but I heard Mini Auntie say, 'Such a sweet boy . . .'

Setting the gin and tonic on the granite counter, I regarded myself in the mirror. I looked like the waking dead. The shadows beneath my eyes lingered even in the hard white glare of the tube light, and up close I couldn't distinguish the leathery purple bags from my bruise. I could, however, perceive fear in my eyes, fear of what would happen tonight and tomorrow and the day after; I feared for my friends, feared telling Ma that I had been fired, jailed, and had to flee; feared for my sanity. Unable to face myself, I undid my trousers and settled on the cold, smooth toilet seat, holding my head, massaging my eyelids, hunched over like Rodin's *Thinker* considering the casual freedom of sitting on a functioning pot.

Dinner had commenced by the time I emerged. Three round tables had been organized like vertices of an isosceles triangle, each adorned with flickering white candles and flower arrangements that obscured the faces of different diners at different angles. Ensconced between the Federal Minister and the venerable American gentleman, Mini Auntie instructed me to sit on a chair wedged between two people I did not know on the other table, the Young People's Table.

The Young People seemed to comprise the sons and daughters of the guests, and Puppies, Pakistani Urban Professionals. They were earnestly discussing the logistics of organizing a charity ball for a leprosy center back home at the once-storied Roosevelt Hotel. Apparently the manager had offered them a discount, but the ballroom wasn't suited to accommodate functions of the size they were planning. 'You *have* to see all the angles,' somebody declaimed.

Slipping into the vacant chair without introducing myself, I helped myself to the lukewarm dishes without delay. There was saffron rice with peas, fried okra with tomatoes, potato cutlets, meatballs garnished with fresh coriander, and in case the menu was in any way deficient, some sort of lamb curry to boot. A cup of diced tomatoes, onions, and coriander in vinegar made its way around the table. It was a royal feast. Piling a hill of rice on my plate, I picked four of the largest meatballs, three of the remaining cutlets, and dug in like an anteater snorting entire teeming colonies of red ants. I popped the cutlets in my mouth and sipped spoonfuls of the thick gravy, and splicing the meatballs open, I unearthed a stuffed core of diced onions and mint.

The conversation had shifted to some engagement party video that featured, toward the end, the belly of a stunning girl dancing in a pink sari. Apparently nobody seemed to know the identity of the girl or the cameraman, personae of certain mystery and diligent speculation. The adults had returned to politics after the imposed hiatus, except for the tubby fellow in the Nehru jacket, who was flirting with the busty divorcée as if his life depended on it. When he paused for breath, she said, 'You certainly are a wily one,' before blowing smoke into the air.

When I finally looked up, I noticed that two boys, whose floppy ears indicated kinship, had watched me wipe my plate clean. 'Hungry?' one of them asked. Reaching for the folded napkin beside my plate for the first time that evening, I dabbed the corners of my mouth in response and slid into my chair. Suddenly, and quite desperately, I needed a cigarette.

Since it would have been ill-mannered for me to disrupt the proceedings to ask around for a smoke, I excused myself with a cough. Discreetly skirting the tables, I jogged down the corridor and scaled the stairs like a ninja, searching the surfaces, drawers, and cabinets for a stray pack. I even lifted the pillows of a chaise, an exercise that yielded an eyeliner and an archaic five-paisa coin. The guests were unusually fastidious that night because, save a quarter-depleted Dunhill, stamped with lipstick on the lip of an ashtray, there were no cigarettes to be had. It would have to do.

As I slunk downstairs, I heard somebody saying, 'We've suffered a singular calamity. Thousands of innocents have died in the most cruel and most spectacular way. Now, we need to take the fight to them. We have to secure our borders and our way of life . . .' Cupping the cigarette behind my back, I followed the voice back to the dining room. It belonged to one of the floppy-eared brothers. 'We need to seek the terrorists in our midst, and if they happen to be Muslims, Arabs, or South Asian, so be it! Security is our inviolable right!'

The audience processed the discourse without protest, but I felt compelled to speak up. I felt hot and bothered. 'Every state has the right to security,' I averred. All heads turned to me: Mini Auntie, Busty, Tubby, Haq, Niggo, the Federal Minister, the American couple, as well as the Young People's Table. 'The point is how do you go about it? In the name of national security, states commit crimes—'

'What *crimes*?'

'You threw a hundred thousand Japanese into camps, whole families—women, children, old people—because *they* posed a security threat. That's not right. That's wrong. And now it's us. *It's me*.' Fueled by adrenaline, I continued, 'I've been in jail for the last forty-eight hours. I was humiliated, starved, physically and mentally abused. Mini Auntie's brother, Ali, is still inside. We're not model citizens—I'm not a citizen at all—but I can tell you this much: we've done nothing wrong. This is no way to treat human beings, and this is no way to achieve security!'

There was pin-drop silence for a few moments. Then Mini Auntie rose. 'Why didn't you tell me, child?' she asked, embracing me in a bear hug.

'I, um, tried—'

'I'm sorry—'

'No, I'm sorry.' I should have said, *I'm an idiot*, but didn't.

We repaired to the kitchen where, among open pots, greased pans, and dirty china and cutlery, she asked me to relate the events that had led to our incarceration, 'slowly and clearly,' as if she were enjoining an alarmed patient. As I narrated the story—minus the cab, the kidnapping, and the porn watching—Mini Auntie listened, arms folded, interrupting once or twice to clarify this or that detail, and when I finished, she hung her head in thought.

I braced for a tongue lashing: *Who told you to go to Connecticut? Who do you think you are? The Three Musketeers? Cops? Robbers? This is real life!* Instead she opened the fridge, scooped a generous helping of homemade mango mousse, and served it to me in a bowl. 'Eat, child, eat.' Swallowing a mouthful, I tasted the sharp tang of guilt. While I was footloose and fancy-free, savoring mousse and meatballs, AC was being treated to interrogations and a meager dollop of prison gruel.

'Go upstairs,' Mini Auntie instructed. 'Call your mother. I'm sure she'll be delighted.'

'What are you going to do?'

'I'm going to go to this Metropolitan Detention Center.'

'Then I'm coming with you.'

'No, you're not, child.'

'Yes, I am,' I protested.

Raising a reproving eyebrow, she persisted in her famous no-bullshit tone. 'You're going to finish your dessert, and then you're going straight home. To bed. Doctor's orders.' She added, 'If you like, we can call your mother together.'

The threat worked. I licked the bowl clean, put it in the dishwasher, and wiped my face with a paper towel. Outside, a hush fell over the dining room when I appeared. Blushing, I escaped upstairs.

⌀

It was already tomorrow in Karachi, already morning and, at nine, probably already hot. The monsoon having passed, the Indian summer would be in full sweaty swing. Not that the weather ever slowed Ma any: she would have said her prayers by now, oiled her hair, lapped the roof in shalwar and sneakers, and bathed, humming, as she was wont, tunes from the Golden Age. She might have been sipping a cup of tea in the veranda or picking at lightly salted pomegranate seeds with the *Dawn* spread out before her. I imagined she would be in her contagiously sunny morning mood. Clearing my throat, I picked up the receiver and dialed. The phone rang once. 'Hello?' I called.

'Shehzad beta,' Ma replied flatly, an acknowledgment of fact. I couldn't tell whether she was groggy or it was a bad line. I waited for her to ask how I was, where I'd been, why I hadn't called, but she said nothing.

'I'm sorry I haven't called, Ma,' I began, hoping that she would interrupt me. 'But ... well ... things have been hectic.' It was a sorry excuse articulated particularly unconvincingly. I listened closely for some softly uttered word, a muted bromide, a sigh even, but Ma steadfastly maintained radio silence. 'Are you there?'

'Haan, beta.'

'Ma, I'm very, very sorry.'

'Shehzad,' she finally said. 'It's been exactly ten days since I heard from you. You have not told me about what is happening over there, so I will tell you what is happening over here. It has rained for weeks. There has been some flooding. The other day I slipped on the stairs outside—'

'Ma!'

'Don't worry, beta. I'm all right. I'm not dying, I'm not ill. It's just a sprain. I wouldn't have even mentioned it, but I do now because ... well ... as I was sitting with my foot in ice water, I thought, surely my son could find the time to ring for one minute, just one minute, just to say a quick hello-how-are-you, for no other reason except that he knows it would make his mother happy. So I sat by the phone, waiting and waiting, hoping you would ring, but you did not. So I did. I rang many, many times, and when I didn't hear back, I began to get worried. I thought, maybe something's happened to him. These days, with all these terrorists running around in America, you don't know. So I rang your work number. I know, I know, I'm not supposed to—you've told me never to call you there—but I had to hear your voice. Instead, a recorded voice told me over and over, *Please check the number and dial again.* I began ringing here and there; I must have spoken to ten, fifteen people. Then somebody told me that your number was disconnected because the building you worked in had collapsed several weeks ago.'

Closing my eyes, I held my forehead and was suddenly the little boy who had broken the expensive crystal vase, hoping, wishing that when he opened his eyes, things would be different, like they used to be. When I opened my eyes, however, perched on the edge of Mini Auntie's four-poster, the room remained the same, still and oppressive, and Ma was saying, 'I told myself, be calm, there must be an explanation for this. I called Mini, and she told me she hadn't heard from you or Ali. I didn't want to frighten her so I acted casual, but I was very frightened, I've been very frightened. I haven't slept for two nights.'

The line crackled, prompting me for an explanation. The moment of reckoning was finally upon me, and it wasn't as if it was unexpected; it had been a long time coming. I wanted to say that I wished I were with her, pressing her feet, applying Tiger Balm, that I had never wanted to leave in the first place, but the moment demanded truth, not sentimentality.

Just as I began to explain, however, Mini Auntie marched in to change into her sneakers and collect her large black Mary Poppins tote and slim cell phone, which was fixed to a socket beside me. 'Still on the phone, child?' she asked, crouching, unplugging the device. 'Tell Bano everything's going to be all right.'

'Everything's all right, Ma.'

'*Is that Mini?*' Ma asked.

'Um, yes, yes it is,' I replied, uncoiling the receiver.

'Can I talk to her?'

There was no defensible reason why Ma could not chat with her old friend, except, of course, that her old friend would tell her exactly what had transpired. With Mini Auntie in earshot, I chose my words carefully: 'I'm actually over for dinner, Ma.'

'Oh. Acha. Mini must be busy. Well, give her my love.'

'Can I call you from home?'

There was a pause, a second or two of deliberation, before Ma said, 'Yes, that's okay, that's fine.'

'I love you, Ma—'

'Beta?'

'Yes, Ma.'

'I don't want to be a bother, but you know . . . I need to bother you once in a while . . . I need to hear your voice. I need to know you're taking your vitamins—'

'I know, I know—'

'I need to know that your office has not collapsed in some terrorist attack.'

'I'm fine, Ma. Don't worry about me.'

'And beta?'

'Yes, Ma.'

'Please say your prayers. You need to thank God that you're alive and happy.'

'Yes, Ma.'

After bidding her khuda-hafiz, I returned downstairs. The guests had dispersed apace, save a gangly, unassuming 'uncle' whom I had met once chez Mini Auntie and once outside Chirping Chicken. One of the most sought-after corporate lawyers in the city, Mr. Azam was accompanying Mini to the Metropolitan Detention Center, presumably for moral support and legal firepower. 'Chalo,' Mini Auntie said, flicking the hall lights and wrapping herself in a beige pashmina. 'Chalain,' chimed Azam.

As we walked to the corner to flag a cab, I repeated my plea to tag along, arguing that I was 'in a way indispensable' because I knew the 'ins and outs of the place,' which was, of course, one hundred percent baloney; I didn't know how I got in or how I got out.

Kissing me on the forehead before climbing into the cab, Mini Auntie said, 'Get some sleep, child.' Then she waved, and I waved back. I watched the cab careen down East End as if watching a departing locomotive train leaving behind clouds of nostalgic smoke. Lighting the depleted, lipstick-stained cigarette, I then ambled up East 86th like a free man.

TWELVE

Any volume on history in AC's extensive library could attest to the fact that over the millennia there have been those who have made a living interpreting dreams—shamans and hucksters, prophets, poets, and psychoanalysts—and although I might have needed to see a shrink at that delicate juncture of modern history, I did not need anybody interpreting mine. They were, from beginning to end, semiotically straightforward.

In halcyon times, my dreams were suffused by a healthy, balmy sensibility that produced images of winged lemurs or igloos wrought of mango mousse. One fine afternoon while dozing in the Great Lawn the summer before I began work, I had dreamed of a busty and decidedly Punjabi mermaid batting her eyelids while bobbing in the frothy wake of the Hudson. It recalled the Hughes verse that went,

> He found a fish
> To carry—
> Half fish,
> Half girl
> To marry.

Lingering like the faint echo of a bubblegum hit, the signified and signifier returned to me throughout the day, refrain by refrain, and at these junctures, I would catch myself smiling and yearning like a hopeful romantic.

In the latter half of 2001, however, my dreams had turned to shit. I suppose everybody's had. I was haunted by earthquakes measuring a full ten on the Richter scale, corpses in a chorus line, by bugs with forty blinking eyes, by pestilence and other signs of the times. And of course from time to time a vivid specter would visit me during my waking hours—as I fed my soiled laundry into the washing machine or bit into lunch—imposing itself on my state of mind and coloring the remainder of the day.

The night I returned from prison, however, I didn't dream. Ensconced in my apartment on the hand-me-down futon, I closed my eyes, attempting to sleep, but like a child in a thunderstorm, I couldn't. There were great matters on my mind—how to break the news of Jimbo's incarceration to the Khans, what to do about the threat of imminent deportation, and how to make amends with my poor, neglected mother—but it was the picayune, the trivial, the stray Gold Toe sock on the floor that ultimately kept me up. I might have been suffering from Baby Bear Syndrome, convinced that somebody had been in my apartment, and though I saw no empty porridge bowls, I found the chairs suspiciously rearranged in a triangular scheme and the toilet seat mysteriously upright. It would have been different had the place been spectacularly broken into and turned upside down, but the evidence was thin, as if the saboteurs had connived to wreak only psychological damage. The strategy worked. Through the witching hour, I tossed and turned, finding meaning in the secret order of household artifacts.

At six in the morning, I drew up a to-do list on the back of an envelope and pinned it to the refrigerator door like Martin Luther, using the tiny banana magnet that came with the apartment:

(1) Go to Khans to break news re Jimbo
(2) check w/Mini re AC
(3) return Abdul Karim's keys

(4)   get job (OR GET DEPORTED!)
(5)   call Ma
(6)   buy TP, hand soap and other supplies

At seven I called the Khan residence to check if I could drop by later that morning, only to get Amo on the line, who cut me off, saying, 'Can't talk now right now,' which was weird, but I didn't give it much thought at the time. And afterward I tried Mini Auntie, but she wasn't home or wasn't picking up, so I left a rambling message punctuated by pauses and apologies. By eight, tasks one and two, despite my best efforts, remained incomplete and unchecked, and I remembered why, as a rule of thumb, I have avoided drawing up to-do lists: to-do lists delineate failure in black and white.

Since the thought of coming clean with Abdul Karim was so distressing, I skipped task three altogether, attempting task four instead, an even more daunting prospect. I had four days to secure employment, four days to find an employer willing to sponsor a work visa—a tall order in the best of times, next to impossible during a financial bloodbath. One day, I reminded myself, had already elapsed.

When I returned the call from the boutique research house that had contacted me earlier, a lady at the other end put me on hold playing some grave symphony, Bach, maybe Beethoven, the telltale theme music of rejection. As I waited, as a familiar sense of dread mounted, the standard industry refrain resounded in my head: *We appreciate your interest in the position but there were many highly qualified candidates at this time.* Instead I was informed that I had qualified for a final-round interview. 'We've been trying to call you for days,' the lady said. 'Today's the last day of the search process. We can squeeze you in at four.'

Putting the receiver down, I pumped my fist like Starks after swishing a three-pointer over the outstretched fingers of Pippen. Perhaps the tide was turning.

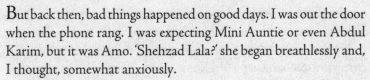

But back then, bad things happened on good days. I was out the door when the phone rang. I was expecting Mini Auntie or even Abdul Karim, but it was Amo. 'Shehzad Lala?' she began breathlessly and, I thought, somewhat anxiously.

'What's wrong?'

'D'you know where I can find Jamshed Lala?'

'I'm not sure,' I replied. 'Why?'

'Baba's had a heart attack.'

I imagined poor Amo finding Old Man Khan slumped on the kitchen floor, dialing 911, attempting coherence between sobs. 'Is he—'

'Barely—'

'Where are you?'

'Christ Hospital, Palisade Avenue.'

'I'll be there as soon as I can,' I said. 'Everything will be okay.'

Rushing out, I calculated that the jaunt to Jersey would take over an hour by subway—that is, if the trains were running on time—but would be less than thirty minutes in outbound traffic. The problem would be flagging a cab, as it was prime time on Broadway. Besuited men and women lined either side of the street at regular intervals, arms in the air. Jogging a five-block stretch, I scanned cabs for heads in the backseat, but there wasn't a single free taxi visible.

Suddenly, the bald-headed profile of a passing cabbie sparked a thought: *Kojo!* I thought, *I'll call Kojo!* Muttering a prayer that he would be close by, I dialed his cell from a phone booth. As luck would have it, Kojo was picking up a ride on Central Park West, the canton he liked to patrol because of 'da rich and da famoos.' When I told him what had happened, I heard him tell his passenger, 'Is emergency, madame. Def in da famalee.' Before I hung up, I could hear a woman in the background crying, 'You can't do that! You won't get away with this! I'll report you, pal!'

Deaf to the threats and bound to duty, to the cabbie brotherhood, Kojo extricated himself in record time, appearing four and a half minutes later, honking a shave and a haircut. With one arm dangling out the window, the other loosely perpendicular to his chest, he reclined in a beaded seat cover sporting an elaborate earpiece and a crisp crimson bandana worn like a crown. 'Thanks so much, man,' I panted, hopping in. 'Is no problim, man,' he replied. And we were off.

When I told him that he was looking good, 'looking prosperous,' he ran a slow contemplative hand over his shapely head and replied, 'You know, Chuck. I wok haad. I makes good monay. I send it to my fada . . . All my life, I take. Now I give.' He had a way of effortlessly and artlessly breaking it down.

Glancing at the molten Hudson, I said, 'I know what you mean, man.'

Zipping down the West Side Highway, however, with the windows down, the stereo on, the sun in my face, I temporarily forgot my anxieties. Kojo jacked up a mixed cassette of Pepe Wembe, Papa Kalle, Kanda Bongo Man, Amadou et Mariam, and sundry Afropop sensations—the variety of sound that Jimbo would, in better days, cut, polish, and string into coherence. Bobbing to the syncopated rhythms, Kojo and I recalled stories about Gator and the backbenchers and swapped anecdotes about our experiences as bonafide New York cabbies. I related an abridged version of the VP episode. In turn, he told me about the night he found himself in Bushwick with a flat: 'Is dark, like Kivu. Any minit, I think, Mai-Mai is comen.' Cutting the air with a karatelike chop, he added, 'But I was ready, like Bruce Lee.'

From time to time, our conversation was interrupted by a sharp synthesized trill, which I initially mistook for a dance-hall touch to the kwassa-kwassa but turned out to be the refrain of the old rap single 'Informer,' the ring-tone of Kojo's space-age cellular phone. After a brief exchange of pleasantries in Lingala, Kojo cut off his compatriot, announcing, 'Is life or def situation,' but as we passed beneath the river, he asked, 'What is da situation, exactly?'

Angling my body toward him, I explained that I had received a panicked call from a close friend earlier informing me that her father had suffered from what I understood to be a near-fatal heart attack. I did not want to get into the mechanics of my relationship with Amo because I did not want to get into why her brother, my friend, was in jail. That might have led to the revelation that I too was an ex-con. The terrorism charges would take some explaining, even to Kojo.

'This Amo,' he began after mulling the situation, 'she is your girlfriend?'

'No, no, no,' I replied, blushing for no good reason. 'Just a girl who is a friend.'

'A girl. Who is a friend,' he repeated, varying meaning with emphasis. 'Is she pretty, this Amo?'

'She's pretty, and intelligent,' I said matter-of-factly, in an effort to compensate for the color in my cheeks. 'She's studying to be an actuary.'

'If ha fada dies, she has som body?' With Jimbo incarcerated indefinitely, she'd have nobody. I shook my head.

When we arrived at Christ Hospital, Kojo asked whether I wanted him to wait, and for a moment I considered the offer, checking the time on the dashboard. It was just about eleven. I would have to leave Jersey by half past two to make it to the city in time for the interview. There was no way I could ask him to wait. 'No, Kojo,' I replied. 'Don't worry about it. I'll figure something out.' Thanking him profusely, I slapped his outstretched palm for a not-so-high-five and disembarked.

The sky above was cloudless and blue.

THIRTEEN

Facing Jersey City on the west and lower Manhattan on the east, Christ Hospital is housed in a tall, gray, oblong building. Angular and clean from the outside, like a suburban three-star hotel constructed in the seventies, the place felt dank and oppressive inside. I thought I could detect the faint riverine smell of a cave as I entered, and imagined the air to be teeming with virulent bacterium, superbugs. I never liked hospitals. Although I had been in one only twice before—once at age four for a virulent outbreak of chicken pox that left a dent on my forehead, and then three years later for tonsillitis—both experiences were sufficiently traumatic because I forever associated hospitals with needles and howls and the stubborn smudges and foul aroma of mercurochrome. At a tender age I had formed the impression that hospitals were populated by the dying and undead alike, that those who went in never really came out.

Such unformed and unfounded sentiments remained lodged in the recesses of my consciousness, but I marched right up to the visitors' desk without betraying them, asking for Khan in the cardiology ward. I was informed by a long-faced octogenarian, 'There's nobody by that name in cardiology.'

The grim pronouncement could only mean that Old Man Khan was already dead, that Amo was somewhere, draped over her father's corpse, bawling unattended and unconsoled because I was late and her brother was wrongly incarcerated. 'Are you absolutely sure?' I persisted.

The man nodded once, slowly and deliberately, in practiced commiseration. 'Okay, so where do they take the dead?' I cried.

'Downstairs,' he tragically replied.

Sprinting down a corridor, I navigated packs of doctors and nurses with tunnel vision and patients on stretchers and wheelchairs, narrowly avoiding what could have been a head-on collision with a rolling cart of stacked lunch trays. Somehow I found myself in a darkened room with a Chinese intern wearing a scowl. Outside I attempted to solicit more accurate directions from a heavyset black lady at the maternity clinic, who asked whether I had a twelve o'clock with a certain Dr. Kahn. 'Kahn?' I repeated.

Then, following a sudden hunch, I retraced my steps, trailed by a pair of concerned orderlies, panting and sweating and cursing the milquetoast who had misdirected me. When I spelled out K-h-a-n, he mumbled that he had mistaken *Khan* for *Kahn*. I was informed that a Khan had indeed been brought into ER an hour earlier and subsequently had been transferred to the operation theater upstairs for an emergency bypass.

Busting into the cardiology ward on the seventh floor like an escaped inmate, disheveled and harried and out of breath, I discovered Amo in the waiting area, hugging her legs atop a hard orange plastic chair. Gently rocking back and forth, she was murmuring something under her breath—the lyrics of a song, the last words she had said to her father, a prayer. When I called out her name, she looked up with startled feline eyes and cried, 'Shehzad Lala!' Springing into my arms, she held me tightly, nuzzling my sweat-blotted chest. 'It's all right, it's all right,' I cooed. We stood glued in embrace for some time until I could hear her heart beating like a clapping wind-up toy. Finally I said, 'Tell me what happened.'

We sat down beside each other. I crossed my legs and produced a folded tissue. Amo wiped her eyes and nose and began: 'So I woke up like I do every day to make Baba breakfast—he has Weetabix and low-fat milk, and a bowl of mixed fruit, and tea, black tea—except, I guess, my alarm didn't go off, so like when I went out, I noticed that the kettle was already on the stove and the TV was on and the phone was off the hook—'

Amo broke off the narration to stare at a weirdly Jersey-shaped dent in the opposing wall. I wondered what could have precipitated the attack—something on the news, somebody on the phone—before laying a reassuring hand against the small of her back. Determinedly pursing her lips, she continued: 'Baba was on his back, and his face was all red and puffy and . . . and the teacup had broken.' Stifling a sob, she rubbed her eyes with the soft of her palms. 'I was thinking, I dunno, if I'd just like woken up earlier—'

'You know, there's nothing you could have done.'

'Y'know,' she continued as if she had not heard me, 'he'd already had a heart attack when I was in junior high, and he's had high blood pressure for as long as I can remember. The doctors always tell him, "Mr. Khan, gotta change your lifestyle"—change of lifestyle is like key with coronary artery disease—but you know how he is, Shehzad Lala. When Ami was alive, he'd listen to her, but now everything's different, and I keep an eye on him, and he listens to me when I'm around, but sometimes it's like he's just humoring me, and I can't be there all the time, I just can't. I wish Jamshed Lala—' Turning to me, she fixed me with a teary, accusatory look. 'I'm so mad at him! Where is he? Why isn't he here?'

Scratching the hook of my ear, I stared vacantly back at her because I didn't have the heart to tell her that her brother had been nabbed on some ridiculous terrorism charge. She might not have even believed me. Clearing my throat, I told her that I had not heard from Jimbo for a few days, that if he knew, he would be here. 'You know that, don't you?'

Amo heaved a sigh in response: 'The doctor's saying he's got something like a thirty percent chance.' Bowing her head, as if peering into the void that was opening beneath her Pumas, she sighed again. We peered in together. I had been there. I decided I was not going to allow her to lapse into despair.

'Look, Amo,' I said in a tenor that made her perk up like a prairie vole. 'All we can do right now is sit tight. It's silly to review and reassess what you could have done yesterday or the day before. You need to be here, right now, alert, in the present. You need to be strong because when Khan Sahab gets out, he'll need you to be strong. Do you understand what I'm saying?' Amo nodded. 'He's very lucky to have you.' Amo smiled for the first time that afternoon. She had a wonderfully winning smile. 'You haven't had anything to eat, have you?' Amo shook her head. 'Wait here. I'll grab lunch.'

'Don't leave, Shehzad Lala,' she said, balancing her chin on the crescent of her open hands.

'I'll be back before you know it.' Taking the elevator back down, I flew through the passage toward the entrance, searching for signs for the cafeteria. The octogenarian was where I left him, misdirecting somebody else. I accosted a passing male nurse, who pointed me in the right direction. The cafeteria was dark and smelled of stale cold cuts, and the lunch fare appeared particularly unappetizing: the soup du jour, Cream of Vegetable, was the color and consistency of soap water, while the Cajun Style Fish Special was baked to a leathery wafer. I decided to try my luck outside. Amo needed sustenance.

Down the length of Palisade Avenue, I happened upon a Chinese restaurant advertising a uniquely revolting American hybrid—Kung Pao Fried Chicken with Cheese Fries—but to my relief, I eventually happened upon a Subway wedged between a condemned three-story Tudor and a hardware store featuring a solitary dungareed male mannequin in the window. There was a line of locals inside, so I dug in my heels and folded my arms, surveying the menu overhead. I remembered that Amo only took halal, so the turkey boloney or roast beef or chicken salad was out of the question. Scrambled egg on a croissant would pass muster. And a cup of minestrone. I picked up a half-foot sandwich and a fountain cola for myself, and a cup of hazelnut coffee for later, in anticipation of my interview and certain collapse.

When I returned, Amo was nowhere to be seen. A wiry mullet-headed man sat in her place. Striding up to him, frowning and mildly mystified, I surveyed the area as if expecting to discover Amo under the row of chairs like a lost pen or a fallen button. 'You got a problem,

amigo?' the man asked. I had many problems, but I didn't want to
add to the laundry list. Raising the flats of my palms, as Jimbo might
have done, I backed into a uniform-clad member of the hospital's
janitorial staff who had been hovering on the floor earlier, trailed
by a squeaky-wheeled pail containing a mop and, it seemed, the
cafeteria's soup du jour. When I asked the lady if she had seen the
girl who had been sitting 'on that chair over there,' she steadfastly
squinted as though I were speaking a foreign language.

'You know, she's about this tall,' I said, raising my hand to my
forehead in a half salute, 'very pretty, wears, um, a thing on her head,'
a description accompanied by a circular motion that might have
suggested a halo, or insanity. 'No se,' she said. 'Okay,' I persisted,
drawing on my Telemundo Spanish, '¿un poquito catalina?'

Just then Amo beckoned from behind a curtain as if playing a
game of hide-and-seek, then guided me past a nurse's station to an
examination room furnished with a bed, chair, and desk. Spreading
the contents of the brown bag on the desk, we lunched hungrily
under a life-size poster depicting cartoon figures administering the
Heimlich maneuver.

Amo told me that she 'came in here cuz that guy was looking at me
kinda funny . . . I get that a lot these days . . . I don't let it get to me.'
Suddenly I found myself empathizing with the hijab. 'I'm so happy
you're here,' she added. 'You're like my knight in shining armor.'

Blushing, I changed the subject. 'How's your father?' I asked.

'No news.'

'Guess we just have to wait.'

'Yeah.'

'Yeah . . .'

'Can I ask you something?'

'Ask me anything.'

'Why do they call you Chuck?'

'You, um, really want to know?' I asked.

'I'm all ears.'

The etymology of my ostensibly all-American sobriquet had been informed by my mythical appetite for mother's milk. Apparently, I was known to feed up to thirteen, fourteen times a day. Although Ma never denied me her sore, bitten breasts, she figured there was something awry, and after consulting with aunts and squawking sundry, she took me back to her old-school Anglo gynecologist at the hospital. 'Madam,' he stated, 'the child latches ineptly. We can work on that. But there is no cause for alarm. You have, I believe, a very affectionate son.'

Ma narrated the story to me before I left for the States. She also told me that the noisy sucking sound that I made might be phonetically transcribed as *chucka-chucka-chucka*—a sound subsequently sweetened and distilled to Chuck. All of this entertained Amo no end, so when I glanced at the wall clock and told her that I had to run, she seemed nonplussed, overwrought even. 'Where? Where d'you have to go?'

'Look, Amo, I'll be back soon.'

'Don't leave, Shehzad,' she said for the second time that afternoon.

'I wouldn't if I didn't absolutely have to, and I absolutely have to.'

Abandoning Amo, I raced out. It was after three. I had less than an hour to get back to the city for my only interview, less than an hour to get my life in order.

I had no suit, no plan, no prayer, and careening toward the city in a cab, I had this sinking feeling that I should have stayed back, because if something untoward happened that afternoon, something tragic, something horrible, I would never be able to forgive myself. As the road blurred by, the yellow dashes merging into one, it occurred to me that I was no longer a good man. In a way, my jihad had stopped short. I was certain that I would fail Amo when she needed me most and fail to make the most important interview of my life. I had, however, promised the cabbie an extra tenner if he got me into the city on time. Miraculously, he did. It was quarter to four when we emerged from the Lincoln Tunnel. Venturing uptown to change was not an option, as the avenues were choked with tourist buses and the beginnings of rush-hour traffic. I had to think of something else, something fast. Crossing Fifth, I yelled, 'Stop here,' and pulling out a fiver, added, 'Be back in four.'

Entering the nearest shop from the corner, I grabbed the first size-thirty-six suit from the rack, then whipped out my only functioning credit card at the counter. 'Would you like to try that on, sir?' asked the saleswoman, which may have been more advice than inquiry, but I waved my hand like *I'm a high roller, darling*. Eyebrow arched, she announced, 'That'll be one thousand nine hundred and ninety nine dollars . . . tax not included.' The figure was greater than my life savings, a month's rent, a round-trip ticket to Karachi, Moscow, and most parts of sub-Saharan Africa. Smiling bravely, I told her to make sure she included the receipt. As she rang me up, I glanced around. I was obviously in the wrong place: the floors were Boticena marble, the ceiling tinted glass, and everything in between, from the curtains to the clothing, was, rather dramatically, either black or gold. On the far wall hung an enormous gilded V, like a totem. 'Come again,' the saleswoman said, handing over the garment bag, probably worth its weight in gold. 'I will,' I replied.

Changing in the backseat like a contortionist, I was careful not to crease or drag the material on the floor mat. The suit appeared to fit well in the rearview mirror—snug on the shoulders and fitted around the waist—but there remained two problems with my attire: I did not possess a tie, and beneath the hem of my extravagant trousers, my lizard-skin cowboy boots were conspicuously visible. Resigning myself to the latter sartorial faux pas, I spent the last three minutes haggling with a rotund security guard in the lobby.

'I wanna make sure I get what you're saying,' he said. 'You gonna pay me three bucks to *rent* my tie for half an hour?' I made an offer for four. I did not have the cash flow to buy it outright. 'This is my lucky tie, bro.'

We settled on five, a handsome return on investment for the doorman, considering that the shiny acrylic number would have fetched an even ten bucks on the sidewalks of Chinatown. It didn't really matter. Somehow I had made it to the interview and somehow looked the part.

The offices of the boutique research house were wood-paneled and spare, suggesting an old-fashioned objectivity, an anomaly in an industry that had contributed to one of the greatest asset price bubbles in recent history. The ambience of the lobby was further defined by a tall, leafy money plant and a realist rendering of a tan colt grazing in a meadow pocked with white pansies. Asked to have a seat, I did as I was told, then promptly nodded off, dreaming of life as a pony. After a fiber-rich breakfast of dewy grass, I might canter over hillocks to hang out with my pals. We would horse around all day, graze some more, and sleep. It would be a genial existence.

When I was finally called, I followed the secretary to a conference room in the back, past a set of cramped cubicles and a half-empty water cooler, a glimpse into the secret lives of analysts. A thin man with a mop of thinning reddish hair got up to extend his hand. 'Last but not least,' he said. We both laughed politely. 'You must be Shayzad,' he continued. 'Why don't you take a seat?'

As he positioned himself at the head of the oval mahogany table before a neat stack of papers and a dog-eared manila folder, I sat diagonally across from him, clasping my hands over my stomach and crossing then uncrossing my legs, conscious of my boots.

'Let me tell you a little about myself,' he began. 'I'm originally from the West, but I joined the firm, oh, in 1991, right after school, so I now consider myself a New Yorker. Over the years, I've worked in the biotech, emerging technologies, and specialty chemicals spaces—traditionally our fortes. We primarily look at middle-market companies, publicly held of course, for institutional investors. We're a niche player, one of few independent research houses left. We're a small shop—I'm one of four directors here—and we've been looking for an analyst to run numbers as well as assist us with the, oh, more qualitative analysis we do here.' Reclining in his chair, the Director said, 'So tell me, Shayzad, what's your story?'

For a moment, I felt myself clam up like a child told to recite verse for a guest. Then, coughing into my fist, I collected myself and began speaking in paragraphs. 'Well,' I replied, 'I arrived in New York four years ago to attend college, which I completed in three. I majored in literature and graduated magna cum laude, then was offered a job at an investment bank. As an analyst, I've closed one acquisition, two debt offerings, and an IPO. I've participated in all stages of M&A transaction processes, from drafting offering memoranda to conducting due diligence sessions to valuation. I've worked with clients' corporate finance departments to develop earnings models and have also created discounted cash flow models, performed comparable company analysis, and run leveraged buy-out sensitivities to value public and private companies—'

'Let me cut you off there, Shayzad,' he interjected, and I was grateful for it. It had, at best, been a lackluster performance. 'I've got an idea of the type of work a financial analyst does on a day-to-day basis. I'm more curious about what brings *you* here, but before you answer that question, I want to know why you decided to get into banking after studying literature.'

The tone and construction of the query seemed benign but wasn't. My VP had been blunt about it: *Why the hell do you want to do banking?* Either way, there was a lot of explaining to do.

'Literature,' I began, 'and banking are thought to be disparate or mutually exclusive but you can make connections. I mean, somebody could teach a course called "Masters of the Universe: The Making of the Myth of the Modern Banker." The course would trace the construction of the idea of the banker in fiction, and nonfiction, and its, um, resonance in the popular imagination. You'd look at *Bonfire of the Vanities*, and *American Psycho* . . . you could even look back to Whitman's Wall Street . . . and then there are canonical treatises on the industry like *Barbarians at the Gate* and *Liar's Poker*. But that's the long answer. The short answer is I needed the money.'

The Director nodded ambiguously, which I understood as an indication for me to continue pontificating. 'And though it was demanding—as you know, we work fourteen-, fifteen-hour days—I did enjoy the work. I enjoyed participating in the development of an idea from the chalkboard to its execution as a tangible event. I enjoyed re-creating a company before me, factoring in everything from the costs of raw materials to macroeconomic forecasts. I enjoyed the caffeine-fueled camaraderie among bankers. I can go on . . .'

Nodding thoughtfully, the Director said, 'That's an, oh, unusual take on the industry. And now, I take it, you're interested in ours?'

'Yes. Very much so. In research I can draw on my background in literature and finance in a way that I couldn't in banking. I believe I write well. I've written essays, criticism, expository papers, research reports, and although they may not be exactly the type of literature that you produce here, I have asked the same questions that any good company or industry report should ask: how and why.'

'How and why,' the Director repeated in agreement. I was finally on a roll.

'And there's more to a company than numbers, a mistake both the layman and the expert make. I mean, you've got to look at more qualitative issues, including the experience and capabilities of its management team, client relationships, potential litigation, issues you can't simply reduce to a ratio or tangible dollar value.'

'You can't, Shayzad, that's right,' he said, jotting something down in the folder before him.

'You can call me Chuck.'

'Chuck . . . Can I ask where you're from, Chuck?'

'Pakistan.'

'Pakistan. Wow. How are things over there these days?'

'Well,' I began like a sententious TV pundit, 'if you really want

to know, there's a war on our border, again. There'll be an exodus
of refugees and fighters, again, an influx of drugs and arms. We've
had a war on our border, on and off, for the last thirty years. We live
in one of the toughest neighborhoods in the world: we're bordered
by Afghanistan on the north, a collection of warring fiefdoms, then
there's nuclear aspirant and fundamentalist Iran to the west, and on
the east there's India, a country with a million-man standing army.
The United States is lucky that way. You've got Canada, Mexico,
and the sea.'

'The sea,' he repeated, as if he had often made the same observation
to unsympathetic audiences. 'Do you like it here?'

'Yes, of course. I mean, some of my fondest memories reside in
the streets of this city.'

'Oh, I know what you mean,' he said with a knowing smile. 'Well,
our time is almost up, but before you leave, I want to ask you whether
you have any questions for me?'

In adhering to the strict etiquette of an interview in the financial
services industry, I asked about the future of the company as a
privately held concern, the nature of the Director's job, about the
responsibilities of an analyst, and the 'career ladder.' Each question
was answered thoughtfully and succinctly. Unlike my VP, the
disarmingly unprepossessing Director didn't particularly care to
listen to the sound of his own voice. I did. It had a slightly high
register, like a yodeler's speaking voice, but resonated with a dulcet
and decidedly American sincerity. 'I apologize we were running late,'
he was saying. 'Thank you for coming by.' Pressing his card into my
palm, he added, 'We'll be in touch.'

We shook hands and were all smiles when we parted, but as
I left the room, the Director called after me: 'Oh, and Shayzad?'
Stopping dead in my tracks, I turned around, shoving my hands
into my pockets as if I had been summoned by a teacher who had
discovered I had not completed the final question on the term exam.
'Are those cowboy boots?'

'Um, yes . . . they are.'

The Director nodded ambiguously.

On the way out, I returned the tie to its rightful owner, the doorman-entrepreneur, but could not return the suit because I had to get back to Amo ASAP. The suit would have to be returned soon because when I checked my savings account balance in the ATM outside, I had the princely sum of seventeen dollars and twenty-four cents, which I could not extract from the machine because the amount was not a multiple of twenty. By all measures, I had slipped below the poverty line. I used the three neatly folded dollars in my pocket to purchase a lottery ticket and a token for the train to Jersey.

It was a trying, tiring journey across the river. Sleeplessness had finally caught up with me and knocked me out for the duration of the commute. I dreamed that I found myself in the same dewy meadow as before, only to discover that the outskirts were bordered by barbed wire and guard towers that appeared to be miniature replicas of the Tower of Babel. And the sinister logic of the nightmare suggested that we were being fattened for the kill. I galloped like Silver to alert Jimbo and AC, but thick fog had swept the countryside, obscuring the well-trodden path back to our grazing patch. Of course, it was too late. Next thing, I found myself skinned and quartered alongside my pals, dangling from a butcher's hook.

I woke with a start, realizing I had missed my stop. Murphy's law was in full effect. Stumbling back, I could only see neon outlines of the local topography in the streetlights. Sleepwalking to the hospital, I somehow had the presence of mind to tell the night guard that my wallet was upstairs with my father, who was on his deathbed. I must have looked suitably derelict, because he waved me through even though it was after visiting hours.

Miffed with my sudden and unexplained absence, Amo coolly registered my presence with a shrug and moue. I wanted to tell her what had happened, but there were more pressing issues to address: although the emergency coronary artery bypass graft had been a success, Old Man Khan had been transferred to the ICU because he had not responded well to the anesthesia. Amo paced the waiting room, cradling her elbows and counting her steps, but at some juncture disappeared. In the meantime, I propped myself up, watching the doors open and close, waiting for Amo to return, then nodded off yet again.

FOURTEEN

On the occasion of my nineteenth birthday, I found myself on that same scarred green bench in the northwest corner of Washington Square, among the malcontents and junkies, feeling sorry for myself, and though it seemed to me that after a year, I was back at square one, ground zero, the year had not been eventless. As my roommate Big Jack often said, I had *worked my tail off*, securing dean's list for two semesters straight. I became financially self-sufficient by securing a six-bucks-an-hour, twenty-hour-a-week-job checking out books at the august Elmer Holmes Bobst Library. I lost my virginity during a brief, desultory dorm-room liaison with a preacher's daughter who wore a wicked pair of cowboy boots. I questioned God after signing up for Philosophy 101, described in the course catalog as 'a survey of major themes and figures in the development of epistemology and metaphysics,' and after listening to the weekly sermons delivered at on-campus Friday prayer by a bunch of crazy Saudis with pubic beards. (I wasn't that big on God in the first place because He had taken my father away.) After a year of a diet of eschatological crappola, I had a shot of Campari at an otherwise unremarkable dorm party because of Campari's association with Kelly LeBrock, and because I wanted to spite the Saudis. It was a seminal shot.

And as per AC's directive, I had lost myself in the city many, many times, and on occasion, I'd even trolled the famous New York nightlife (armed with a fake state ID, furnished by AC, that claimed I was born in '74 and christened Papadopoulos). The only time I met with success on my forays was the night I unknowingly wandered

into an Aztec-themed bar in Alphabet City and a handsome man
offered to buy me a Greyhound. It would have been impolite to
decline. As we made small talk, he asked if I had *been here before*,
and I had replied *yeah, all the time*, 'but there sure are a lot of men
here tonight.' My generous, gregarious patron would turn out to be
my first homosexual friend, one Lawrence né Larry. Laughing, he
asked, 'You don't get out much, do you?'

At a certain juncture in New York, after you have discovered
that the city's like a grid, and that the best goddamn falafel joint in
the city is Mamum's in the West Village, and after you have forged
relationships with the local newspaper vendor and the good folks
at the twenty-four-hour Duane Reade, you get this feeling that the
inner life of the city still eludes. You feel that you're missing out, that
at any given moment, day or night, there's an epic party taking place
to which you have not been invited. On the night of my nineteenth
birthday I felt this way. Since there was nobody around—Big Jack
had gone to China Grove, TX, for the Columbus Day weekend, and
AC had sworn off revelry in preparation for the heroic defense of his
much-delayed dissertation proposal—I treated myself to a dinner at
the legendary Les Halles brasserie—*yes, table for one, please*—and
thought I would treat myself to a drink at a chichi downtown venue.
But after taking one look at me, the bouncer asked me to try my luck
somewhere else. Lucklessly, I retired to Washington Square.

As I sat twiddling my thumbs (steadfastly refusing offers to
purchase 'sweet ganja' and trying my damnedest not to listen to a
high-pitched evangelical standing on a soapbox, preaching the End
of Days), a motley horde of musicians began converging around
the fountain in twos and threes, in wigs, in dresses, topcoats, and
Unionist uniforms, and one guy, wearing a homemade percussion
kit, was fixed on stilts. It was the strangest thing. Some appeared to
hail from the back streets of New Orleans; others could have been
from the front lines of the Great Suburban Rebellion. A few had
arguably escaped from a traveling circus. They greeted one another
like lost tribesmen, swigged booze from flasks and Gatorade bottles,

and noisily tuned their instruments—tubas, bugles, trombones, and honkers, as well as xylophones and recorders. At the appointed time, at the beck of some secret call, the percussionists began beating a consensual *dum, da-da dum*. Then all of a sudden there was a musical explosion. Washington Square regulars rarely bat an eyelid. That night they did. It was like midnight mass; it was like band camp on crystal meth. Later I'd learn that the event constituted the closing night ceremony of some annual horn festival spanning the coast.

They played jazz riffs and Afro jazz, klezmer music, gypsy music, show tunes, marching band tunes, 'When the Saints Go Marching In,' 'Sinnerman,' and a crazed rendition of 'Take Five.' They glide-stepped, high-stepped, boogied. At one point, a nymphet in a gold cheerleader's uniform jumped into the fray, twirling a flag like a bo or kendo warrior. Then a clarinet player started break-dancing. Onlookers joined in. It became a free-for-all. Drawn, I followed, clapping along, qawwali-style, then dancing, like Rumpelstiltskin, yelling *Yahoo!* and *Wah wah wah!* and *Bohaut khoob!*

That's when one of the tuba players, ostensibly a Samoan Rastafarian, pulled me aside. 'You from the homeland, dude?' he yelled over the noise.

'What?' I yelled back, wondering *what homeland would that be? Samoa? Jamaica?*

'You from the Pac Land?'

'Pakistan?' I yelled.

'Knew it,' he said grabbing me. 'You a Pac-Man.'

'I'm Shehzad, but they call me Chuck,' I said, shaking his free hand.

'Yeah well, I'm Jimbo, a.k.a. Jamshed, 'cept tonight I'm Jumbolaya. Know what I mean?'

I had no idea, but I nodded like I knew who was who and what was what. I knew this much: at that moment, I was attending the best party in the city.

Later I would realize that the best parties in the city took place in the great outdoors, in parks, on sidewalks and boardwalks; and that there's a party on the street every day. Later I would realize that I was already part of the inner life of the city. That's how things worked here. You had epiphanies and that led to other epiphanies.

'Here, dude,' Jimbo said, proffering a triangle and stick.

'What do I do?' I asked like an idiot.

'Beat it like a mofo.'

Later that night Jimbo and I would exchange stories, cigarettes, numbers. We would become the best of friends. He would invite me to Thanksgiving dinner in Jersey, where I would be introduced to his father and kid sister (and soon after, his new-found love). That's how things worked in the city. You met somebody, then somebody introduced you to somebody else, and then they would become part of your story.

When a swarm of flies entered my reverie, I woke, swinging my arms and swatting the air, before realizing that the peculiarly stubborn fly that had entered my ear was in fact a pudgy, probing finger. *That's strange*, I thought in my soporific stupor, *I've got a finger in my ear*. Then somebody exclaimed, 'Banzai!' Looming above me, blocking the tube light like a solar eclipse, stood a smiley behemoth, a Sasquatch in a track suit, offering his hand. 'Jimbo?' I said, as if in a dream.

'Dude,' he replied, lifting me up like a duffel bag and mashing my face against his fleshy chest. We hugged like a couple of ex-cons. Jimbo smelled like an ex-con. He must have come straight from the slammer. 'I'm born again,' he announced, 'like 'em Watergaters.'

'I can't believe it . . . it's great to see you, yaar . . . how'd you know to come here?'

'Myla told me, y'know, Myla and Eddie Davis from upstairs?'

'You been inside yet?'

'They ain't lettin' me in. They say he's, like, under the influence—'

'Anesthesia—'

'Yeah, that's it, that's right. That's the word. Besides, I don't wanna give him another attack.'

'Don't say that, yaar.' I wasn't sure if Jimbo was serious, but he was anxious. So was I, but I said, 'He's fine, he'll be fine.'

'My old man, he's tough as nails,' he declared unconvincingly.

Blinded by excitement and Jimbo's bulk, I did not notice that there was somebody else in the background, craning for attention, like a familiar but distant relative at a family reunion. At first I thought I was still dreaming, but in my dreams Jimbo would be followed either by loping Munchkins on a good day or by the Wicked Witch of the West in the buck. Instead, he was followed by the Duck. I regarded her for a few moments, sheepishly, perhaps a little idiotically, because her appearance seemed more astonishing than a visit from the fanciful denizens of Oz. 'Hiya, Chuck,' she said. It was a little weird—we had, after all, exchanged words and parted unceremoniously—but I figured that the best way to approach the situation was with a kiss. 'Hiya, Dora,' I replied, planting a wet one on her cheek. 'Have a seat.'

Save a venerable Puerto Rican couple nestled ear to ear at one end of the room and a nurse-on-duty enthralled by a romance novel at the other, we had the place to ourselves. Rearranging the seating, we took a hard orange chair each, but when the Duck squirmed, Jimbo grabbed her by her love handles and valiantly plopped her down in his lap. Lassoing her arms around Jimbo's neck, she asked, 'Are you being frisky, Mr. Khan?' Jimbo nodded. 'I be frisky, miss.'

It was great to see them together. I felt warm and giddy like a night out at Tja!, and like on a night out at Tja!, we traded stories. From Jimbo's monosyllabic responses, however, it seemed apparent that he was not particularly eager to relive his experience. When I inquired whether he had come across a certain Grizzly, he replied, 'Dunno, but there was some dude who sounded like what's-his-face—'

'Mick Rooney?'

'Yeah,' Jimbo replied with uncharacteristic vehemence, '*Micky friggin' Rooney.*' But if Jimbo had not come across the eminently sensible and empathetic Grizzly, I wondered how he had been released. 'I get my phone call,' Jimbo said, 'so I call Dora—'

'And,' Dora interjected, 'he's like, "Hiya hon, I'm in the joint. You think you can drop by for some conjugal lovin'." I was totally flabbergasted. I was livid. Jimbo's many things—a great DJ, a bad drunk—but he's no terrorist. Everybody knows he's like a teddy bear, a lamb—'

'"Baa Baa Black Sheep," baby.'

'You're a stud, sweetheart.' Jimbo nodded in agreement. 'Anyway,' the Duck continued, 'first I thought I'd get to Brooklyn, but then I'm like, *What am I going to do?* so I call the one person I turn to when things seriously go wrong—'

Before she could say more, the Duck abruptly slid off Jimbo's lap, as if suffering pins and needles, and before I could ask her to continue, I realized that Amo had materialized before us. She must have escaped the recesses of the cardiology ward for air, or company. In the furrows across her brow, I could read that she was unimpressed by the belated appearance of her big brother and an unfamiliar, pot-bellied girl perched happily on his thighs. Digging her fists into her slender waist, she cried, 'Where've you been, Jamshed Lala?'

Jimbo stood up but did not dare approach her. She looked like she was going to spontaneously combust. 'In the joint, sis,' Jimbo mumbled.

The claim sounded preposterous, and Jimbo didn't immediately elaborate. 'Yeah, right!' Amo yelled, startling everybody: me, Jimbo, the Duck, the nice Puerto Rican couple in the corner. Before things could get out of hand, however, I interjected. 'Actually, Amo,' I started, 'we were both in prison.'

'Wait! *What?*'

'We were arrested, over the weekend, on terrorism charges, or suspicion of terrorism, or something, I don't know. Anyway, it's a long story.'

'*Terrorism?*'

'You know AC, right? He's still inside. You should be happy your brother's out and here now.' Amo processed yesterday's news with rapid blinks of the eye, and all of a sudden she cupped her mouth and bowed her head to hide her face. Then Jimbo jumped up and hugged her as if she were a bouquet of long-stemmed flowers.

In the meantime, the Duck had been standing perfectly still, watching the Khan reconciliation with one hand on her nape and her head slightly tilted to one side. I suppose she would have remained that way had I not intervened. 'Um, Amo?' I said. 'Let me introduce you to the Duck, I mean, Dora . . . and Dora, this is Jimbo, I mean Jamshed's sister, Amo.' It wasn't one of my better introductions.

'Aamna,' Amo corrected me.

'Hiya, Amina,' said the Duck. 'I've heard a lot about you. It's so nice to finally meet in person.' Amo offered a gelid smile as a reply but, because she had been brought up well, managed a quiet, cordial, 'You too.' And with exclamations, explanations, and introductions out of the way, Jimbo asked, 'What's the lowdown, sis?'

We were informed that Old Man Khan was recovering from the anesthesia and, courtesy of the nurse-on-duty, could see family. 'I came out to get Shehzad,' Amo said, 'but I guess now we can all go in.'

'Don't think that's a great idea, sis.'

'What d'you mean?'

'Think about it for a second. The old man's had a heart attack. He don't need to see me. What if he, like, freaks out or somethin'?' I agreed. Trooping in together did not seem particularly prudent at the time. 'Chuck, dude. You up for a reccy?'

'Sure thing, yaar.'

Squirting a dollop of hand sanitizer into my palms in preparation, I dutifully followed Amo past the examination room where we had lunched earlier and down a wide corridor patrolled by shuffling nurses to a room divided into four quadrants by floor-length vinyl curtains. It was humid inside and smelled of unwashed feet and Vicks rub and something like mercurochrome. Two of the four beds were occupied, and I could discern from the prone silhouette of the patient on my left that he was tall, bony, and friendless. I found myself muttering a prayer for him. That's all one can really do.

Amo parted the curtain on the right, and there lay Old Man Khan, like Christ on the cross, connected to tubes and drips and pulsing machines. A tube dangled from his lower lip so that his gaping toothless mouth drooped to one side while his dentures swam in a half-empty glass of fizzy water on the table wedged between the bed and the wall. Although his eyes were swollen and mostly shut, you could make out a horizon of white below each lid. Like a wounded buffalo on the Serengeti, he breathed heavily, only dimly aware of the vultures circling above.

When I took the chair beside him where Amo must have spent the night, half awake and hunched over, Old Man Khan stirred: raising his stubbly chin by a few degrees, a gesture that seemed to be more a reflex than an acknowledgment of our presence, he extended the curled fingers of his right hand as if reluctantly displaying his palm to a palmist. Taking his hand in mine, I uttered salam, and when he didn't readily respond, I repeated the greeting in a louder voice. In response, Old Man Khan issued something between a growl and a groan, causing one of the machines to beep like the metronomic soundtrack to a horror flick.

'What's wrong, Baba?' Amo cried. 'What d'you need?'

Old Man Khan attempted to articulate the thought again, and again the thought came out mangled, but when I picked the tube from his mouth, he gasped, 'Beta.' At first I thought he had mistaken me for Jimbo, but even in his condition that was not plausible. Crushing his fingers into a fist, he cried, 'My son . . . they took my son . . .'

And suddenly it all made harrowing sense: it was not the tea or the news that had caused the seizure but the phone call. At seven in the morning the day before, Old Man Khan had learned that his son had been jailed. As the machine continued to beep like an electronic countdown, I told Amo to call the doctor.

'But Jamshed Lala's here—'

'Just *do* it.'

As Amo grudgingly sidled away, I leaned into Old Man Khan and said, 'Khan Sahab! Jamshed is okay. Your son is fine . . . I've spoken to him . . . he's actually on his way over right now.' It was the truth, or very close to the truth, though I was not sure whether or not Old Man Khan heard or understood. The exertion had strained him. Shutting his angry blue eyes, he had lapsed back into a stupor.

It was unnerving to see the grand old man reduced to an animal state, half-conscious and half-naked: the spotted green hospital gown had come undone at the back, and the baby blue blanket that had shrouded his body from the waist down had risen to his knees to reveal surprisingly small, bunioned feet. I could not help but marvel at them. They had hauled him from the rocky Pathan heartland to the port city of Jersey City, from boyhood to manhood, from ruffian to family man. It was too early for the journey to end.

Tucking the ends of the blanket under his heels, I raised my hands and bowed my head and mumbled a prayer that began, 'Allah Mian, please help Khan Sahab get back on his feet. His family needs him.' While I was at it, I added, 'You took my father away too soon. Don't take Khan Sahab yet.' Before I could complete the plaint, God dispatched a doctor. A red-headed lady with an attractive mole on the crease of her mouth charged in with a stethoscope, asking *if I'd mind waiting outside.*

I found Amo rocking against the wall in the corridor, studying the ceiling like an amateur stargazer connecting cosmic dots on an overcast night. When she saw me, she began talking. 'Thought Baba's diet was flavonoid poor, or he wasn't watching his HDL—you know, variables you can like, manage—but it wasn't just that. To think that Baba coulda been home, gardening, or soaking up the sun—he likes to do that after breakfast—or cookin' up a storm, if . . . if . . . statistically, this totally doesn't make any sense. You could like run a regression analysis on the different variables but the correlation between random events would be kinda meaningless . . .'

Although I did not have an appreciation for the actuarial sciences, I understood what Amo was getting at, but before I could get in a word edgewise, the doctor emerged. 'Different people respond differently to anesthesia. Your father hasn't responded well. He needs rest. I suggest you wait—what's the time now?—at least two hours before seeing him.' Slipping her hands into the pockets of her scrubs, she rhetorically said, 'Okay?' as she turned to leave.

'Actually,' I began, 'I need to talk to you, doctor.' Pausing, she glanced at her dangling locket watch, then uttered a noncommittal *un-huh?* 'There are some issues that you may want to consider. You see, I'm pretty sure Mr. Khan's seizure was triggered by the news that his son had been imprisoned, except now he's free, but Mr. Khan doesn't know—'

'Wait a minute. *You aren't the son?*' I shook my head. 'Where *is* his son?' When I replied that he was in the waiting room, she pinched the bridge of her nose, stating, 'Only family's allowed back here.' I offered to take her to the correct family member. As she followed us to the waiting room, the doctor half-jokingly asked, 'He's not an ax murderer, right?'

'No,' Amo blurted exasperatedly. 'He was in for like, terrorism!'

Stopping dead in her tracks, the doctor said, 'Beg your pardon?'

'It was a mistake,' I interjected, frowning at Amo. 'That's why he was released.'

'So he's *not* a terrorist?'

'You can judge for yourself.'

It took us a while to spot the prodigal son. The waiting room was bustling like a vegetable market in the morning. Entire clans were lodged in or around the orange seats. Three generations of a family of Cambodian descent congregated along walls in the far corner as if they had laid claim to the land. A diminutive Greek grandmother beat her chest as her burly sons argued throatily among themselves, and a brood of four adorably well-behaved, well-dressed black children sat in a row according to age or size beside a lady in gold-sequined headgear. Mercifully, Mullet Man had not returned, but the elderly Puerto Rican pair continued their solemn vigil.

There was an amorous couple in the mix, oblivious to the activity surrounding them: the man, a block of flesh sprouting dreadlocks, stood over his partner, massaging her shoulders like he was playing a grand piano. Amo pointed them out. The doctor did a double-take as we made our way across. 'Mr. Kahn?' she asked.

Disengaging from the Duck, Jimbo asked, 'How's my dad, doc?'

The doc officiously repeated the prognosis, reiterating that he should wait two hours before visiting with his father. 'But you *must* see your father.'

Jimbo considered the entreaty before replying. 'Our relationship's kinda funky,' Jimbo said. 'You don't think I'll trip him out?'

'You'll make him *very happy*,' she replied, smiling sternly before turning to leave.

'My old man's tough's a nut, huh, doc?'

'He's a survivor.'

The four of us stood around because there was one chair between us. Then Jimbo and I managed to secure another, and the Duck and Amo tentatively settled down next to each other like children told to make conversation. We had an hour and forty-two minutes to kill before the Great Khan Reconciliation. In the interim, I decided to make another brunch run.

Jimbo's stomach had been rumbling like distant thunder all morning. I felt for him; he had been on the famous carbonly Metropolitan Detention Center Diet for days. Before heading out, we took orders from the ladies—another scrambled egg on croissant and cup of minestrone for Amo, a Granny Smith and a small bottle of mineral water for the Duck—and I mentioned the Kung Pao Fried Chicken with Cheese Fries to Jimbo. 'Sounds tight, dude,' he said, cradling his belly like a pet hippo left with negligent neighbors for the weekend.

'Beats prison gruel.'

'Fo shizzle, ma nizzle.'

'Hey,' I began as we marched into the afternoon, 'what happened back there?'

'Dude, I'm here. Don't wanna go back in the hole. Know what I'm sayin'?'

I imagined he had had it rough. The good folks at the Metropolitan Detention Center must have treated him like the Incredible Hulk, even though he was more like his mild-mannered doppelgänger.

'Okay, fine, but at least tell me how you got out?'

'The Drake, dude,' he replied, teetering on his toes. 'The Drake came through.'

I should have guessed. I had met him once because I happened to be over at the Duck's after a crazy night of merrymaking to retrieve my wallet (which, after a hard target search, was excavated with the use of a broom). Striding in with his latest acquisition tucked under his arm—it might have been a minor Whistler—the Duck's dad (whom Jimbo naturally christened the Drake) observed me with absinthe eyes and academic curiosity. Although nobody really knew what he did for a living—one had heard in passing his association with fund-raising, philanthropy—he cut the figure of that rare breed of man known as the gentleman adventurer: he wore a double-breasted raincoat and a rabbit-hair Trilby that he removed to reveal a full head of white hair.

'You must be the Pakistani,' he had said by way of introduction. 'I've been to the Kaalash Valley. Remarkable place, remarkable people. Descendants of the armies of Alexander. Pakistan's fascinating, fascinating. I can tell you stories. I've trekked to the foothills of K2, which, Dora, is the second tallest mountain peak in the world. I've traded vodka with the Chinese border guards at the Khunjerab Pass, played polo with the Mir of Nagar . . . Did you know Bob vacations there?' I didn't know if he meant Bob Hope or Bob DeNiro, and although impressed with his knowledge of my homeland, I got the sense that had I been a Masai tribesman in full warrior regalia, he would have related the history of my people to me.

Later I was told that the Drake had called me a fine young man but, mistaking me for the boyfriend, added that I seemed 'somewhat tender' for his daughter. When he finally caught up with Jimbo one night at the Oak Bar, he reportedly found him to be 'not entirely oafish,' inadequately exotic, and definitely not his daughter's type. And when the Duck tried to enlist him in the Free Jimbo Effort, he did not readily oblige. 'Who knows what evil lurks in the hearts of men?' he allegedly asked. Not the sort to take no for an answer, Dora called her godfather, Drake's college roommate who, luckily for Jimbo, was the serving state governor. It was a matter of time before Jimbo's case would receive due scrutiny.

Though I would have liked to probe the matter on the way back, Jimbo had started talking to himself: 'They never lost their way an' they were mad focused, stone cold, dude, rollin' dirt balls like it's nobody's business, carryin' foodstuffs on their pinheads, like leaves and biryani bits from the night before.' It took me a while to get what he was saying. 'I'd watch 'em in the garden every morning, solderin' on, hut hut hut hut. It'd wake me up. Old Man Khan would be like, "Look at 'em ants, beta. Look at 'em ants."'

'Jimbo, yaar, I told you once, I'll tell you again: Old Man Khan will be happy as hell to see you.'

The Kung Pao was still warm and gooey upon our return, and dispensing with formality, Jimbo wolfed down his share standing up. After the famous carb-only Metropolitan Detention Center, it must have been the first square meal he'd had for days. Amo and the Duck, on the other hand, lunched like picnickers, crossing their legs and spreading paper napkins across their laps. I could hear them whispering among themselves about the vitamin value of the Kung Pao, but Jimbo seemed unperturbed and unrepentant, pleased with himself and the novelty of the dish. Afterward he wandered off toward the general vicinity of a broom closet and then disappeared. He returned not more than ten minutes later bearing a sorry-looking, hand-picked bouquet of dandelions. It was time.

Leaving the Duck behind, we headed to the room. When we entered, the machines beeped, the air-conditioning whirred, the neighboring patient wheezed, and Old Man Khan stared at us vacantly as if we were a trio of straggling Cambodian orphans. Then, raising his arms, he boomed, 'Why are you all around standing like this?'

Amo leaped to embrace him, while Jimbo and I lingered by his feet because there was no way the two of us could negotiate the alley between the bed and wall without knocking over Amo, the drip, the breakfast table, and the empty vase on the breakfast table. In the meantime, I squeezed another transparent glob of clinical-strength hand sanitizer from the dispenser on the wall. Jimbo followed my lead, rubbing his fleshy palms together as if in prayer.

When beckoned, the prodigal son lumbered toward his father, presenting the dandelions like a repentant child. Old Man Khan pulled Jimbo to his chest and wept. I had never seen anything like it.

'I thought I had lost you, beta,' said Old Man Khan.

'Thought I'd lose you, Baba,' Jimbo said.

'Tell me what happened. Tell me everything, beta.'

Settling on the perimeter of the bed, Jimbo and I took turns relating the wild and woolly story of our incarceration, pausing intermittently to clarify facts (*wait, the raccoon was AC?*), opinions (*d'you think they had already decided they were going to arrest somebody that night?*), or to question the momentum of inevitability: what if AC had cooperated with the feds like a sane human being or Jimbo had not come charging down the stairs like the Light Brigade? What if we had left earlier? What if we hadn't left the city at all? And although nobody said it, I am certain that the following question was in the back of everybody's mind: what if 9/11 never happened?

According to AC, serious historical inquiry incorrectly considers the question *what if* to be the turf of Philip K. Dick or comic book titles like *What If the Incredible Hulk Had the Brain of Bruce Banner?* Although historians were not in the business of assigning probabilities to historical events, AC opined they should. 'Look, chum,' he once expounded, 'it's not like anything can happen at any time. You have to consider the *conditions of possibility*. When a power forward goes up for an offensive board, for example, the probability of scoring a bucket increases. If you have a center in the paint, the odds increase further, and if it's, say, 1993, the Eastern Conference Finals, twenty seconds left on the shot clock, Charles Smith with the rebound, the sound of the ball ricocheting against the hoop has, ah, historic resonance.'

The question in the back of my mind was closer to home: what if AC had been present, perched on the bed among us in his ostrich-skins and velvet jacket, waggling his lounge lizard mustache? By now he would have smoked a fatty in the men's room, banged a nurse, played hide-and-go-seek with the kids in the waiting room, disposed of Mullet Man, and shared the murky and potent contents of his pewter hip flask with the lonely man in the adjacent bed. Moreover, he would have negotiated a private room for Old Man Khan, the penthouse or presidential suite, and filled it with tiger lilies, tulips and gardenias because that's the way he was—charming and roguish, thoughtful and unhinged, a man of incongruous and incommensurable qualities.

'So, wait,' Amo was saying, 'if Ali's still in, how'd you guys get out?' I told her I owed my freedom to a burly and sympathetic guy who was at once my interrogator and benefactor. 'And you, Jamshed Lala?'

All eyes turned to Jimbo who cleared his throat, probed the corner of his eye for the possibility of dirt and then mumbled something about an old friend springing him. It was the kind of reply you might offer when interrogated about the missing cookies in the cookie jar. 'Which friend?' Amo asked.

Attempting to signal to Amo that this line of questioning was unhealthy, I discreetly karate-chopped my throat, the universal signal for *cut it out*, but because she was angled away, she missed the gesture. 'Which friend, Jamshed Lala?' she persisted.

Jamshed Lala did not immediately reply, probably because he was considering his limited options. He could have lied. I would have. The truth was so damned tiring. It might have made life easier for all of us. We could have amicably continued our lives without fear or reproach. Instead, he said, 'Dora, sweety.'

'How'd she do that?'

'Dad's pals with the governor or somethin'—'

Suddenly Old Man Khan growled, 'Dora? Who is this Dora?'

Amo and I exchanged panicked glances. I checked the heart monitor.

'My friend, Dora,' said Jimbo.

Old Man Khan sat up and frowned as if he had just inhaled the rank fumes of mercurochrome. 'Your *friend* Dora? That girl! Where is she?'

'In the waiting room.'

'Waiting room?' Old Man Khan repeated. '*Here?*' Jimbo nodded. 'What is she doing here?'

'She's here 'cause we're here.'

'I want to meet this *friend*. Call her. Bring her to me!'

Immediately volunteering to fetch her, I scurried out of the room and down the corridor, inhaling and exhaling methodically like a marathon runner pacing himself for the interminable last leg. Just as I neared the waiting room, however, I heard somebody holler after me. At first I thought it was a member of the hospital staff reproaching me for not adhering to the hospital's visitation guidelines, but it was Amo.

Tapping the rubber soles of her Pumas against the linoleum, she panted, 'Hiya.' There was a flush of color in her cheeks recalling cotton-ball rouge on a doll. She looked different, like somebody else, probably because her headscarf had slid off her head. It was only then that I came to appreciate why some interpreted the Koranic injunction concerning adornments to include hair and head. 'Hiya,' I repeated breathlessly.

'They needed to be alone.'

'Oh . . . right . . . okay,' I stuttered. Amo smiled as if I had said something amusing; I smiled back; and then a moment passed during which we said nothing but maintained eye contact as if mesmerized by the fluorescent light reflected in each other's pupils. It might have been nothing or it might have been the sort of moment that had passed between Begum and Old Man Khan one fateful night many years ago in a hospital in Karachi. He might have held her. She might have allowed herself to be held. Amo took a step closer. 'I'm . . . I'm glad you're here, Shehzad,' she said. 'Y'know, every time you leave—to like go get lunch or wherever you went yesterday—I feel I'll never see you again.'

We were close enough to kiss. We could have, we should have, but fate intervened in the shape of the Duck. I had seen her from the corner of my eye, pacing back and forth like Hager between the hills. 'Hiya guys,' she said. 'What's going on?'

Recalling my urgent mission, I reported, 'Khan Sahab's summoned you.'

'Now?'

'Now,' I confirmed.

The Duck swallowed. Then she scratched the tip of her nose, licked her lips. In all the time I had known her, the Duck had never lost her decidedly queenly cool. At Christ Hospital, however, she seemed to be on the verge. Pulling her aside, I said, 'You okay?' The Duck shook her head. 'Okay, listen. This is what you do. When you walk in, right, raise your hand, preferably your right hand, to your head, bow slightly, and say *salam*.'

'Say it again,' she said mouthing the greeting.

'*Salam*, like *sholom*, but sharper,' I said, but then added, 'or like *salami*, without the *i*.'

'Salami. Salam. Got it.'

Then the three of us walked back together like tourists at the Jersey City Museum, pausing outside the room to exchange sighs and skittish smiles (and the Duck tied her dirty blond hair into a neat bun, which she then pierced with an unused chopstick). When we entered, Jimbo took her by the hand like a proper gentleman and presented her to his father like his bride. 'Baba Jan,' he said. 'I'd like to introduce you to Dora.'

Old Man Khan scrutinized the Duck with fierce blue eyes. We all did. I thought I saw the Duck mouth 'salami.' That would have been that. Raising her hand to her head like a native, however, she managed salam, adding, 'I'm honored to meet you, Mr. Khan.'

The gesture had a salutary effect on Old Man Khan because the lines that marred his sandpaper brow vanished, and he beckoned to her with an open hand. 'Come,' he said, patting the bed. 'Sit down.' The Duck did as she was told. 'I am very grateful to you for what you have done for my son.'

'You don't need to thank me, Mr. Khan—'

'Your eyes tell me you are a good person. That is what matters. It doesn't matter if a person is Eastern or Western, black or white, from New York or from New Jersey. In my experiences, each human needs the same things: food, water, shelter, loving. Will you agree with me, Dora beti?'

'Yes, Mr. Khan . . . You know, my father would agree with you.' Pausing to think about what she was going to say next, she added, 'When you're better, I'd like you to meet him.'

As Old Man Khan mulled a response, I imagined the epic tête-à-tête: Pathan and Anglo-Saxon, Muslim and Episcopalian, immigrant and son of the soil, making small talk at a mutually agreed upon forum, perhaps a quiet corner booth at the Oak Room. It would be the first time in nearly a decade Old Man Khan would traverse the Hudson and probably the first time he would dine at a Zagat-rated establishment. The situation would require feats of diplomacy. Old Man Khan would sample the braised swordfish with couscous because he only took halal, and the Drake might deferentially forgo his evening Glenfiddich. Then they would discuss the relationship of their progeny together, knowing in the backs of their minds that the future was a fait accompli.

Placing his hand on the Duck crown, Old Man Khan turned to Jimbo. 'Jamshed beta,' he said, 'it's tea time. We must offer our guest a cup of tea. And biscuits. We must find biscuits!'

At any other time, I would have volunteered for a biscuit run, but at that juncture, I couldn't stay to avail of the famous Pathan hospitality because I remembered I was on the run. In seventy-two hours, life as I knew it would come to an unceremonious end. It was time to leave.

After asking Old Man Khan for permission, which was reluctantly granted, I offered a round of 'byes and bows from a distance. The Duck kissed the air. Amo frowned. Jimbo offered to walk me out. 'I'll pray for you, Khan Sahab,' I said before heading out.

'I am alive because of your prayers, Shehzad beta.' And as always, he said, 'You must give my salam to your mother.'

As we cut through the attendant hordes in the waiting room to the visitors' desk, I realized I had lost my fear of hospitals. Things sometimes worked out. Before parting, I asked Jimbo if he had a place to stay. 'You know you're always welcome to crash with me, yaar.'

Mauling me sentimentally, Jimbo said, 'You're a good man, Charlie Brown. Thanks for lookin' out for the family and everythin'.' When I told him he didn't need to thank me, Jimbo mauled me again and said, 'A real civilized soonker.'

'What's going to happen to our friend, yaar?'

'That governor guy's lookin' into it, dude.'

'What? Wow! Why didn't you tell me before?'

'Just keep your fingers crossed,' he said, demonstrating, 'and thumbs, like this.'

'Well,' I sighed, 'at least *he'll* be okay.'

'What's wrong, dude?'

'I'm okay. I'm fine. It's just that back there they told me, I've got to leave the country.'

'Whatchu talkin' 'bout, Willis?'

'My visa. It expires in three days.' Jimbo slapped his forehead loudly. 'Everything hinges on me getting this job—'

Grabbing me by the lapels with uncharacteristic alacrity, Jimbo said, 'Do what you gotta do!' Then, unzipping his track jacket, he exhibited pink welts on his rounded shoulders. It was a jarring display. Tracing the tumid outline of a lash just above the shoulder

180   H. M. NAQVI

blade, it occurred to me that if Jimbo had been beaten, AC would
have been left for dead. He wasn't easy. 'You survive, dude. Like my
old man. We're survivors.'

∾

It was a fine sentiment, except that survival is a material exigency.
Food and shelter are contingent on liquidity, but my cash was tied
up in a lottery ticket and a two-thousand-dollar suit. Pawning the
latter would free up the nominal cash flow for subsistence, but there
were already creased stripes running down the spine of the jacket that
would have to be ironed out with delicate, deliberate strokes. And I
possessed neither iron nor ironing board. It would have been grand
to return the Amazing Technicolor Dreamcoat, then idle away the
waning afternoon among the multitudes on Fifth, window-shopping,
sampling colognes at Bergdorf, appraising fake-diamond-encrusted
Rolexes from West African hawkers, touring FAO Schwartz like
the man who refuses to grow up. Instead I found myself pounding
the paan-stained streets of Jackson Heights, Queens, clad for a soirée
at a Texan country club, Abdul Karim's keys jangling in my pocket.
I had some unfinished business and a half-baked if not entirely
harebrained plan.

FIFTEEN

The air was cool and smoky like November in Karachi and, as usual, wafting mutton biryani. The aroma reached the height of the el and extended across this side of Roosevelt Avenue. Little Pakistan was unusually tranquil, as if the natives, bracing for a hurricane, had left town in a hurry. Every other shop seemed shuttered, and the sidewalks were mostly abandoned by the aunty patrols, the layabouts huddled at corners pushing calling cards, the dark-eyed Bangladeshi busboys sucking beedis during bathroom breaks. Save a couple of Lincoln Continentals—one defiantly blaring *dil bolay boom, boom*—the main drag was also mostly deserted like an obscure landing strip.

Later I'd learn that in the sweeps following 9/11, many had fled across the border, to Canada, to Mexico, with not much more than the clothes on their backs. Many would leave for the homes they had left decades ago, never to return. There was, however, some activity on 37th Avenue: the ramshackle Palace—a hardcore porn theater that had been reborn as the neighborhood Bollywood venue—remained operational for the matinee, a 'hair-raising' musical remake of *Ghost*. And the Sikh-owned liquor shop where we had been known to congregate for assorted nips and aperitifs was open for business, as was Kabab King next door.

Once upon a time, we would make a fortnightly pilgrimage to the legendary Kabab King for late brunch or early dinner, dragging with us insular denizens of Manhattoes that had included on occasion Ari, Lawrence né Larry, the Duck and her urban tribe. By the time we arrived, we would be famished, sometimes still hung over from the night before, and though the uninitiated were known to get the proverbial strangers-in-a-strange-land feeling, they would be welcomed by the mustachioed majordomo like lost relatives from the homeland and extended VIP treatment: the frayed floral-patterned curtains of the designated family area in the back would be parted, additional chairs would be arranged, dusted; the unctuous glass table tops would be cleared, wiped. Salad would arrive, soda would be served. Then came the feast of meat: bihari kabab, seekh kabab, chicken tikka, chicken boti.

According to a *Times* food critic, whose besmudged photocopied review could be found sandwiched between the table and glass, 'The kabab rarely receives its due respect. Dismissed as simple, sneered at as primitive, the kabab sizzles through life unappreciated, just as cars and buses rumble into the unconscious sonic background of city life.' I had read it so many times that I could, for a time, recite it at will like doggerel committed to memory by rote during a young and impressionable age, and what irked me was not so much the misconceived analogy but the whimsical, vaguely Orientalist characterization of the kabab: 'The kabab . . . is simple and primitive—as old as the day the first ancestral hominid stuck a piece of meat on a stick and held it over a fire.'

There was no doubt in our minds that the piece was penned by a white man, not an erudite Jeffrey Steingarten or an urbane Tony Bourdain but the Sam Huntington of food criticism. After all, the steak is considered primitive in most parts of the world, thought to be cut by Neanderthals from the rumps of roving buffalo and slapped unceremoniously on the fire. Although Sam might have traced the antecedent of the kabab to the neighborhood of Paleolithic Age, its preparation is an evolved exercise that requires parboiling meat, mincing it, marinating it, spicing it, and finally grilling it over coals. The critic, however, managed to get the ambience of the place right:

$25 AND UNDER

JUICY KABABS TUCKED AWAY IN A QUEENS CABBY HAUNT

Perhaps it's fitting, then, that a place celebrating the humble kabab is itself as humble and unprepossessing as Kabab King Diner, a bright and cluttered Pakistani restaurant, which occupies one point of the five-point intersection of 37th Road, 73rd Street and Roosevelt Avenue in Jackson Heights, Queens. It looks like a cabby haunt, with a big steam table and communal tables set with pitchers of water, where diners eat with plastic utensils from plastic foam plates. But behind the steam table, where assorted curries and stews sit warming, and behind an aisle, where cooks dart back and forth filling orders, dozens of skewers hang from a rack, waiting to be inserted into one of the tandoor ovens. And from these ovens emerge kababs as moist and succulent as you can imagine, layered in a thick yogurt marinade, well-herbed and intensely spiced. These kababs do not fade into the dry background babble. They shock you into taking notice.

We would be more stuffed than shocked afterward, sluggishly eyeing each other, the cabbies, and their families on the adjacent tables, and the gutted Styrofoam plates before us. Somebody would inevitably inquire about the dessert menu before being told that taking dessert at a kabab joint would not be advisable. Somebody else would inquire about the restroom and would be promptly and vigorously discouraged. Then we would pay at the counter before shaking hands all around, and return the way we came.

～

It would have been wonderful to revisit the old haunt, but I had not traveled to Jackson Heights for the proverbial kabab, shabab or sharab. Those prelapsarian times were far, far away. Skirting Kabab King, I turned the corner and walked three-quarters of the block to the somber brick walk-ups on the right-hand side of the street. I had decided to come clean with Abdul Karim.

When I rang the buzzer below the rusty copper-plated mailbox, sometimes left unlocked for the weekly exchange of keys, Abdul Karim answered the door, wrapped, as usual, in his royal blue bathrobe. In the background, I could hear the squeaks and whistles coming from a TV, the telltale sounds of Looney Tunes, and for a moment I imagined everything was fine, like before; but then I noticed that Abdul Karim had shaved his mustache—a dried dab of shaving cream still smudged his earlobe—and his eyes were cherry red and veiny, as if he had a nasty case of conjunctivitis.

'Dare you!' he cried, jabbing me with his finger as if intending to puncture my sternum. 'Dare you show your face? Do you know how much suffering you are causing?'

Staring at him blankly, I apologized profusely—'I'm sorry, I'm sorry, I'm sorry'—for what, I wasn't sure. I didn't have to guess. 'The FBI came into my house. They were waking up my six-year-old daughter, treating us criminally. They were asking, "What your relationship to the Shehzad boy? You are knowing he is terrorist?"'

Rendered speechless, I hung my head. I felt like bursting into tears.

'I was trusting in you,' Abdul Karim was saying. 'I was taking you in, giving you work, but you betrayed me! You betrayed us. You are the betrayer.' Nodding to myself, I agreed with the accusations. It was my fault. I should not have dragged the Family Karim into the stormy seas of my life. 'We are decent people. We don't want your types. You go do jihad some other place else!'

'I'm sorry,' I slurred, 'I'm sorry, I'm sorry,' and would have continued to inanely spout apology upon apology but was interrupted by a voice ringing from inside: '*Aray bhai, kaun hai?*'

It was Mrs. Abdul Karim. A big-boned lady defined in part by a formidable greased, hip-length braid, she was at once an efficient homemaker and a demanding wife, determined on keeping up with the Joneses or, as it so happened, the Garcias. I had met her only once before, the very first time I had fetched the keys, and though she had been cordial and had served a cup of Kashmiri chai, I got the impression that she was not sold on me, perhaps because like her husband, I had come down in the world.

'You go now,' Abdul Karim instructed, jabbing me again. As I stumbled down the stairs, he said, 'You see, you are upsetting Mrs. You go now. Go, go, go.'

'I'm sorry,' I said, repeating the words like a mantra as I retraced my steps to Kabab King. I needed sanctuary, a reprieve, a moment to collect my thoughts. Sidling in like a supplicant, I found a spot by the window and a discarded scrim of cracked naan to chew on. I toyed with a saltshaker. I folded paper napkins into origami hats. I reread the *Times* review. And I conversed with Abdul Karim in my head while fending off waiters with tight smiles and half-truths. Although I claimed that I would order a little later—*I'm actually waiting for someone*—I could not afford the entrees on the menu. In time, however, I ordered some water, which was splashed like a half-hearted favor into somebody else's plastic cup on the table. The staff was worn down and on edge like Abdul Karim, like me, like everybody else. The majordomo was nowhere to be seen. Maybe he too had fled across the border. Maybe it was time I fled as well.

After spending the better part of an hour in deliberation with the saltshaker, I was virtually escorted out by the staff, but instead of returning to the city, as I might have once upon a time, I decided to return to Abdul Karim's. I had to speak up, explain myself. I couldn't simply up and leave. Returning to the scene of disaster, I determinedly rang the bell again, but this time Mrs. Abdul Karim attended the door. She stood in the doorway as if guarding her home and hearth from an intruder intent on thieving and pillaging. It was the pose Ma would strike when some stranger rapped on our door: a beggar, a cook-for-hire, somebody collecting for the neighborhood madrassa or on my father's debts. Ma would hear each unexpected visitor out with her fists on her hips but would always have the last word. Nothing got past her.

'Get out!' Mrs. Abdul Karim suddenly yelled, waving a wooden stirring spoon in my face. '*Duffa ho!*' Somehow I stood my ground, and before she could whack me with the spoon and send me packing, I pleaded with her in Urdu to hear me out: '*Aik minute,*' I said, holding up a quivering finger, '*mujhay bus aik minute ki mohlat deejiay. Phir main aap ko kabhi tang nahin karoon ga.*' Mrs. Abdul Karim frowned as if she'd heard it all before, as if I were parroting the promises her husband had made about making a better life in the United States of America. Clasping my hands, I repeated, '*Aik minute, bus aik minute.*'

'*Aik minute,*' she groaned, hands on hips, spoon in hand. 'Only *aik minute.*'

'Madam,' I began, 'I'm truly, truly sorry for what has happened. I'm sorry for the pain I've caused your family. It's completely my fault. I feel ashamed, horrible, guilty. I'll do whatever it takes to make things right.'

'You will do nothing,' Mrs. Abdul Karim said. 'You will get out.'

'Okay, but I just want you to know that your husband shouldn't worry. I'm not a terrorist. I was wrongly accused, wrongly imprisoned—I spent days in jail—but they realized they made a mistake, they let me go . . . The cab must have been impounded, but I've been too afraid to make inquiries. I'm even afraid to call my mother.' Looking at my feet, I continued, 'I mean, what am I supposed to tell her? "Everything's changed, Ma, everything's changed for the worse."'

Mrs. Abdul Karim watched me with hawk eyes, processing my sorry spiel with the same severe frown, but then to my jaw-dropping astonishment, she rather abruptly proclaimed, 'I will make one cup of tea.' Scanning the length of the street for signs, shadows, FBI agents, she ushered me inside with a quick, sure wave of the spoon. Perhaps she felt sorry for me or bound somehow by etiquette; either way, I felt touched and grateful, and I entered before the offer could be rescinded, almost tripping on the welcome mat. Abdul Karim was out. I was told to take a seat while chai was prepared. I did as I was told.

Cramped and cozy, the two-and-a-half-bed-one-bath always reminded me of our apartment in Karachi, although the aesthetic of the Abdul Karim household would not have cohered with Ma's sensibility. The drapes, for instance, were a shade of magenta and trimmed with gold tassels. There was a framed calligraphic piece on the wall paired with an oil color that recalled that famous Frost poem. Notably missing was the mammoth color portrait of Altaf Bhai, the leader of the thuggish but fiercely secular Karachi political party. Over the course of the preceding few months, I had gleaned that Abdul Karim was an MQM man who had fled his beloved city and declared political asylum in the early nineties when the establishment flagrantly persecuted the constituents of the party. He could not have anticipated then being persecuted again.

Before taking a seat, I surveyed the collection of blown-glass figurines and hand-painted porcelain dolls on display in a solid sheesham cabinet, the centerpiece of the room: an angel befittingly strumming a harp, a leopard in repose on a rock, a gaunt couple ballroom-dancing, a life-size hummingbird in midstroke sucking nectar from an orchid, a barefooted child wearing a raccoon felt hat and sporting a musket on his shoulder. I nearly knocked over the vaguely African statue brushing my elbow, which on closer inspection turned out to be a replica of the famous dancing girl of Mohenjodaro.

When I sat down, I discovered that the raised footstool at my feet opened like a book to yield Abdul Karim's royal blue slippers, a smoking pipe, a bag of tobacco, and a pair of reading glasses. I felt like Goldilocks, and like Goldilocks I peered into the smallest room, a storeroom of sorts that housed, among other items, a hamper and an ironing board. There must, I figured, be an iron somewhere.

As I manhandled Abdul Karim's intimate possessions, I noticed that I was being observed by a very cute, bright-eyed, ponytailed six-year-old, now swinging by an arm from the doorframe, now bunching her pink corduroy frock. She wore matching pumps and the curious smirk of a painted porcelain figurine come to life.

'Hello, beautiful,' I said, beckoning to her with an open hand. 'What's your name?' When she refused to divulge it, I told her mine.

'Chuck,' she chuckled. 'What kinda name is Chuck?'

'Well . . . I suppose, it's American.'

'Are you American?'

'Um, no . . . I'm actually Pakistani.'

'Why d'ya have an American name when you're Pakistani?'

I shrugged.

'Papa's Pakistani.'

'What about you?'

'I'm Pakistani-American.'

'So what's your name?'

'My name is Tanya.'

'Tanya,' I repeated. The name not only worked on either side of the civilizational divide but possessed a pleasant resonance. 'You know,' I said, 'you have a really lovely name.'

Grinning ear to ear, Tanya gamboled over, laying her hands on the armrest in a gesture of good faith. We discussed which cartoons she watched—Pokémon, Tiny Tunes, Bugs Bunny, in that order—and which school she attended, and I correctly guessed her favorite color. We became the best of friends. As I chatted with her, I realized I had not interacted with a child since leaving Karachi. In fact, I had not attended a baby shower or funeral for that matter. It was, in some ways, a strange, disconnected existence.

When Mrs. Abdul Karim returned balancing a tray of chai and vanilla cream wafers artistically arranged around a lemon tart, she found Tanya perched on the armrest, legs kicking the air, holding forth happily on this and that.

'Are you troubling the guest?' Mrs. Abdul Karim asked, setting the things down. The reality could not have been more different: Tanya had been roused by the Federal Bureau of Investigation because of me. The child hopped off the armrest and darted to her mother's lap to burrow her face in the folds of her dupatta. I used to do the same when I was her age and wished I still could.

'Now you go do homework,' Mrs. Abdul Karim instructed. 'I will come soon.' It was either the appointed time for homework in the Karim household, or I was unsavory company. Returning to her parents' bedroom, Tanya turned up the TV to what sounded like Tom and Jerry.

'You have a lovely daughter, madam,' I remarked.

'She is the apple of her father's eyes,' she said. 'We are living for her only. She will have good life here. It is too late for us.'

The thought made my heart sink as I burned my tongue sipping the piping tea. After some time I asked, 'Where is Tanya's father?'

'He is trying to release the cab. I am worried all the time. If there's no cab, there's no job, and if there's no job . . .'

The worry was infectious. When I offered to help, Mrs. Abdul Karim pinned me with a look that made me feel sheepish and small like a barefooted child wielding an unwieldy musket. Downing the milky, saccharine chai like medicine, I understood that the best service I could offer was to leave the family alone. I also understood that my brief but eventful career as a New York City cabbie was over. I laid the keys on the footstool.

Before I could be escorted out for the second time that afternoon, I screwed up the courage to ask Mrs. Abdul Karim for a 'small favor,' and though she met the request with an understandable sigh, I persisted: 'This is going to sound a little strange—and you can say no if you want—but may I, um, use your ironing board?'

Mercifully, Mrs. Abdul Karim agreed. Consequently, the suit was duly returned.

SIXTEEN

When my father returned from work, I would observe him wash up, change, take his tea, and watch the evening headlines on PTV. Then as Ma prepared dinner, he would mount me on his shoulders, and we would embark on our customary stroll to the nearby mangrove park. On the way, we would pass the open-air barbershop under the cedar tree and the family cobbler on the corner. We might pick up a couple of spiced charcoal-grilled corns on the cob or a packet of steamed water chestnuts. And my father would point out passing cars, motor cycles, bicycles, and the odd donkey cart, as well as the neighborhood flora and fauna, from jasmine bushes and bougainvillea vines to crows and mynahs and white-tailed kites turning languid circles in the sky. Everything, I learned, had a name, and every name held meaning. *Bougainvillea is a flower. Mynah is a bird.* There was, I learned, a scheme, an order to things, to the world.

As soon as we would arrive at our destination, my father would put me down so that I could jump, run around, or roll on the grass. There were no swings, ladders, or monkey bars back then. The topography of the park encouraged grown-up activities: after-meal strolls, newspaper reading, cigarette smoking, contemplation. The area was divided by a narrow pebbled path lined with palm trees that had been painted red and white to deter termites. On one side there was an esplanade, and on the other a swath of reeds. I stayed clear of the mangrove brush. It stirred with movement. On occasion, we spotted a mongoose or a feral tomcat within the grassy interstices, creatures that populated my earliest nightmares.

Exhausted after displays of great athletic prowess, I would join my father, who would be enjoying a cigarette on one of the two functional concrete benches. Then, when the evening call to prayer would resonate from tin loudspeakers, he would return me to my perch and we would make our way back. I would run my hand in the hairy gyre of his crown, and squeeze his rubbery ears, and we would continue our discourse.

Streetlamps, I learned, would be lit only on the walk back. 'The world is always turning, Betu,' he'd say. 'Now the sun's on the other side of it.' In this way, my father introduced me to the Copernican model of the solar system, the Food Pyramid, the Karachi Art Deco movement. Legs dangling, I'd take it all in.

One evening in autumn '85, Ma told me that my father had gone on a trip abroad, and that I would be spending the night at the neighbors' house. As she packed an overnight duffel bag, combed my hair, and dabbed my face with cream, I remember asking her, 'When will he come?' *He will be gone for many days.* 'But who will take Chuck to the park?' *Somebody will take Chuck to the park. There will always be somebody who will take Chuck to the park.*

Central Park is heavenly in the summer: golden pools, dandelion spores carried by the breeze, monarchs aflutter, wet dogs, angels in unfastened bras, open shorts, baring their pink limbs. On Sunday afternoons, a jazz ensemble gets going outside Strawberry Fields, and down the road, throngs of Rollerbladers attend the Roller Disco. They spin round and round like dervishes, like there's no day, no night, no today, no tomorrow, just the Beat. I'd aspired to join the movement, to get a pair of blades and spin around, but never had the time, and then when I had nothing but time, I found I had no inspiration.

After soaking up the music, you can head north, circumnavigating the Lake, to soak up some sun at the Great Lawn. Along the shaded asphalt path, there will always be a couple of kids dipping makeshift fishing rods in the water, fashioned from sticks, string, and paper clips, and though there were plenty of meaty worms and beetles in the topsoil, what they caught with them, God only knew. On occasion, I would pause in wait for the Big Catch but never saw anything happen. I suppose I did not possess the temperament of a fisherman.

There are two routes to the Lawn from there. You can hang a right and take the scenic route through the labyrinthine dirt paths, schist corridors, log bridges, Kentucky coffee tree arbors, and thickets of wild blackberries that is the Ramble, where at dusk you may happen upon fumbling lovers, a gay tryst; or if you are inclined to believe that the shortest distance between two points is a straight line, you would follow the drive past the Tavern on the Green to the Delacorte Theater. In the morning, you happen upon hundreds of dedicated tourists and Shakespeare enthusiasts snaking up the hill in the back for tickets to the evening performance, some of whom, having camped since dawn, breakfast, play Scrabble, or bird-watch. I had lined up twice in vain for a production of *A Winter's Tale*—if I'm not mistaken, starring Balki from *Perfect Strangers*—without breakfast or board games or binoculars. Serendipitously, however, I was offered scalped tickets for a nominal five bucks a pop by a German au pair in the Ladies Pavilion. It was a spectacular show.

Beyond the Delacorte, the great sprawl of the Great Lawn beckons. As you approach it, you can see kites in the sky, Frisbees tossed in the brilliant sunshine. You can see the red uniforms of weekend softball players, the white wedding gowns of the lean Taiwanese catalog models posing by the willows. On a summer afternoon in the park, you can feel the intimation that God is in Heaven and all is well with the world.

~

But all wasn't well in the world. When Mini Auntie called at the crack of dawn, I knew something was wrong. She sounded choked up, like she had caught a cold overnight, and proceeded to mumble an apology for not getting back to me. 'That's okay,' I replied, 'that's fine.' It had been a mere twenty-two hours since I had left her a message. Then she delivered the following news concerning my best friend: although the terrorism charges against AC were dismissed—the bomb-making manual and the sinister Arabic literature turned out to be *The Anarchist Cookbook* and Ibn Khaldun's *Muqaddimah*, respectively—the authorities found four and a half grams of cocaine *on his person*. 'The penalty for possession in New York is the same for second-degree murder . . .'

When I put the receiver down, the walls of my apartment closed in on me. *Fifteen years to life*, I mumbled, gobsmacked. *Fifteen years to life*. I needed to get out, get to Mini Auntie's. Racing out in my pajamas, cowboy boots, and hunting hat, I figured I would cut through the park to the East Side. I sprinted two and a half blocks crosstown, a desperate, flailing two-hundred-yard dash, until I could feel my lungs constrict and my legs turn to lead. I stumbled past the Natural History Museum, entered the park, and considered collapsing on the undulating green. Instead I found myself drifting.

I drifted south, in the general direction of the Pond. It wasn't to ponder the age-old question: where do the ducks fly in the winter? It wasn't even winter yet, though the leaves were changing color. In another couple of months, everything would be black and white. Children were already being dispatched in woolen hats, the odd scarf, but they marched on unencumbered. They played in the leaves. They would play in the snow. When I was their age, I had played in the sand, building dikes and sand castles, digging tunnels, packing balls of silt. For a moment, I thought I whiffed salt in the air, realizing the morning breeze reeked of the sulfurous, rotten egg smell that suggests a fundamental imbalance in the stratosphere.

I drifted past Tavern on the Green, Strawberry Fields, the Sheep Meadow. The last time I had been to the Meadow, I had accompanied one Ali Chaudry. The week after I was fired, I holed up at my place for days. One fine day, AC showed up at my door in a beige safari suit, bearing two six-packs of Bud in one hand, and what appeared to be an aerodynamically compromised homemade kite, in the shape of a JF-17 fighter jet, in the other. 'Get dressed, chum,' he said, 'I've come to spring you.' I remember I was so excited to see him that I threw my arms around him, almost crushing the thing.

It was a hot, still afternoon, so he suggested that we suck down the brews first and shoot the shit before the breeze picked up. Perched on the shaded incline that overlooked the meadow, AC explained that the JF-17 is a third-generation fighter jet, coproduced by Pakistan and the People's Republic, and that the kite was jointly invented in the fifth century by two Chinese philosophers, Lu Ban and Mozi.

'The Middle Kingdom,' he said wistfully. I nodded as if I knew what he was getting at, but didn't, though it didn't matter. 'Back in the sixteenth century, a traveling Italian monk presented the old Mings with a map of the known world. At the time, cartography could be said to be, ah, sophisticated technology, like fuel cells, gene splicing, et cetera, et cetera, but instead of accepting the gift graciously, the Ming emperor threatened to disembowel the fellow.'

Naturally, I asked why.

'The map put Europe smack in the center, shoving China into the border and splitting the Pacific, when for the Chinese, China was the center of the world, the Middle Kingdom.' AC took to a frothy sip of Bud. 'The emperor proclaimed he'd allow the monk to retain his genitalia only if he produced a more accurate representation of reality.'

When I asked if a more accurate map was furnished, AC replied, 'The monk kept his yang.'

The episode might have suggested something about the construction of history, or the intimate connection between manhood and discourse, or something like that, but it did not really matter because I was four beers into the afternoon, and the afternoon was simply splendid. When the breeze finally stirred, I scrambled down like a child, circling and zigzagging barefoot on the grass before AC called after me, explaining that I had to be stationary to launch the kite. Taking the JF-17 from my hand, he began walking away, downwind, counting a hundred paces. 'Now tug!' he yelled. I tugged. The kite rose like magic.

On the periphery of Cherry Hill, I had a brilliant idea. It was so brilliant that I slapped my head: *I'm going to spring AC from prison.* As I started to jog, I thought through the logistics of the plan. After fetching Jimbo from wherever he was at the time—the Duck's or Christ Hospital—I would stop by a hardware store for necessary supplies: rope, a roll of duct tape, Ping-Pong balls, aluminum foil, paper matches, a couple of cans of spray paint. I was thinking *Anarchist Cookbook.* I was thinking sabotage, acts of terrorism. We would arrive at the Metropolitan Detention Center after making an appointment to meet AC—people meet friends and relatives in prison all the time—and on the way up, we would make a pit stop at the nearest john. There we would detonate several rudimentary smoke bombs: pierced Ping-Pong balls wrapped in foil. Then the fire alarm would ring. There would be panic, pandemonium. We would take advantage of the situation. We would move in like ninjas.

That's how far I got when I started to feel tired, really tired, faint, perhaps because I had run all the way from Cherry Hill to the Children's Zoo, a distance of three-quarters of a mile if not more. When I began to see red and yellow dots like snowflakes, I parked myself on a bench outside the seal enclosure, slumped and swollen eyed. I felt the urge to retch, but the only garbage can being at least fifty yards away, I imagined myself spewing all over the place, scarring the early development of the children playing tag in the vicinity. Their mothers were already glancing at me over the horizon of their glossy magazines like gazelles. I was the spotted-back hyena in their midst. Except that hyenas are survivors; hyenas hunt in packs. I was *tout seul.*

Propping myself up against the wood armrest, I attempted to sit up but crumpled like a brown paper bag. I kept saying to myself *sit up, goddamn it, sit up, the kids are watching*, even though the kids weren't at all interested. They were ruddy-faced with exhaustion and had started to play a new game that involved spinning in place, yelling 'Sheep, sheep.' As I watched them with vicarious thrill, I figured that the only way to turn back time, to be a kid again, was to have my own. Of course, I'd need to get hitched first. Perhaps to Amo. We would make a good couple. We would have healthy, handsome children. We would bring them to the park on the weekends in carriages, in pushcarts, on our shoulders. Uncle Jimbo and Aunty Duck could join us. We would all saunter en famille, picnic, people-watch, feed the ducks. It would be grand.

While I entertained notions of becoming a family man, the famous musical clock above the northern entrance to the Children's Zoo struck eight. Turning to watch the dancing animals atop, I noticed a short black female cop in the arch below. Although there was nothing unusual in her appearance, nothing threatening in her manner, I instinctively shrank within myself and looked away, looked at the sky. It was cloud-swept and gray, and since I hadn't watched the weather forecast, I couldn't tell whether or not it would rain. When I glanced back nonchalantly, I saw the cop making her way to me, gesticulating wildly. Then I saw the snowflakes again. It was a goddamn blizzard.

When I returned to consciousness, I was on my back with several diapers cushioned beneath my bruised head, surrounded by eyes bearing down on me belonging to one of the mothers—a brunette in culottes—an octogenarian in a Panama hat hunched over a walking stick, and the cop who had frightened the living daylights out of me. 'You all right, honey?' she asked. I wasn't all right. I felt panicky, paralyzed, and there was a ringing in my ears like rattling chandeliers. 'You need an ambulance?' Shaking my head, I muttered, 'I'm okay, I'm fine.'

'*You on drugs?*'

'No ma'am!' I exclaimed with a start as if I were a Mormon. 'I'm clean, I'm sober.'

'Well, you don't look so hot, honey.'

Forcing a self-assured smile, I sat up and said, 'I . . . I get a little epileptic in the morning.'

Helped up by the arm, I dusted my clothes and fixed the hunting hat on my crown. 'Thank you, ma'am,' I said. 'Thank you for everything.'

As soon as they dispersed, somebody tapped me on the shoulder. 'She wasn't comin' forya, Mac,' explained the old man in the hat. 'She was comin' for the kid.' He further clarified by pointing at a five-year-old with a runny nose prancing by, waving a twig like a conductor. The child did seem mildly menacing. 'There's rat poison in the grass. See the signs?'

It was later that I realized that I had been in the throes of some sort of culture-bound psychosomatic psychosis, like the hysteria in fin-de-siècle Vienna that had inspired the Great Quack, or brain fog in West Africa that periodically turned men and women into zombies, or anorexia and bulimia that ravaged prep-school and party girls in Manhattan. The authorities gave me existential heebie-jeebies. They had become what scarecrows or clowns were to some kids, avatars of the Bogeyman.

At that moment, however, I realized I couldn't take a walk in the park, much less walk into a prison, with or without duct tape and a box of Ping-Pong balls.

SEVENTEEN

When I entered my apartment that afternoon, I didn't feel so hot. I was trembling. The place was cold and dark, and I felt that damp, drizzly November in my soul. Suddenly I had the urge to escape, make a clean break, skip town. In the movies, people skip town all the time. You see recalcitrant teenagers, eloping lovers, ex-cons violating parole rattling drawers and armoires, scavenging for money—spare change, hidden wads of cash—in piggy banks, cookie jars, or under sofas and mattresses. You see them stuff attaché cases with undergarments, clothes on hangers, and cast one last glance upon the wreckage before dashing out. You see them sticking their thumbs up curbside or jumping into jalopies and heading out west or across the border, into the sunset.

When you think about it, the peculiarly American trope of escape has informed narratives spanning the western to the road comedy, from *Butch Cassidy and the Sundance Kid* to *Thelma and Louise*. It puts the old literary archetype, whether Mesopotamian or Greek, starring that old British knight or the legendary Omani sailor, on its head. The protagonists, often paired, are not in pursuit of golden fleeces or holy grails, like the heroes of yore, but are pursued, usually by the long arm of the law. They are outlaws or are rendered outlaws by the whimsical, uncharitable vicissitudes of the modern world. Like the residents of New Hampshire, they aspire to live free or die.

And though you root for the youthful antiheroes, you know damn well they cannot, will not succeed. In fact, you realize that they were doomed from the word go. They will never make it to the Promised Land.

~

Escape is not so much a destination as a frame of mind.

I was there.

Picking the hunting hat off my head, I flung it across the room, pulled off my boots on the way to the bathroom, peeled off my ribbed T-shirt, and stripped down to my hairless, tawny birthday suit. I figured the best way to get rid of the shakes was to take a nice long hot bath. Parting the shower curtain, I deployed the stopper and turned the faucet, but when I stepped into the tub, piping hot water scalded my sole. Hopping out, toes splayed on the slick tiled floor, I mixed hot with cold before lowering myself inside again. As the water lapped my legs, hips, the small of my back, my belly, my chest, I shut my eyes, searching for pinholes, penumbral shapes, streaks of light, but there was nothing there, not even a shadow or suggestion of a silhouette. I could only make out an expansive vista of darkness. I felt I was teetering on the ragged edge of the universe. One misstep, one slip, and I would totter, I would fall.

Suddenly I remembered I was all out of soap. At any other time, it wouldn't have been a big deal, but at that instant, soaplessness became an epic, existential issue, one that demanded action, immediate resolution. Dripping and pocked with goose bumps, I hauled myself to the cabinet, where I surveyed the shelved supply of mistakenly acquired, malodorous deodorant sticks and a collection of spiky old toothbrushes I had not disposed of because of a middle-class childhood grounded in frugality. There were several cardboard rolls of toilet paper, a fat, rusted can of Barbasol, and a blunt, hairy disposable razor. There was, however, no sign of soap. Instead, I came across an unopened, gift-wrapped box of Ativan, Lexotonil, Klonopin, or something like that, presented by AC after I had been fired.

Inside I found three strips, a year's supply as far as I was concerned, embedded with twelve oval tablets each. Dumping the contents onto the faux-marble countertop, I came across the accompanying prescriptive literature. STORE AT CONTROLLED ROOM TEMPERATURE 20°C (68°–10°F), it began. KEEP IN COOL DRY PLACE. My gaze was drawn to the warning below:

> Pre-existing depression may worsen during use. This drug is not recommended for use in patients with a depressive disorder or psychosis . . .

There was no doubt that I was quite delicate. Flipping the leaflet over to the other side, I read the section pertaining to overdose:

> In mild cases, symptoms may include drowsiness, mental confusion, paradoxical reactions, and lethargy. In serious cases, and especially when other drugs or alcohol are ingested, symptoms may include ataxia, hypotonia, hypotension, cardiovascular depression, hypnotic state, coma, and, death.

The label might as well have read eat me. Peeling open twelve tablets one by one as if I were shelling pistachios, I crushed them in one hand and, leaning over the sink, bared my soul in the bathroom mirror. It was a futile exercise: as the steam swirled in ghostly configurations, I kept wiping the surface of the mirror with my free hand as if to perceive something real, corporeal, but there was nothing there. I began to bawl inconsolably, like a grieving child. Snot seeped into my mouth, and warm tears ran down my cheeks and dripped down my chin into the sink. It was a pathetic display. It had to stop. Licking my hand, I chewed several moist tablets as if I were chewing Tic Tacs. They tasted like aspirin, like chalky mush. I remember taking note of water cascading over the wall of the tub and spilling and spreading across the floor. Straddling the divide, I responsibly turned the faucet clockwise before losing my balance. I tumbled for the second time that day.

❧

I felt numb, dead, like my father.

EIGHTEEN

The world had turned upside down; up was down and down was up, and I lay curled like a fetus on the floor, clutching the shower curtain as if it were the holy shroud of Turin. Unable to stir, I lay for a long time—I don't know how long—like a fish out of water, wriggling one foot—I didn't know which one—to make sure that I still could. I had water in one ear and a ringing in the other like a fire alarm. By the time I finally picked myself up, using the can for a crutch, and dried myself with a hand towel, I realized that the ringing was not in my head. Following it to the phone, I mechanically held the receiver to my ear. Somebody was speaking to me in a thin voice, in laudatory tones, but I was unable to follow. It was as if I were still under water.

Instead, I dimly remember regarding the concrete courtyard outside my window, taking stock of the changes in the topography: the barbecue grill had been put away, as had the other seasonal fixtures: the tiki torches and the two striped deck chairs where my squirrelly neighbor wiled away midsummer Manhattan nights, sometimes alone, sometimes with company, sucking cigarettes, sipping wine coolers, and gazing at the sky. All that remained was a thin strip of Astroturf, a pair of cigarette butts, a limp potted umbrella plant, and a bag of charcoal. The weather for cookouts and making out had passed. Thanksgiving was practically around the corner. Soon the city would become deserted as the natives traveled to laden tabletops in the hinterland. After the leftovers and heartburn, about the time the nostalgia settled, Christmas preparations would be in full swing: giant snowflakes hovering above Fifth Avenue, miniature worlds at display in the windows at Saks, and at Rockefeller Center, the massive fir would be lit by a million flashes.

The year before, I had watched a neighboring family of three from my windowsill perch, assiduously arranging bows, baubles, candles, and strands of silver and gold tinsel on the boughs of a Christmas tree. Presents were wrapped, eggnog and cookies were circulated at regular intervals, and once the decorations were secure, the prematurely balding thirtysomething father got up on a stepladder and picked up his child, who in turn strained to deposit a glass angel on the leafy summit. I thought I got the hang of it. In fact, that year I had resolved to get a tree myself. Although I did not really celebrate Christmas, I figured I could participate in the associated rituals.

The rituals of the only holiday I religiously commemorated were as familiar as the city: party-hopping, boozing it up, kissing strangers at the stroke of midnight. Although I did not have any plans for the big night yet, it was still early. I was quite sure that I wouldn't be attending the festivities at Times Square to watch the apple drop. I had been only once, and it had been deathly cold, and crazy: people crushed against one another with pretzels and beer on their breath, yelling and blowing whistles into the subway, as if heading to the next party—Superbowl Sunday perhaps, or St. Pat's Day, the Halloween Parade in the West Village. There's always a party in the city.

All of a sudden I registered the voice on the phone. 'Congratulations,' it said. 'Expect a letter in two to three weeks outlining the terms.' Rhetorically muttering thanks, I hung up.

It took me several moments to appreciate that I had been duly notified of a fortuitous, unexpected development. It took me several moments to appreciate that the afternoon I attempted suicide, I had been offered a way out. Then I puked all over the place.

Although still dizzy and nauseous and sore, I threw on some clothes and grabbed the famous to-do list from the refrigerator door and dashed to get a phone card from the neighborhood bodega. It was time to call Ma, buy soap, TP, time to make things right. *When you fall*, Ma once told me, *you get up, and when you fall again, you get up again.* Racing down the block with her dictum in mind, I turned the corner, narrowly avoiding collision with a family of three, only to be intercepted by the Moroccan, who, it would seem, had been lying in wait.

Blocking my path like a telephone pole, he extended his hand, proclaiming salam-alikum. Mumbling walaikum, I offered mine. 'I not see you for long time,' he began.

'Yes,' I replied.

'I worry for you, brother.'

Attempting to extricate myself from his iron grip, I said, 'That's very kind of you.' I wasn't in the mood for chitchat but he wouldn't let go.

'I brayed for you.'

Nodding as if I appreciated the tacit conversational subtext, I wondered if I really owed my emancipation to the Moroccan's prayers, to divine intervention. 'Thank you—'

'You bray too. Allah looks after His children.'

Although I had always believed that I had more in common with somebody like Ari or Lawrence né Larry than the Moroccan, I was reminded that we shared the same rituals, doctrinal vocabulary, and eschatological infrastructure, even if we did not read the same books, listen to the same music, hang in the same watering holes— I'm sure he did his hanging elsewhere—or subscribe to the same interpretation of history. Peering at me through the same round professor's glasses, he asked, 'You go somewhere?'

'I go somewhere?' I repeated.

'You go home?'

'Oh, no, no. I, um, was out of town.'

Sucking his teeth, he crossed his arms and tapped his feet, gestures that could be interpreted collectively as *yeah, bullshit*. Figuring that it would be easier to disclose the nature of my absence to my sole well-wisher than to spin an elaborate web of lies, I leaned into him and said, 'If you really want to know, brother, I was in jail. That's why you haven't seen me.'

The Moroccan's eyes widened. 'In the Bassaic County?'

'No,' I replied, taken aback, 'in Brooklyn.'

'In the Metropolitan Detention Center?'

'How do you know?'

'My wife's cousin. They take him.'

'*My* friend,' I said, 'is still there.'

Shaking our heads, we both commiserated in silence for our fallen comrades, our brothers in arms. Then, glancing at the sky, he rhetorically asked, 'What can we do?' I looked up as well. I imagined God looking down on us through the cloudy veneer. 'Is in Allah's hands.'

There was nothing more to say.

The Moroccan thrust a copy of the *Times* in my hand. 'Take it, take it,' he said, even though I didn't care for the news. I tried to return it, but he was insistent. 'Bresident Musharraf give speech today,' he said. 'Read it, read it.'

'You are too kind.'

'You are my brother. You want something more?'

'Actually,' I replied, 'I need a phone card, brother.'

As I dialed home from the only functioning public phone on 79th, I recalled the nine-hour time difference in the summer separating the Atlantic and Arabian coasts. Although it was after midnight in Karachi, there would still be traffic on the streets, and roadside diners on and off Bandar Road—Bundoo Khan, Student's Biryani—would be chatting over milky tea. Above the fray, our ninth-floor apartment would be dark and still. The windows would be open, the faint caustic smell of mosquito repellant in the air. Ma would be asleep draped by a sheet, arm crossed over brow. If I were home, I'd be sleeping beside her.

The phone rang. A crosstown bus thundered past. 'Hello?' I said.

After a pregnant pause, Ma replied, 'Beta?'

'*Ma—*'

'Is everything all right?'

'Well . . . everything wasn't all right . . . but now it is . . . so don't worry—'

'Shehzad,' Ma interrupted, 'it is nearly one in the morning. I am a little slow, and you are talking a little too fast. Now tell me again: why should I not worry?'

'Me,' I replied. 'You shouldn't worry about me.'

'You are calling at one in the morning just to tell me that I should not be worried about you?'

Taking a deep breath, I attempted to organize my thoughts. 'Yes,' I began, 'kind of. I actually have something to tell you. About three months ago, in the first week of July, I was let go, you know, fired. There were companywide layoffs. There's been a downturn in the market, an economic recession, and after 9/11, well, companies have mostly stopped hiring.'

I could hear Ma breathing. I could see her massaging her eyes. She was probably sitting up by now, hunched and cross-legged.

'But don't worry, Ma. About fifteen minutes ago, I was offered a job. It's with this research house. I like the people. They want me to write financial reports. It's something I can do and do well. They told me I'm a "great fit." It's very promising. It's a wonderful opportunity.'

My disclosure was met with silence, and for a moment I thought the line had dropped. Then Ma said, 'If it is such a wonderful opportunity, beta, why do you sound unhappy?'

'I do?'

'Are you?'

'I don't know,' I said, then blurted, 'yes, yes, I am. I would have been okay, but there's more.'

'More?'

'More I haven't told you,' I replied, clearing my throat. 'Last week Jamshed, Ali, and I were arrested on terrorism charges—'

'What?'

'We were arrested, interrogated, thrown into solitary confinement. It was crazy. They kept saying we were *in possession* of bomb-making manuals, terrorist literature. They kept telling us that we were *in for life.* I was certain that I wouldn't see the light of day. But somehow, somehow, they let Jamshed and me go—'

'*Thank God!*'

'Then Khan Sahab had a heart attack—'

'*Oh God!*—'

'Don't worry. He's okay. I went to see him—he's recovering—and he sends you his salam.'

'Inshallah!'

'But Ali, he's still inside. Mini Auntie's in a state . . . I've been in a state myself. I've been feeling so helpless. There's nothing I can do. What can I do?'

'Why didn't you tell me, beta?'

'What do you want me tell you, Ma? That life's changed? The city's changed? That there's sadness around every corner? There are cops everywhere? You know, there was a time when a police presence was reassuring, like at a parade or late at night, on the street, in the subway, but now I'm afraid of them. I'm afraid all the time. I feel like a marked man. I feel like an animal. It's no way to live. Maybe it's just a phase, maybe it'll pass, and things will return to normal, or maybe, I don't know, history will keep repeating itself . . .'

I stopped. I was talking to myself. Ma had fallen silent. She was probably standing, regarding the city lights through the lattice circumscribing the balcony. Although the brightest blazed from the

Dentonic-Once-A-Day-Everyday billboard welded to our building, our balcony offered a panorama of the old city, from the great white modernist dome of Jinnah's mausoleum in the north to the spire of the grand neo-Gothic colonial relic, Empress Market, in the south. Bandar Road cut past below, connecting the landmarks and ferrying traffic to and from the sea. I could hear the purl of rickshaws over the clamor of crosstown buses; I could almost smell the smog, feel the breeze against my cheek. I heard myself say, 'I want to come home, Ma.'

NINETEEN

In the end you make your peace and say your goodbyes, not necessarily in that order. You improvise because you didn't anticipate the end, just like you were unable to anticipate the beginning. You procure several cardboard boxes—three or four will do—and dump things in unceremoniously: textbooks, papers, porn, picture frames, winter clothes, hunting hat, linen, Tupperware, stainless-steel lota, wash 'n' wear pajamas, stale Chili Chips, one opened box of Ativan. You find you are unsentimental about the bricolage that contributed to the infrastructure of your formative years. You make one box for the good folks at the Salvation Army, you mail another to an address in your hometown; you prepare a care package for a friend or two, and whatever doesn't fit, you pitch. You leave nothing behind. It takes a mere afternoon to wrap things up. You don't even break a proper sweat. Three efficient, limber-limbed Brazilians show up at the appointed time, address you in Portuguese, and stomping in and out in workman boots, haul everything else away. You pay them extra to haul the futon to the street, without scratching the floor. You sweep the place with a borrowed broom, you mop the bathroom with a kitchen roll. The place looks no different from the day you arrived, as if you were a squatter all this time, not an original settler. It's easy come, easy go. You settle down on the floor, legs crossed, eyes closed, like an ascetic. You sit mute and motionless until there's no feeling in your legs and time ticks to the sound of your heartbeat. When your good friend's sister shows up unexpectedly in the evening, presenting a dish of gulab jamuns and a chaste, experimental kiss on the cheek, you are elated, you are touched, because genuine manifestations of kindness are infrequent. In turn you offer to take her out to the three-star Italian bistro around the corner because downtown seems far away.

∽

The sun was setting on the West Side, catching windows and storefronts, and burnishing the streets with a rosy veneer. The natives ambled back from work, some in sneakers, some with ice cream cones, some with slim briefcases slung by their sides like schoolchildren. They stopped at bars along Amsterdam for happy hour, spilled into outdoor patios, and sipped sangria, soaking up the evening. It might have been the last nice day of the fall.

We decided to sit outside as well, legs crossed, hands clasped in laps, not talking, not meeting each other's eyes, sipping tap water at regular intervals as if it were Brunello. I consulted the menu, unfolded my checkered napkin, rearranged the cutlery. I avoided looking at Amo because I was afraid if I did, I would stare. She was turning heads.

She had arrived in a denim jacket, a white T-shirt, an ankle-length chiffon skirt, a sequined satchel, and trademark red Pumas. She had arrived sans hijab. Her straight, brown, shoulder-length hair cut across the forehead like a Japanese schoolgirl's wafted jasmine and cloves. When I politely inquired about the recent changes in her sartorial regime, she asked, 'You mean the skirt?'

'Um, no,' I replied. I didn't know if she was messing with me. 'I meant—'

'Lemme guess, Shehzad. You mean the hijab?'

Folding my arms, I expected an exposition on identity, though I had always suspected that Amo had swapped teenage angst and Britney Spears posters for religion. Instead she said, 'I've been, like, kinda overweight forever—guess I took after Begum—and for the longest time, I didn't care, but then life got kinda rough in junior high—it was always like, "Hey, there's marshmallow girl," whatever—and got rougher in high school.

'Then all of a sudden, guess it was beginning of senior year, I started to change—don't know how, don't know why, it just happened—and the same guys who were calling me names back in the seventh grade were hitting on me and everything. I was so disgusted by the whole thing that I was like, bring it, bring on the hijab. And it's not like I'm not Muslim. I've been to Sunday school all my life, and I say my prayers and everything and am proud of who I am.'

'Wow. Well. That explains a lot. But it doesn't really explain why you—'

'Took it off.'

'Yeah.'

'Your guess.'

'Well,' I stuttered, 'I don't really know, but I do know that you're looking, um, quite beautiful. Very beautiful.'

Amo blushed and beamed as if my compliment were news or a revelation, then rather unexpectedly asked, 'What do you want, Shehzad?' I was rendered speechless by the bold query. Smiling, she added, 'Like on the *menu*?'

'Oh,' I mumbled, 'right.'

I was pretty sure she was messing with me.

We ordered primo staples of Italian-American cuisine—penne vodka for me, and spaghetti, no meatballs, for her—and munched on olive-oil-dipped sourdough slices while we waited. When I asked after Old Man Khan, Amo told me that he was not convalescing as well as expected: not only had the procedure left him weak, but his blood pressure had been acting up again, posing a heightened risk of stroke. 'Baba blanks out after dinner, which is like, really scary.' I said, 'I can imagine,' but I couldn't. 'I pray every day,' Amo continued. 'God has to listen to me. God will.'

She told me Jamshed Lala was with him. In fact, he hadn't left his father's side since my stay at Christ Hospital, and though he had planned to visit me after learning of my imminent departure,

Amo had insisted on coming instead. 'Baba needs him,' she said. 'I asked him why you're leaving, but he told me to ask you myself. So why're you leaving?'

Avoiding her attentive eyes, I attempted a doughty smile, then toyed with the saltshaker and took a generous swig of tap water. It would have been nice to have had a glass of wine, perhaps a whole carafe, but I deferred to propriety, to Amo. 'I don't know, Amo,' I began. 'It's complicated.'

If I had had a couple of drinks in me I might have told her about the fear, the paranoia, the profound loneliness that had become routine features of life in the city, about my undistinguished career as a banker and a cabbie. If I had a couple of drinks in me, I just might have spilled my guts. But I didn't. Dinner was served, a fine excuse to drop the subject. Besides, I was ravenous. I hadn't eaten all day. I requested parmesan, the pepper mill, and more water, but dispatched the dish before the waiter returned.

Amo, on the other hand, took her time, chewing her food, wrapping strand after strand of spaghetti around her fork. 'Well,' she said, looking into her plate, as if commenting on the consistency of the tomato paste, 'I'll miss you.' I felt my ears burn, my heart beat faster. It was perhaps the nicest thing anybody had said to me in ages.

'I'll miss you too, Amo.'

'Is there like, any way I can convince you to stay?'

The query might have been whimsically sentimental, something friends say when friends leave, but I was pretty sure I heard the suggestion of marriage in the tenor, and for a few moments, while chewing the last piece of sourdough in the bread basket, I found myself considering the possibility, the conditions of possibility. I would have to be employed and prospering, and Amo would have to complete her studies before the subject could be officially broached. Then one day I would travel to Jersey City on the train, sweaty and anxious and dressed in my Sunday best, to ask Old Man Khan for his daughter's hand. When I thought about it, his avid interest in me, in my professional trajectory, might have been the attention of a potential father-in-law. Assuming that he would bestow his blessings on us—you never knew with Old Man Khan—Ma would be called, and sweetmeats would be distributed all around.

Next, the logistics would be hammered out. The event would take place at the banquet hall of a hotel on the periphery of the city, a Holiday Inn or even a Sheraton. It would be attended by Mini Auntie, the likes of Kojo, Ari, Lawrence né Larry, and prominent members of the community—the consul general of Pakistan, the editor in chief of the *Urdu Times*—and the not-so-prominent, like Ron the bartender, who would attend as a civilian because the festivities would be dry. There would be a consensus among the guests that Amo was the most beautiful bride they had seen in a generation. Dinner would be catered by Kabab King. Jimbo would deejay. And the limo would hopefully be organized by Abdul Karim.

Afterward we would rent a junior one-bedroom on the Upper East Side before applying for a mortgage on a more accommodating apartment, and in a decade or so, with both of us earning six figures, we might move to the suburbs, like the Shaman, Scarsdale perhaps, *because of the schools*. After producing progeny, we would live out the rest of our days with an SUV in the garage, assorted objets d'art in the drawing room, and a view of a manicured lawn.

At the end of the day, it was a vision I found I could not quite commit to. 'Maybe you could visit me in Karachi,' I said. 'You'll like it there. It's a lot like New York.' That was the truth.

Amo didn't respond. Perhaps she had her mouth full; perhaps she didn't agree. After polishing off the remaining spaghetti with quiet diligence, she dabbed her lips with a starched napkin, then politely refused dessert. And when I asked for the check, she dug into her satchel, offering to pay, but I reached across the table and held her hand. I didn't let go till the waiter returned with the change, then persuaded her to accompany me on a stroll.

We sauntered side by side like an old couple, rubbing shoulders but not holding hands. Crossing Broadway and West End to

Riverside, we could sense the river beyond the sliver of greenery. The soil was wet and fragrant beneath our feet. The sky was murky. I thought I glimpsed a yellowing crescent among the clouds, but when I pointed it out to Amo, there was nothing there. 'It's getting late,' she said.

'Guess we should head back,' I said. My flight was in less than four hours.

'Guess so.'

Turning around, we headed back to civilization; at the entrance of the 72nd Street stop, we said our goodbyes. I told Amo how wonderful it was to see her and that I'd keep in touch. 'You promise?' she asked. I pecked her on her cheek and hugged her casually, but my heart sank as she turned her back and disappeared into the multitudes.

The apartment was bare, save my father's suitcase and Amo's gulab jamuns. While waiting for the taxi to JFK, I wrapped the dish with the *Times* like a cheap present. My glance fell on a section of the paper entitled A NATION CHALLENGED: PORTRAITS OF GRIEF, a regular feature those days.

MOHAMMED 'MO' SHAH

NO FRIEND OF FUNDAMENTALISM

Mohammed Shah enjoyed driving around in his Mercedes 500 SEL. He was a Muslim from Rawalpindi, Pakistan, and worked for a life insurance company based in Hartford, Conn., where he was said to be 'on the fast track.' Mr. Shah, 40, also enjoyed reading and eating out.

'Everybody thinks all Muslims are fundamentalists,' said Michael Leonard, a coworker. 'Mohammed wasn't like that. He was like us, like everybody. He worked hard, played hard.'

But according to Mr. Leonard, Mr. Shah wanted to settle down. 'I didn't know him for a long time, but I know he wanted to get married, start a family, and all that good stuff. He just hadn't met the right girl.'

Mr. Shah was attending a conference at the World Trade Center when tragedy struck. He called Mr. Leonard to ask him to cover for him. A plane had hit the building, he said. He was going to be late.

It was the oddest obituary. Perhaps all obituaries are fundamentally odd. There was no mention of the ship jumping, gas pumping, porn watching, cigarette running—*de mortuis nil nisi bonum*—and there was no mention of us. The story was simple, black-and-white: the man was a Muslim, not a terrorist.

After reading it over, I did what we do at times like these. I took off my boots, tucked in my shirt, and rolled up my sleeves. I washed my face, arms, and feet and parted my hair with wet fingers. I spread the rug from the suitcase that Ma had dispatched four years earlier, stood, heels together, arms folded over stomach, and, positioning myself generally east, toward Mecca, recited the call to prayer.

In the name of God, I began, *the Beneficent and Merciful. God is great. I bear witness that nothing deserves to be worshipped but God. I bear witness that Muhammad is the Apostle of God. Come to prayer. Come to prayer. Come to success. Come to success. God is the Greatest. There is no God but God.*

Raising my hands to my temple, I murmured, 'Accept these prayers on behalf of Mohammed Shah.'

Then, when it was time to go, I left.

Epilogue

You take a flight from Karachi to Manchester to New York. Stretch your mouth at Immigration when you say, 'Haya doin'?' This may expedite the process. They appreciate familiar idiom. Don't get into a car with the man with sunglasses. Hail a yellow cab at the curb. You will cross miserable swaths of Queens: empty playgrounds bordered by barbed wire, boarded-up rowhouses, signs for MOT LS. You will glimpse broken, blurred images framed by graffiti and rubbish and cut by underpasses: a homeless man lurking, the contents of his life spilling from a shopping cart. This will jar your sensibilities. You will think: *Is this it? America, land of the free, from sea to shining sea? Where are the skyscrapers? The long-legged blondes?* Your cabbie drives as if he is late for an appointment and from time to time observes you through the rearview mirror. He is also Pakistani and knows what you are about: an off-the-boat student, a bacha. He will dispense unsolicited advice. Secure a Green Card. Stay away from long-legged blondes, unless you can't secure Green Card. You suspect that he's taking you for a ride, but you listen raptly. He tells you about the dhaba in Jackson Heights that serves the best plate of nihari this side of the Atlantic. You find comfort in his familiarity with the American Way of Life or, as he says, with *livin' in Umreeka*. 'Down the road,' he adds, 'you will find out who you are.' The bumper-to-bumper traffic on the Brooklyn-Queens Expressway reminds you of Tariq Road at night. The cabbie turns up the radio: *'1010 WINS: You give us 22 minutes, we'll give you the world.'* You repeat the curious phrase while attempting to compute how far you have traveled. Your mind drifts back to the memory of your mother's last embrace, your clan waving from behind tinted-glass doors. Karachi's energy, noise, hoards, billboards, and sandy aesthetic stir profound sentimentality. There you were yourself and you were alive. Now you feel lonely, you despair. Now you are tired and the airplane meal has given you dyspepsia and the novelty of the New World has already worn off. You massage your eyes, hide your face, look down at the yellow lines on the road blurring into one. Then the road inclines, and when you look up, you see spires and masts and growths of iron. You recognize the Empire State Building from the movies, the Citicorp Tower, the Chrysler Building, and when you glance south, you see the world-famous World Trade Center. The sky shimmers; three streaks of white jet smoke disappear above Midtown; a helicopter descends in slow motion over the Hudson. 'IT's 72 DEGREES AND SUNNY IN CENTRAL PARK, GOING UP TO A HIGH OF 77. IT's GOING TO BE A BEAUTIFUL SEPTEMBER DAY!' You are elated. *This is it*, you think, *America, land of the free, from sea to shining sea*. You roll down your window. A warm breeze ruffles the hair. You start humming, 'Start spreading the news . . .' You realize you never knew all the words.

ACKNOWLEDGMENTS

I would like to thank Sarwar Naqvi, the first writer I ever knew, for instilling in me a fondness for literature, and Asad for purchasing a laptop for me when I was broken and broke. I would especially like to thank the indomitable Zafar Iqbal for his mysterious, implicit, and explicit support of this project.

I'm grateful to Afshan, Vineeta, Jason, and the handful of others who read the manuscript at various junctures, John Mac for allowing me to use his office in the summer of '07, and Asad Hussain and Nadia for allowing me use of the cave at North Hoyne Street earlier in the year.

I would also like to mention playwright John Glavin, whose extraordinary intervention allowed me to complete my education once upon a time, Leslie for allowing me to continue it in the recent past, and my dear friend and guardian angel, Akhil, without whom I would, in many ways, find myself bereft.

Above all, I would like to thank the brilliant and evergreen Lee and the ever optimistic Gary Morris, without whom this project probably would have remained confined to a cocktail napkin.

He just wanted a decent book to read ...

Not too much to ask, is it? It was in 1935 when Allen Lane, Managing Director of Bodley Head Publishers, stood on a platform at Exeter railway station looking for something good to read on his journey back to London. His choice was limited to popular magazines and poor-quality paperbacks – the same choice faced every day by the vast majority of readers, few of whom could afford hardbacks. Lane's disappointment and subsequent anger at the range of books generally available led him to found a company – and change the world.

'*We believed in the existence in this country of a vast reading public for intelligent books at a low price, and staked everything on it*'
Sir Allen Lane, 1902–1970, founder of Penguin Books

The quality paperback had arrived – and not just in bookshops. Lane was adamant that his Penguins should appear in chain stores and tobacconists, and should cost no more than a packet of cigarettes.

Reading habits (and cigarette prices) have changed since 1935, but Penguin still believes in publishing the best books for everybody to enjoy. We still believe that good design costs no more than bad design, and we still believe that quality books published passionately and responsibly make the world a better place.

So wherever you see the little bird – whether it's on a piece of prize-winning literary fiction or a celebrity autobiography, political tour de force or historical masterpiece, a serial-killer thriller, reference book, world classic or a piece of pure escapism – you can bet that it represents the very best that the genre has to offer.

Whatever you like to read – trust Penguin.